ALEXA HAYES

VAMPIRE BEACH

If a vampire's existence or the existence of his family was threatened, the life of a single human became meaningless. What were a few years in the greater scheme, anyway? Their life spans were fleeting. What was wrong with giving one a little push?

But Rafferty O'Neill couldn't bring himself to imagine killing Alexandria Hart, ripping out her throat and draining her dry. Something about the woman pulled at him in a way he couldn't remember since he'd first been turned. Just smelling her scent made his gums ache and challenged his ability to keep his fangs in check.

Whenever he pictured himself bending over her bare neck, he saw the rest of her nude and writhing in his arms. She would beg for him to enter her, with teeth or manhood. His fangs weren't the only things he wanted to slide into her body.

Worse yet, from the smirk on his friend's face, Thane knew it.

VAMPIRE BEACH

ALEXA HAYES

new york

DEDICATION

To my husband and daughter for their constant patience and support. Thanks for putting up with the growling woman typing in the den and for knowing when to lure her out.

Chapter One

When will that asshole take no for an answer? Lexi Hart thought while taking more than a little glee in crumpling the offending certified letter in two shaking fists. She closed her eyes and took a deep breath, letting the scent of lavender that permeated her shop soothe her anger-filled nerves. She murmured a mantra the beachfront yogi taught her last year when she started joining him for his morning sun salutations.

Calm. Controlled emotions. Lexi refused to let the man, the money-grubbing developer, get to her.

"Okay, not a love letter from a steamy, secret admirer or even some nice, tame junk mail. What's up with the postal massacre?" a deceptively young voice teased between the annoying pop of ever-present gum.

"Take a wild guess," Lexi snapped, her large, dark eyes glowing with anger. Her petite form shook, causing the shot of metallic thread in her long, flowing skirt to shimmer as her pent up frustration fought to break free. She hated being powerless, and the jerk hadn't broken any laws. There was nothing she could do.

Her friend and employee, Stella Jones, rolled her eyes, twisted her lips and tapped one purple, French-manicured finger on the glass of the counter in front of her. "Hmm, let's see. It's been two days since the last time this 'land-grabbing, blood-sucking, corporate bastard' made a generous offer on your lovely beachfront home. How much did he up the price this time?"

Lexi sighed and leaned against the counter display-ing various colored crystal sun-catchers. She thrived on the stress-free existence of the little piece of nirvana she'd carved for herself in this California town, exist-ing out of time. The newest member of her community made it hard to remember that.

"He's offering enough to make it tempting if it wasn't my dream home, my auntie's beach retreat, that he was talking about." Lexi turned to take a proud look at her eclectic decorator shop, packed with bright colors and exotic pieces. "I'm glad *Afterthoughts* has been in the black and growing steadily for the last few years. If he'd caught me back in the lean days, I'd be homeless and guilt-racked right about now."

Stella stared at her from beneath jagged, rainbow colored bangs, concern marring her cheerful, devil-may-care face. "Are you sure it's worth it? It *is* only a house. I remember your great-aunt Becca as well as anyone else in this town. She loved that house, but she was one of the few down-to-the-bone practical people living in wonderful Santa del Sol. She wouldn't want you holding onto a windfall for sentimental reasons."

"And I wouldn't," Lexi replied, certainty ringing clear in her soft voice as she let her gaze flicker to the window, watching the tourists and townies ambling down the boardwalk. "I know that's not what she'd have wanted. I loved Auntie Becca, but money is money. My parents succeeded in drumming *that* into me. But I love that house. It's everything I've ever dreamed of having. I'm comfortable financially, and getting more so every year I'm in business. I'll be ready to expand the shop into a true interior design company any time now, all on my own merits. I don't *need* to sell my house."

Stella nodded, understanding in that way only someone who'd known you for years could have, laughter lighting her eyes. "And Rafferty O'Neill pisses you off."

Lexi opened her mouth, ready to defend her high moral ground, but closed it with an audible snap. If she couldn't be honest with herself, what was the point? "More than I can say," she grumbled. "It's not his superior attitude. Hell, with four older brothers, I'm used to that. He comes into my hometown, buying up everything left and right. It makes me nervous. *He* makes me nervous. And don't even get me started on his business associates, like Thane Erikson or any of the bands he brings in. They make *you* look normal."

Stella ignored the jab with another roll of her eyes, and a pop of a large, pink bubble. "And worst of all, he and his people have been making a real go of it. You have to admit, tourism is up, unemployment is down, and whether you like it or not, Rafe O'Neill is the one to credit."

"But I don't have to like him, or sell my house to him." Lexi pursed her overly lush lips into a pout no one but her closest friend ever saw. "He can build his mansion, tract housing, or fancy resort around me. I'm not selling." She crossed her arms defiantly, but relaxed. "Now, I'm heading over to Neon for a bite. Do you want me to bring you anything?"

Stella shook her head, and let the subject drop. "Well, they do have that new pad thai bowl I've been meaning to try. Tell 'em not to be stingy with the meat or the spice and bring me a pint of their coconut ice cream. I'll keep it in the freezer in the back until closing. Nothing like fancy boardwalk ice cream before you go to bed to bring sweet dreams."

"You haven't met a dessert you didn't like," Lexi teased, flipping her long, spiral black curls over her shoulder as she walked around the counter to get her purse.

Stella wagged a finger at her, sending her multitude of metallic-hued bangle bracelets jingling. "That's jealousy talking, my friend. You wish you had my metabolism."

"Nah, I like being able to stop eating for a minute or two, unlike some people. I don't want to spend my life chained to an éclair," Lexi shot back as she danced out the door to the tinkle of tiny chimes.

She stood in the doorway, letting the cool dusk air embrace her. Purples and deep reds washed the clouds that hung in the sky over the ocean as the last glimmer of sunlight slid into the water. Lexi loved Northern California sunsets and had from the first moment she saw one, when she was a wild little hellion banished to her great-aunt's home to straighten out and get away from the dicey crowd she'd fallen in with. One look at the sunset from the boardwalk, and it had been love at first sight.

She strolled across the walkway and leaned against the bright-red, wooden guardrails to gaze over the beach as the tide rolled in. She sighed, letting the muscles in her shoulders relax, allowing a day's worth of stress to ease. Peaceful moments like this were why she never looked back once she came home to stay in Santa del Sol after her Aunt Becca's death. She closed her eyes, listening to the steady beat of reggae music farther down the boardwalk and inhaling the sweet smell of cinnamon and sugar from the shop next door, which specialized in funnel cakes and churros.

God, she loved this town.

That was the real reason O'Neill got under her skin, like a festering splinter. It wasn't that he kept pushing her. It wasn't that he had more money than one man should be allowed. It wasn't the Irish accent. It wasn't even because he was handsome as sin, and probably expected every woman to fall at his feet and give him what he wanted.

He wanted to change *her* town. He'd bought most of the beachfront properties off of the boardwalk area, several from key businesses in town, and a large portion of the boardwalk itself. He'd opened the hottest new after-hours club, Nocturne, just off of the beach. With its constant influx of live music and funky atmosphere, Nocturne attracted people from out of town, as far as the Bay Area, Reno, and even L. A.

He brought Santa del Sol to life in a way it hadn't been since its heyday in the 60's, long before Alexandria "Lexi" Hart was a twinkle in her father's eye.

While Lexi appreciated what O'Neill had done, from a civic point of view, her heart ached at the change. Growth was life, survival. Growth equaled change.

But that didn't mean she had to like it. Or the person who brought it.

As the last of the colors dancing above the water faded to gray, Lexi turned back to the mile-long stretch of boardwalk.

It was a nice stroll to Neon; the beginnings of a beautiful night. She smiled and waved at the regulars, humming along with the carousel tune as she passed it. But as she walked the last block, she heard a sound; something discordant, out of place.

Lexi peered into the dark alley. The strange sucking sound raised the hair on the back of her neck and had her reaching for her cell phone.

Something wasn't right.

A man held a young blond woman across his arm in a deep dip that would have done justice to the cover of an 80's era romance novel, one of those bodice rippers with the heaving bosoms. No one in their right mind believed people did things like that in real life. But here Lexi was with a ringside seat.

The woman didn't put up any type of struggle. That stilled Lexi's finger on the buttons of her cell. The moans coming from the woman's throat had nothing to do with pain and everything with pleasure, sending answering quivers through Lexi's form. The blonde was a willing, eager victim, reaching up and sliding her fingers through the man's dark hair, pulling him closer.

His hand moved upward, slithering beneath her

shirt and kneading her breast as his lips caressed the arch of her neck. The blonde arched forward, wrapping one leg around his hip and grinding herself against his pelvis with desperate, pumping jerks. Her tight mini-skirt hiked higher, giving Lexi a glimpse of a crimson garter belt framing deeply tanned, firm skin.

Lexi started to step back, ease out of the alley before the couple noticed they had an audience when the man swept the woman back to her feet, leaning her against the wooden wall. The woman sighed and wobbled on her high heels. The man propped her up and, giving a deep chuckle, slid a strong thigh between her legs for support.

The man nuzzled her neck, whispering something too softly for Lexi to hear. He glanced over his shoulder, directly at Lexi. His teeth gleamed wet in the scant light, sending chills down Lexi's spine.

Lexi stumbled back, falling into a hard, warm barrier. A sharp, spicy male scent surrounded her as strong arms wrapped around her waist, sending a weak, fearful yelp to her lips. For one splinter of a moment, her eyes closed and her body embraced the feeling of security that masculine presence gave her.

"I didn't take you for the timid type," a deep, familiar voice rumbled against her ear. "Afraid of the dark?"

Lexi's face tightened, her back straightening away from the body behind it. She shook off the chills his closeness sent skittering through her body, refusing to acknowledge any interest in the bastard, no matter how attractive he was. She clenched her fists and turned to look up, way up into the face her savior/tormentor.

"O'Neill, fancy meeting you in a dark alley," she sneered to hide the blush tinting her cheeks, cursing her milky skin that refused to tan and left her vulnerable to fiery reddening with the slightest provocation. And here was the last person she would want to catch her in an accidental act of voyeurism, the situation reeking of a weakness she didn't want to acknowledge. She smoothed out her fitted top before delivering her first volley. "Looking for little old ladies to trick out of their nest eggs?"

A glint of humor and perhaps respect shined from his deep, emerald green eyes as he flipped a smooth, silky lock of auburn hair behind his ear. "No, I save that for Sunday evenings. It's a Friday night. Obviously, I'm on the prowl for sweet, young virgins to defile." He sneered and twirled an imaginary mustache. "Oh, what you think of me."

Lexi resisted the urge to stamp her foot and toss her head. How he made her feel like such a petulant child, she'd never know. "Well, you don't take no for an answer. What else am I supposed to think?"

"That I'm offering you well above fair market value for a piece of land easily replaced a few miles up shore?" he asked, head tilted and that superior smirk sliding across his chiseled face. Lexi couldn't decide whether she wanted to scratch his eyes out or chew on his lower lip.

No wonder the man pissed her off.

"Then why don't *you* buy there, if it's all the same?" she snapped, wincing at the whine in her voice.

Rafe crossed his arms, lounging against the wood and brick building. "Because your lot is right in the middle of the land I plan to build on. I don't want to rearrange my design plans to reflect a crescent moon surrounding your property. And from this conversation, I take it that you're turning down my latest proposal?"

"My, you're smarter than I gave you credit for." But Lexi had to admit, for once she was glad to see the man. If nothing else, he distracted her from the strange tableau she'd witnessed. She felt guilty about spying on the couple, but the whole situation felt off somehow, on an instinctive level.

Unfortunately for her peace of mind, Rafe noticed her preoccupation. "What is it?" he asked, looking back to the alley. "Did something frighten you? You're not your usual, biting self. A little off your game."

She shrugged, keeping her face blank. "It's nothing, just a couple of tourists who need to get a room. I thought someone was in trouble at first. Don't worry. Give me a minute to recover, and I'll be ready to take you down a peg."

She walked on, hoping he would follow and not go check things out for himself. It was embarrassing enough seeing what she saw, but to have Rafe O'Neill see it too? She could imagine the condescending smirk and comments carefully chosen to slice through her. She'd burst into flames on the spot.

Damn him.

She turned back to him, a brow raised askance, tapping a foot for good measure. His face tightened, eyes narrowing for a moment so brief she wondered if she imagined it. Then his expression smoothed out and he sauntered over to her. "I'd offer to walk you back to your shop, for your own protection, but you'd only find some ulterior motive in the offer. So I will leave you here, at least until the next round. Stay to well-lit areas, if you'd please. I'd hate to lose a worthy adversary this early in the game. So few people are willing to cross swords with me these days."

"I'm not selling you my home," she whispered at his retreating back.

"And I'm not letting you stand in the way of building mine," he tossed over his shoulder before disappearing around the corner.

Chapter Two

Rafe stalked into Nocturne, an aura of anger and violence shimmering around him keeping even the humans at bay. Customers packed the circular dance floor in front of the large stage as well as the surrounding tables, something a part of Rafe appreciated. The good food and intoxicating music pulled in the crowds, as intended. But tonight he wished all the careful planning hadn't done the job so well. He would've liked more privacy for the now inevitable confrontation.

Green sparks danced below the surface of his emerald eyes as he scanned the crowd for his erstwhile minion, the man who would break his rules. Given a closer look, the red glow of the beast he held within pulsed deep below the green.

It didn't take him as long to find the young man as he feared it would. The fool had the gall to stand at the black and chrome bar, cheeks flushed with his recent feeding, laughing and flirting with one of the new waitresses.

Rafe glided across the dance floor, feet skimming the floor as his temper rose, straining his control over his human mask. His gums ached and throbbed as he slid behind his minion. "Jordan, we need to talk."

The man continued laughing at his quarry as he turned to face Rafferty. "Can't it wait? I haven't started work yet."

"That's not what I've seen," Rafe growled, letting the other vampire feel a tinge of his power, pushing his will and compelling the fledgling. "Meet me in my office."

Rafe turned and walked to the back rooms, not trusting himself to talk to the man any further, not in such a crowd. After the danger Jordan had put them all in, Rafe knew there would be bloodshed when he confronted the loose cannon. He wouldn't exacerbate the situation by shedding it in plain sight.

Rafe felt Thane, his second, slipping in behind him, a dark shift of power flowing through the room. Thane must have sensed that something threatened and came to lend Rafe support or control. Either way, the master vampire was thankful for the presence of the other, calmer head. It might keep him from ripping Jordan to shreds.

And they needed every member of the family alive if they hoped to survive in this new land, even the idiots who couldn't keep their fangs to themselves.

Rafe took his seat behind his huge, oaken desk, with Thane standing at his side. His friend's face remained an impassive mask while Rafe allowed his rage to fill his features as Jordan stepped into the darkened room.

For the first time, the younger vampire had the good sense to look frightened.

"What?" he asked, his eyes flashing back and forth between the two older vamps. "What's wrong?"

"What's wrong?" Rafe asked, the tenor of his voice causing every piece of crystal and glass in the room to tremble. His knuckles whitened as he gripped the edge of the desk in an effort to keep himself from launching across the room. "Are you such an imbecile not to know what you have done wrong?"

Jordan opened his mouth, but must have thought better of whatever he was about to say. Instead he stood, hands clasped behind his back, waiting for Rafe to continue.

Whether he would ever realize it or not, that trusting, submissive act saved him from the worst of his punishment. Had Jordan shown the slightest hesitation, Rafe would've put him down. He might not agree with all of Edmund's tactics when it came to keeping his nest in line, but Rafe realized a certain amount of fear and intimidation was necessary. Nothing was more important than the safety of the whole nest.

Rafe laced his fingers together, tapping the tips against his chin. "When did you last feed?"

"Within the last half hour," Jordan stammered. He made eye contact with Rafe for a moment before gazing deeply at the plush white carpeting.

"The last half hour? Would that have been the young woman you left on the boardwalk not a mile from this place?"

Jordan's eyes darted back to Thane's silent, menacing presence before answering. "Yes. But I made certain her mind was wiped clean of all memories of me. She'd been drinking and will blame any loss of time on the alcohol."

Rafe felt the muscles in his jaw clench and release, clench and release. "That's good. If true, I may not have to kill you. Thane or Shanna will check your story later, and you'd best hope you are correct. But for now, you and I need to have a little discussion about priorities. Do you know what our first priority as a family is right now, Jordan?"

If a vampire had the ability to sweat, Jordan would have been wiping his brow as he stammered his answer. "To build a safe home, a place where we don't need to worry about attacks from other nests or from outside threats."

Rafe grinned and nodded, urging the young fool on. "And why do we need this?"

"We no longer rest under the protection of the gracious Eldora and those of her blood," Jordan recited in a tight voice, the tension in the room rising by degrees.

"Correct." An icy smile formed on Rafe's lips. "Now for the hard question. What did you do wrong tonight, Jordan?"

Jordan stared at Rafe, eyes blank, clueless. The idiot had no idea what he'd done.

Rafe was across the room before his chair hit the back wall, his fingers wrapping around the other vampire's neck. Jordan's toes skimmed the carpet as Rafe dangled him above the ground. He trembled, waiting for the deathblow to snap his neck like a twig, sending him into the dark embrace of true death.

Rafe let his fangs slide out to their full, two-inch length, his lips peeling back in a snarl that would've done justice to a lycanthrope. "Know this, Jordan. I am your master now. You chose to follow me here, to start a new nest. It was your decision. But there are rules you have to follow, rules that keep us all alive. You broke one of the first rules, a rule that even a dumb animal would understand."

Rafe carried Jordan to the other side of the room, slamming him against a wall, the impact causing a colorful summer landscape to fall to the floor. Rafe ignored the sound of breaking glass, leaning forward, letting his fangs graze the other man's jugular. "You don't foul your own nest, Jordan. You don't feed within walking distance of one of your safe houses. As long as you are under my rule, you don't feed within a ten-mile radius of our new hometown. You want some warm blood, straight from the vein, drive up the damn highway. Otherwise, you drink the pre-packaged stuff we get from the blood banks or don't feed at all."

Rafe broke the skin on the other vampire's neck, letting a thin rivulet of blood trickle down beneath his collar. "Otherwise, you're meat," he whispered into Jordan's ear. "I won't allow you to jeopardize what I fought to gain for us. I'll drain you myself and offer your body up to the local werewolf pack for a fun, sturdy new chew-toy. Do you understand?"

"Yesss," Jordan hissed, fingers clawing at the wall behind him, leaving deep furrows in the hardwood.

Rafe smiled, letting Jordan slide back down, supporting him until he gained his feet. He reached forward, smoothing the man's collar and adjusting his jacket. "Good. You may go."

Jordan gave a wavering smile and turned for the door, no doubt happy to make such an easy escape.

"Oh, one other thing," Rafe said, hand covering the other man's on the doorknob.

Jordan looked up. Rafe's fist plowed into his face, the force of the punch flinging the other vampire through the air to slam into the opposite wall. He crumpled to the floor, his face not as beautiful as it had been, most of the bones crushed. For a fledgling like Jordan, only sixty years old, it would take days to heal completely.

Wiping his hands against his thighs in disgust, Rafe nodded to Thane. "Get someone to drag him to the basement and make certain he's secure for the day. I don't want him turning to ash because he was too weak to care for himself. He's an imbecile, but he's part of our family."

"And we care for our own," Thane answered, the first hint of a smile dancing in his eyes as he reached for the intercom.

"Always," Rafe sighed, the weight of leadership lying heavily on his shoulders.

He allowed himself a moment to sag against the wall. With Thane, Rafe could show the momentary lapse without it being thought of as a weakness. "I need a drink. Threatening children gives me an appetite. You want one?"

Thane arched an eyebrow and tilted his head. "As I have a feeling you have something to discuss, yes. Is it going to be a long night?"

"Not necessarily. But you might want to have Shanna check on Jordan's early evening snack before she leaves to meet with the northern pack. I want that covered before the werewolf talks."

Thane gave a sharp bow from the waist and clicked his heels. "As you wish, Master."

Rafe resisted the urge to laugh or take a swipe at his friend. There was no room in the life of a master vampire for humor. No cause for personal happiness. But for his sanity, Rafe knew that having someone he could depend on to treat him like normal kept him from becoming a monster like Eldora or Edmund. "Drop the Master crap. I may be a Master to Jordan and the others, but you are my friend and brother."

"We've been through too much together for me to be anything else, but you are Master of this nest." Thane bent forward again, letting his pale brown hair fall away from his neck, a perfect, ritualistic offering. He looked up at Rafe with trust and acceptance. "You won't get any challenge from Shanna or me over that. I want you to know you have our support."

Rafe gave an uncharacteristic snort, and grimaced. He waved Thane up, walking across the room to lean against the desk and reaching for a blood-filled brandy glass. He took a deep, soothing drink before striding for the door. "You just don't want to deal with teaching the fledglings how to survive. You're as strong as me. Don't think I don't realize it. You just don't want to work."

Thane laughed, nodding as he turned and hoisted Jordan into his arms, ready to pass the deadweight to whomever he chose for cleanup duty. "Someone else can handle the hassle of ruling us, keeping us safe and in line. You do it so well. Me, I want to spend eternity wrapped in my mate, not thinking three steps ahead in the political and strategic nightmare that is our existence."

Rafe scowled as he stepped out into the cacophony of Nocturne nearing full swing. "Lucky bastard," he whispered just loud enough for Thane's inhuman ears to catch. His friend's laughter followed him out to the bar.

It was barely ten o'clock and people packed the darkened club. Humans and inhumans rubbed shoulders and partied in safety amid the black lacquer and chrome. It never ceased to amaze Rafe. If one half of Nocturne's patrons ever figured out what the other half were, a panicked stampede would rip the place apart.

Instead, a chaotic peace existed.

The Others in Rafe's club followed the rules under severe, bloody penalty. This was a safe house, a sanctuary. Any who crossed the threshold were under the protection of the young nest of vampires who now called Santa del Sol their home. And while they were juvenile for their kind, only a fool would challenge almost a dozen vampires ranging in age from sixty years old to well over three hundred.

Rafe and the others had the home they'd always dreamed of, a place far from the whims of older, more psychotic vampires. They made certain it stayed safe.

Rafe nodded to one of his family, Claudette, who served as the hostess of Nocturne along with Rafe's human assistant, Patricia. Physically, the young female vampire had completely recovered from the savage attack that instigated the family's break with their former nest. Still, she felt more comfortable around the human patrons of Nocturne, beings she could control if she felt threatened. Rafe couldn't convince her to leave the sanctuary, even for a short stroll down the beach in their new hometown. He hoped once he'd built their compound and put in the tight security planned by several top human and vampire-run agencies that she'd feel safe. That they'd all feel safe.

Rafe vowed to undo the damage inflicted by the elder Edmund, with Eldora's indifferent acceptance.

Lennox had two bottles waiting for him as Rafe slipped behind the bar. The other vampire nodded towards the stage, his brown hair sporting the surfer cut he had to redo every evening. "The new lycanthrope band you hired sounds awesome. If we sign them for a long term, they'd develop a strong following in the human community and keep the customers coming. Between their look and exotic riffs, they'd be a huge draw for the club."

"You'd know best on that one," Rafe replied as he snagged the bottles. Lennox had been part of the beginning of the music industry, in the days of the phonograph, before he was turned. Rafe relied on Lennox to keep him current on the music trends. If the other vampire said the wailing and gyrating of the werewolves on stage qualified as quality entertainment, Rafe would take his word for it. Personally, the organ music piped out of the carousel down the boardwalk was closer to what Rafe enjoyed. He was of the opinion that music should soothe and seduce the senses, not incite a riot. But what did he know? His age was showing.

Rafe shimmied past couples locked together as the dance floor spread out to the tables. He held the innocent-looking wine bottles over his head, so no humans would get too close a glimpse at them. He staggered back into his office, now Jordan-free. Thane sat in the chair across from his desk, feet propped in the other chair. Rafe lowered himself with a groan into his large leather throne, a gag-gift from Thane and Shanna when they first decorated his office. To their disgust, he enjoyed lounging in it, acting the emperor. He said it was because he loved lording it over his new minions. Actually, he enjoyed teasing his only friends. The years stretched on eternally without people to embrace the moments with you.

"Notice, my feet aren't on your desk." Thane pointed out before he shoved his feet deeper into the upholstery.

"Thank goodness," Rafe replied, keeping his face blank as he pulled a second glass out of his desk drawer to join his still half-full one, putting the empty one along with a bottle in front of Thane. "It took forever to get the scratches out the last time. I had to ask some of the wolves for advice on wood care."

Thane reached for the bottle, pouring the thick, ruby liquid into the fine crystal. "I'd love to have seen *that*. So, what's on the agenda?"

Rafe leaned forward, rubbing his temples with his thumbs. "I need advice from someone I trust who won't spread word to the others."

Thane froze mid-drink. He lowered his arm and whispered all their worst fears. "Is it Edmund?"

Rafe blinked at his friend, shocked that Thane could even think he wouldn't want to bring a threat that serious to the attention of the others. "God, no. If the problem was Edmund, I'd have a full meeting, a call-to-arms. Edmund's not the kind of thing to keep secret. It would endanger the whole nest." Rafe took a deep breath and poured his own drink. "No, it's the other, more attractive thorn in my side."

Thane sagged back in the chair, a smirk crossing his stoic features. "The human woman," he said, eyes dancing. "She turned you down again, did she?"

Rafe sipped from his glass, his tongue licking away a small, escaping drop. "She has no intention of selling me the land, Thane. I could offer her ten times what it's worth, and she wouldn't sell. The woman is entrenched."

"So, what are you going to do?"

"I don't know," Rafe answered. He wouldn't admit doubt to any other member of his family, but he could be honest with Thane. Thane would see it as honesty, not weakness. Without honesty about all the factors, strategy became pointless. "We need that land. Without it, we'll be left with a major hole in our security. I can't have that."

Thane shrugged, ever the realist. "So, we kill her. It may be 'fouling the nest,' but you know what they say about drastic times."

Rafe avoided Thane's gaze as he considered the suggestion. It wasn't as if he hadn't thought of that himself. It was the practical solution. Living under Eldora's rules and whims for hundreds of years left him with a very pragmatic outlook on the lives of humans. He'd watched Edmund bleed children dry in front of their parents to enforce silence in an entire village. He'd seen Eldora rip through towns, a demon of vengeance at the slaying of one of her pets. He'd even felt the bitter heat of their displeasure when he thought to question their decisions, spending agonizing nights strapped to a table as others feasted on his flesh and blood, rejoicing in his pain.

If your existence or the existence of your family was threatened, the life of a single human became meaningless. What were a few years in the greater scheme, anyway? Their life spans were fleeting. What was wrong with giving one a little push?

But he couldn't bring himself to imagine killing Alexandria Hart, ripping out her throat and draining her dry. Something about the woman pulled at him in a way he couldn't remember since he'd first been turned. Just smelling her scent made his gums ache and challenged his ability to keep his fangs in check.

Other parts of his anatomy, he had no control over in the woman's presence. Whenever he pictured himself bending over her bare neck, he saw the rest of her nude and writhing in his arms. She would beg for him to enter her, with teeth or manhood. His fangs weren't the only things he wanted to slide into her body.

Worse yet, from the smirk on his friend's face, Thane knew it.

"I don't want to kill her," Rafe admitted, reaching for the bottle again. "I will if I have to, but I wouldn't enjoy it."

Thane stared at him for a long time, the only sound being that of Rafe's throat as he swallowed.

"It's more than not wanting to be like Eldora and Edmund, isn't it?" his friend finally asked, a huge grin cutting across his face, flashing his fangs.

Rafe glared at his amused friend. "Yes, I'm attracted to her. I'm not fool enough to deny it. I'm also not fool enough to let it endanger my life and the life of my family."

Thane shrugged, throwing back the last of his glass and pouring another. "Then seduce her. Screw her and bend her to your will. You're a three hundred-year-old vampire. With years of experience alone, using no mind tricks, you have it over any other male she's met. Using your powers, how hard could it be?"

"Harder than you'd think," Rafe whispered with a grimace. He raked his fingers through his hair as he let his old friend absorb his reply.

"You can't control her mind?" Thane swung his feet off the other chair. He leaned forward, propping his elbows on the desk. "Is that what you're saying?"

"I can't control her mind."

Thane leaned back again, considering the ramifications. "That puts a different spin on things. Even Edmund wasn't completely immune to your powers. If Lexi can't be manipulated, she has the ability to become one of us." Thane narrowed his eyes before putting voice to Rafe's temptation. "Have you considered turning her?"

Rafe shook his head, trying to shake the idea out of his mind, though it clung with the tenaciousness of a weed. "I've never made another vampire. I could do it, but I have enough trouble keeping the fledglings I inherited from Eldora in check without adding one of my own."

"Well, that leaves binding her. You could do that without completely changing her. We already have several human servants bound to us. What's one more?"

What was one more? Rafe thought to himself. Then

he pictured Lexi obeying his every command, every whim, without the ability to resist. He could have her any way he wanted her, any time, anywhere. He didn't like the fact that the thought speared him with guilt at the same time it sent ribbons of desire surging through him.

"You're right," Rafe sighed, holding his glass in one hand and the bottle in the other as he tried to convince himself. "I should bind her to me and be done with it."

Thane smirked, his voice carefully neutral as he fed Rafe his most attractive option. "Of course, you could always give seducing her one more chance. I mean, you don't want to give up before you've given every option a try, right? No point denying yourself pleasure."

Rafe raise a single eyebrow at his friend before he tossed back his bottle of blood. He slammed the bottle back down on the desk with a dull thud. "If I didn't know better, I'd say you sounded like an old married woman trying to pair off one of her single friends. You wouldn't be trying to shackle me to a life-mate, now, would you?"

Thane held up both hands. "Oh, I wouldn't think of it. That's Shanna's job. I know better than anyone that mating isn't something you can force. It's either there, or it's not. I just think it would be a shame if it was there for you in this woman, and you made her a slave instead of a queen."

Rafe hid his flinch as Thane's barb struck deeper than intended. "She wouldn't be a slave. She would be one of our servants. Our humans are not slaves to our whims. They are cared for and protected."

"But do you think she would see the difference?" Thane shot back. "Our servants know the difference. They've seen what other vampires do to their humans, how little respect they're given. Alexandria Hart doesn't even know vampires exist."

Rafe stood, towering over his friend. "Then let's hope she's strong enough to face it."

Chapter Three

Lexi sat in a full lotus position on her towel, letting the sounds of the waves crashing against the shore and her *Krishna Das* CD soothe her ragged emotions. Breathe in fresh, salty, sea air and picture the flame of the candle dancing toward you. Breathe out and picture the flame dancing away. Keep your mind clear, focused on the moment. Exist in the present.

Though it was a ritual she did every morning since she'd run into the fifty-something sixties-devotee who'd done yoga on the beach, Lexi's twenty sun salutations followed by a fifteen minute meditation session was a struggle.

Her recent dreams had been disturbing, too disturbing. Flashes of blood, water, sand, and more blood hit her randomly and uncomfortably even now. A good, deep sleep eluded her until well past three o'clock. She shouldn't be surprised that she'd slept through her alarm, putting her behind schedule. Normally she would've skipped the routine to go straight to work, but after the nightmares she needed the centering before facing her workday.

She'd say the stress was getting to her, pulling her

mind in dark directions, but she didn't have that kind of stress. The fact that she couldn't think of a good reason for the nightmares disturbed her almost as much as the images themselves.

As the music ended, she started moving her fingers and toes, and then rolling her neck. She raised her arms and opened her eyes, watching the sun sparkle on the waves, smiling at the early morning wind-surfers already fighting for dominance over nature. The not-so-musical squawk of seagulls punctuated her feeling of centered peace, of home.

God smiled down on Santa del Sol.

Lexi hopped to her feet, wiggling her toes in the coarse, rocky sand as she scooped up her flowing, tie-died skirt. She pulled it on, and then slithered out of her tights beneath and stuffed them into her straw beach bag. She piled her towel and CD player on top, grabbed her sandals, and headed for the road and her little VW bug.

She swung her bag, whistling, when her toe snagged something in the rocky sand, sending her to her hands and knees. A sharp sting zipped through her palms, and her elbows popped. Lexi gave a decisive curse as everything rolled out of her bag. She started shoving clothes and discs back in, muttering under her breath.

As she grabbed her towel, she shoved a few rocks and sand out of their position. Time stopped, and the blood drained from her cheeks. Her hands trembled and her stomach heaved.

There, lying not a foot from where she knelt, laid a ravaged human leg.

The police arrived within minutes, not an amazing feat considering the station was less than three miles from where Lexi discovered the body. A group of surfers and sun-worshippers had already gathered around her, forming a wall of support as the police asked their questions.

No one had much to say. There wasn't any blood or sign of a struggle. No one recognized the young woman as the coroner bagged her. The police didn't have to tell Lexi that the poor girl had been dumped there. Someone further south, maybe in San Francisco, would be getting a call that afternoon, one filled with condolences, but delivering only pain.

Lexi was allowed to leave the crime scene, after giving the police her address and phone number for any further questions. As it was, for the first time in two years, Lexi staggered through an unlocked door into an open shop, clutching an extra-large Styrofoam cup. The scent of fresh roses overpowered the wonderful, life-giving smell of coffee.

"It's the first sign of the apocalypse, you know," Stella told her, her face and voice a perfect deadpan. "First you come in late for work, then the plagues start. Next thing you know, we're ice-skating in hell. It'll be all your fault."

Lexi glanced over to a young couple poking around her display of real and reproduction Tiffany lamps. She felt pale and drained. She shouldn't have come in at all, but she didn't have anywhere else to go and couldn't face her empty home, not after her grizzly discovery. "Just because you can get away with six hours or less of sleep a night and still be chipper in the morning, you don't need to rub it in on us lesser beings. If we didn't have customers, I'd really tell you what you could do to yourself."

"You're just mad because time didn't stop and no great cataclysms occurred without you being here." Stella patted Lexi's hand, the picture of sympathy. "I opened the shop. People came in and even bought things in the half hour you weren't here. You're still the driving force behind Afterthoughts, but you aren't so indispensable that you have to be here every morning. Your business is well established enough to run smoothly even when you are unexpectedly detained. Be proud, your baby's growing up."

Lexi smiled, but felt a little pang. She *liked* being indispensable. She enjoyed knowing something needed her, that she had a purpose. Stella was right. *Afterthoughts* was her baby. She'd pushed it past the simple knick-knack and curio shop her auntie ran into a burgeoning interior design shop, a place to come and put the finishing touches on your home or pick up a reminder of your visit. Pride filled her every time she thought of all she'd done for the dim little corner store.

But Stella had a point. Here Lexi was, at work as planned, after finding a woman's body. How sick was that? The only way to forget something that unsettling happening to her was to go to work and pretend it never happened, that her beautiful morning getaway hadn't been marred by evil.

After seeing how fragile and temporal life could be, Lexi knew she needed to do something to lighten up. Starting with giving her friend a hard time about her fast-paced love life.

She walked to the counter and plucked a rose from

the crystal vase in prominent display by the cash register. The sweet floral scent filled the air as she twirled the long-stemmed beauty between her fingers and forced a grin. "So, who's the newest love-struck victim? The drummer from that band you keep talking about? Someone from the Community College?"

Stella matched her grin for grin, grabbing the envelope tucked between the blossoms and shoving it at her. "I don't know. You'll have to tell me. I don't read other people's love letters, but the curiosity's been killing me."

"Huh?" Lexi stared at her own name in flowing, gold-script on the card. Who would be sending her flowers? And who would call her Alexandria? No one called her by her full name, not even her own parents. The only time she ever saw her first name was on her income tax forms.

Last time she checked, the IRS didn't send roses.

She ignored her snickering friend, tearing open the edge of the thick, white paper and pulling out a gilded card. She blinked at the message, handwritten in elegant calligraphy, her brain trying to grasp the unexpected words.

"Okay, this is a different angle," she said after several seconds passed.

Stella waited for three whole seconds before jumping at her. "That's all you have to say, 'This is a different angle'? What kind of a response is that to two-dozen, long-stemmed roses in a cut crystal vase? The least you could say is 'Oh, how romantic,' or bat your eyes and sigh while holding the card to your heart or something. What kind of a girl are you?"

"The kind that doesn't trust two-dozen, long-stemmed roses in a cut crystal vase and an invitation for a date at one of the most expensive restaurants in town from a man who's been hounding her for months now, and not in the fun, I'm-attracted-to-you kind of way."

Stella raised a single brow and started to say something.

Lexi stopped her with a chop of her hand. "No, not hounding me for a date, or even a quick fling. Hounding me for my home. That's not very flattering."

"Oh, the capitalist pig, beachfront property snatcher," Stella replied, ever agreeable. "Hell, girl, after all the aggravation he's given you, he owes you a dinner at the nicest place in town."

Lexi wrinkled her nose and tossed her head. She couldn't take Rafe on top of her Twilight Zone morning. "You're just saying that because he's rich and he's hot."

"No, I'm saying that because he's hot and he's rich," she teased Lexi, a flash of humor crossing her face. "You have my priorities completely in the wrong order. Hot is definitely more important than rich. You can't sleep with money, the paper gets itchy and the coins are too cold in the winter and too hot in the summer."

"Stella..." Lexi warned as she felt the muscles in her shoulders tighten.

Her friend raised her hands to ward off the tirade bubbling up. "I'm not saying you should sleep with the man. Not right away, at least. But going out to dinner with him isn't the same as selling him your house. Maybe you could even get him to listen to you and stop making the offers."

Lexi shook her head in disbelief. "He hasn't stopped yet, and I've talked to him about it more times than I'd like to think about."

"Yeah, but you weren't wearing the scorching little red dress I plan on lending you," Stella answered. The evil little smile spreading across her face sent chills down Lexi's spine. She remembered that look on Stella's face from her misspent youth, and it never boded well for Lexi.

"Let me get this straight," she said, trying to ward off her impending doom. "You not only expect me to go out with the guy, you expect me to let you dress me for the occasion?"

"Yeah, and you know what the worst part is?" Stella asked, cocking her head to one side.

"No, but I'm certain you're dying to tell me."

"I expect you to enjoy yourself. Live a little. Hell, make him feel as uncomfortable as he's made you feel." Stella stared straight into Lexi's eyes, making her squirm. "You can't tell me that doesn't appeal to your feminine side. You may not date much, but I know you. You like the male attention. Otherwise, you'd wear jeans everyday, not your flowing hippie/gypsy wear. Let's pull up your skirt and pull down your neckline and let him see how it feels to be the main course."

Lexi's stomach clenched, and she could feel a cold sweat breaking out on her forehead. But Stella was right. A little voice hiding deep inside her, that part of her that ran wild in Las Vegas during her teen years, wondered what it would be like to pull the tiger's tail, to tempt fate. She hadn't done anything crazy in a long, long time.

What could a single dinner with a gorgeous—albeit conniving—man hurt? If nothing else, she could order the most expensive items on the menu and stick him with the bill.

And she could forget how the sand clung to pale, young, dead flesh.

"Maybe I will, but no red dress," she blurted before she could change her mind. God help her, but she needed to do something, and she didn't care what it was as long as it drove that image from her mind. "I don't need to wave a cape in the man's face. I'm thinking something more subtle, more like me as opposed to you."

Stella pulled herself up to her full five foot two inches, plus three with the stiletto heeled boots. With her hands on her magenta latex-covered hips and her chest thrown back, she looked down her nose at Lexi. "Are you saying that I'm not subtle?"

Lexi raised one eyebrow and stared at Stella. "You wouldn't recognize subtle if it bit you on your punk-Goth butt. You can advise, even make suggestions. But if I close shop early to go on a mad shopping spree with you, I expect to be the one making the decisions."

Stella shrugged, trying to look unconcerned, but the cat-that-ate-the-canary grin gave her away. "Hey, anything you say if I get off work early."

"Then it's a deal. You take care of these customers, and I'll call him and finalize the plans. As soon as I know when he's picking me up, I'll let you know when we can leave."

Lexi spun on her heels and started for the back. But Stella hadn't had the final word yet. "Which will be at least thirty minutes to an hour earlier than you'd plan," she called out at Lexi's retreating form. "You'll wait until the very last minute, and we won't have enough time to buy the dress, much less shoes and matching purse."

"Whose money are we spending here?" Lexi tossed over her shoulder. "Now get back to work."

"Right. Anything you say, Boss Lady."

Lexi shook her head at her friend's need for the last word in any conversation, but smiled as the other woman walked up to the young couple still looking at lamps. Poor little lambs wouldn't know what hit them. Stella might look like an apathetic, anarchist ne'er-do-well, but she was one hell of a saleswoman. It didn't matter if the customer was a gray-haired octogenarian or a sixteen-year-old high school quarterback. Stella worked her magic, and they all left with something within their price range that they honestly enjoyed.

It was a weird gift, but one Lexi was more than willing to take advantage of.

Whatever the reason, Stella was better off here than living on the streets in Vegas or L. A. That was the true reason Lexi looked up her old friend after inheriting the shop, not just to have someone she trusted working for her. She wanted to make certain the one friend from her youth that honestly cared about her didn't end up in jail, or worse, just because she didn't see any other options.

And Lexi never regretted her decision, even when

Stella talked her into doing things that went against her better judgment.

Lexi glanced back once more as Stella led the couple to another display, and then ducked beneath the heavy velvet curtains that separated the shop from the hallway leading to the office, bathroom, and storage room. Even if Stella had talked her into agreeing to go out with O'Neill, she deserved some privacy when talking to a man about a date, especially if he was trying to get his hands on her deed as opposed to her.

A wave of depression swept through her at the thought.

Lexi grabbed the receiver and dialed before she could over-think and talk herself out of it. The phone rang long enough for Lexi to start preparing the message she'd leave for the machine.

"Hello, O'Neill residence," a husky Kathleen Turner voice answered.

Lexi felt the blush moving up her face. Her low opinion of Rafe took a greater nosedive. It was bad enough that he tried to romance her home out of her, but to do it when he was already involved with someone? That reached new pits of disgrace as far as she was concerned.

Lexi cleared her throat, scrambling for a neutral reply. "Hello, may I speak with Rafe O'Neill?"

"He's occupied at the moment. May I take a message?"

I'll just bet he's occupied. "My name is Lexi Hart. Please tell Mr. O'Neill that I won't be able to meet with him this evening or any other. He knows my answer, and it won't change."

The other woman started to say something, but

Lexi hung up before she had a chance. The hell with what the woman had to say. If she was dumb enough to fall for O'Neill, she deserved whatever she got from him.

Lexi walked around her desk and sagged into her embroidered wingback chair, kicking her feet up on the ottoman. She could delay the inevitable discussion with Stella for a few more minutes. She wished she could see the look on Rafe's face when he got her message. She'd bet he didn't get turned down often. And he didn't look like the type who'd enjoy it.

She grinned at the thought, closed her eyes, and leaned her head back.

Chapter Four

The automatic lights flickered to life as the furnace began blasting warm air through the cool, underground chamber. Soft classical music filled the air, the volume increasing every thirty seconds. Rafe's chilled, lifeless body absorbed the warmth and the comforting sounds, coming to himself in a slow ease. The old adrenaline-filled rush, claws extended and fangs gleaming, that once shot him out of his coffin while living in Eldora's keep didn't exist here. No fledgling or elder sought his blood, for vengeance or pleasure. His new battles, while still violent, weren't so deadly.

For the first time in over three hundred years, he relished the simple joy of lazing around in bed.

But even in his new situation, he couldn't lie in bed all night. In some ways, maintaining peace for this small community took more time and effort than surviving in the principality under Eldora's control. But she used terror and bloodshed to demand obedience, not treaties and diplomacy. Rafe had things to take care of daily, business transactions to oversee, negotiations with a werewolf band for headliner status.

And a date with an obstinate human woman to prepare for, a seduction to plot.

He stood naked, shrugging on a robe from the leather recliner by his bed, and padded to his large walk-in closet. One of the biggest advantages of being the offspring of the oldest living vampire in the world had to be access to large amounts of money. And learning the necessity of a proper wardrobe. Eldora came from an older time period, but embraced the later conventions when clothing and money made the man as much as raw power did. Rafferty had neither advantage as the second son of a poor Irish farmer.

While it wasn't worth the blood he shed after Eldora turned him over to the sadistic Edmund for guidance in his new life, he had every intention of using the money and training to his advantage now.

He shoved his arms through the racks, looking for something elegant, but not too off-putting for a modern woman. It was a difficult balancing act that fashion today put both men and women through. A century ago, dressing hadn't been a difficulty, when roles and expectations were rigid and choices limited. Then, everyone knew what to wear. Rafe liked his modern freedom, but missed the security of past beliefs.

He closed his eyes, bringing back to mind the elegant balls of nights gone by; dances with graceful, regency ladies followed by hours gorging on their pale, swan-like throats. He always felt his age weighing most heavily on him when he first woke. Whether it was because he was alone, or not having yet fed, the years bothered him. He worried that he would end up like many others who let the world outpace them, who met the sunrise rather than change with the ages.

It was the fear of ending his own existence that forced him to challenge Edmund and Eldora and form a new nest, his own need for freedom as well as that last bit of humanity that compelled him to protect his new family was almost secondary. With others depending on him, though, he wouldn't allow himself the luxury of wallowing in self-pity. He would be compelled to keep up with the times.

One advantage of the times being the wonderful security systems, panic rooms and the like available; especially if you knew which companies to go to, the ones who understood special needs.

Some might consider his choice paranoid. Maybe the guard dogs and state-of-the-art security system were a bit much. Maybe having three panic rooms in the basement of Nocturne set up as bedrooms for his vampires while allowing a pack of displaced were-wolves to live upstairs for extra protection went too far.

In the end, he didn't care.

Wait until he built his beach compound. The plans he and his security team had developed would give new meaning to the word 'safety'. Only the most powerful supernatural being would be able to break through, and even then the system would slow them down long enough for a mass evacuation, day or night.

His team blocked every avenue Rafe could imagine Edmund and his minions using to harm his people.

It took skill, creativity, and a whole lot of cash, but the plans were set. All he needed now was to secure the property.

Including the small sliver owned by a stubborn, raven-haired, mortal beauty.

Rafe pulled himself together and checked the security cameras showing the empty hallway outside his door. Seeing everything clear, he opened the door and stalked up the long staircase, too hungry and weak to glide gracefully. At the top of the stairs, he opened the door leading to the back storage room of Nocturne.

Silence held reign; the club wouldn't open for another hour. Two hours after sundown was the only set time for opening, a little eccentricity that titillated the public, but gave the management time to wake, feed, and prepare for the crowds. You didn't want a crew of hungry vampires waiting on a club packed full of warm food.

Patricia, a young brunette with her long hair pulled back in a neat bun, waited at the other side of the storage room door with a bottle full of crimson liquid and a crystal glass sitting on a silver platter.

Being the boss had its privileges.

"Anything happen that I should know about?" he asked, following the ritual he'd set up five years before after recruiting the efficient Patricia as his human servant.

"Nothing out of the ordinary, with one exception," she replied, a hint of unease lingering in her eyes, her heart giving a slight shudder. Even after all this time, that instinctive fear of giving bad news to a man lingered. Putting her and her daughter under his protection and getting rid of her abusive husband had freed Patricia physically, but the stain remained on her soul.

Rafe had enjoyed ripping open the bastard's throat, feasting on his hot blood. Knowing his victim was a strong man, a man who rejoiced in his own brand of violence, made feeding and killing the man all the sweeter.

That wasn't why he'd chosen Patricia for his servant, of course. It was for her loyalty, fierceness, understanding nature, and competence. That coupled with her need to provide for her child made her the perfect servant. The fact that Patricia's situation reminded him of his own, that of his family and Edmund, had no bearing on the decision.

But her fear of him after so many years pained him. Humans were such fragile creatures permanent damage, an easy feat.

"What is it?" he asked with as much gentleness as a hungry predator could muster.

"Miss Hart called." His servant bowed her head, unable to meet his red-rimmed gaze for long. "She has declined your invitation for this evening."

"Did she give a reason?" Rafe growled, incapable of softening his angry voice.

Patricia shook her head, but Rafe could sense that she held something back. A human servant could no more lie outright or lie through omission to a master than they could do him harm. It was one of the many reasons a human servant was so valuable.

He stared at the woman, his eyes glowing red. She stared at the area above his shoulder. "I believe it may be my fault, sir."

A brief moment of shock stilled Rafe's hand on the crystal glass mid-way to his lips. Patricia rarely made mistakes. Her meticulous nature made her a wonderful, organized assistant. She feared reprisal too much to be anything but cautious.

"How so?" Rafe questioned before taking a deep drink of the electric crimson liquid. Patricia looked too tasty at the moment, and he needed the control satiating his hunger provided. "Alexandria Hart has proven to be sufficiently obstinate on her own. How could you have caused this latest, and not unexpected, refusal?"

"I can't say for certain, sir," she mumbled, refilling his glass. "It's a feeling I have."

Rafe waited for his servant to gather her courage enough to continue. She wiped a ruby drop with a crisp, white linen napkin before speaking. "I got the impression that she called intending to say yes."

"Oh?" Rafe raised a single eyebrow, surprised. Even he realized the odds were against Alexandria's acceptance.

"It was the sound of her voice, sir. She sounded positive and upbeat when I answered the phone. It wasn't until after I spoke to her that her tone changed."

Rafe took another drink, using the moment to mull over her words. It didn't sound like the Alexandria Hart he'd come to expect. "And you think what exactly?"

"I think she may have gotten the wrong impression of my position here," she whispered, taking the empty glass from his hand and placing it beside the empty bottle. "I didn't have time to tell her I was your assistant."

Rafe toyed with the idea. "And you think she might be jealous? I hardly credit that. No, the woman is being her usual, headstrong self. I'll have to take a more personal, hands-on role. Now, don't worry. There was nothing you could have done."

"If you say so, sir."

"I think he's losing his touch and doesn't want to admit it," a snide voice remarked from the darkened stairway.

Rafe turned to the petite, blonde vampire stepping out from behind Patricia. Young for a vampire, but always an early riser, Claudette took great pride in getting up before the master. The skill hadn't been enough to save her from the worst of Edmund's treatment, but that singular talent saved her undead life all those months ago.

As she stepped closer, the overhead lights shined off her black leather cat suit. Her light blonde hair, pulled back from a fragile, pale face with a red silk ribbon, accentuated the long line of her neck. Her drawn face, along with the dainty tips of her fangs peeking out along her lips, hinted at the fact she had not fed yet tonight.

Rafe took a deep breath and waited. Claudette lashed out at anyone and everyone with her sharp wit since her time as Edmund's toy. Rafe wondered if she would ever heal from the abuse. Physically, she had fewer scars than any of them, but internally, she was a mess. Edmund dispelled her of any pride, leaving only her body as a source of power. She used sexual attraction to control her situation. When that didn't work, she resorted to sarcasm and anger.

Rafe couldn't fault her for her anger at the world and tried to be patient with her. But her moods plunged to dangerous lows when she hungered.

Rafe knew she'd force his hand before long. He couldn't keep allowing his authority to be flouted in public by her, not without risk of losing the precarious hold he had on all the vampires beneath him. He walked a thin line, not seeing a need to be as vicious as his predecessors, but also having to keep a tight rein on a group of headstrong youngsters tasting freedom for the first time in decades, even centuries.

Balancing his options, he stared at Claudette, willing her to stop now. "You have something to say to me?"

Her lilting, humorless laugh echoed in the small room and down the stairs. "It sounds as though you're losing your magic touch. I've never known you to have problems drawing women to you, controlling them. Male vampires excel at that, the use of sex against women."

"I don't have to explain myself to you, Claudette," he growled, letting his fangs flash. "I will handle things. I will safeguard this nest. That is all you need to concern yourself with."

Claudette fluttered her eyelids, becoming the image of an innocence he hadn't seen in her since Prohibition. "I just wanted to offer my services, help however I can. I'm able to do more than serve drinks and show humans to their seats, you know. Perhaps you aren't the mortal woman's type."

Rafe kept close hold on his temper, letting

Claudette hang herself. "And what do you mean by that?"

"Maybe you're a bit too masculine for her," she answered, sliding her hands along her leather-encased form and licking her lips. "Have you considered that? If so, I could give it a go."

Rafe thought of the look he'd seen in Lexi's eyes whenever he stood close to her, that little flash of desire quickly hidden. "I don't think that's the problem. But thank you for offering your services."

"Oh, I try to please." Claudette stepped forward past Patricia, as if the other woman wasn't there. She stood a hair's breadth away from Rafe, her chest almost grazing his. With her arms hanging at her side, she looked up at him, running her tongue along the teeth between her fangs. "I really do try to please," she whispered, arching towards his lips.

Rafe felt his face harden, as opposed to any other part of his body. Unlike Lexi, Claudette left him cold. He leaned down until his nose and forehead brushed hers. She smiled, eyes falling closed as she tilted her head up, ready to meet his passionate kiss.

"I'll keep the offer in mind, but I don't let anyone control me. Not through pain, hunger, or sex. Don't play with me, little girl."

Claudette jerked back and snarled, fangs flashing.

Rafe brushed her aside, stepping around her and out into the hall. If Claudette said one more thing to him, tried to seduce him again, he would hurt her. He didn't want to do that, not after what Edmund had already done to her.

But she was right. He hadn't turned on all his charm with Miss Hart, hadn't had a chance to. But human women hadn't given him a challenge in centuries, not since he'd survived his feral stage, regaining his mind enough to put on a human façade and rejoin civilized society. And while they hadn't fallen all over themselves to get to him when he was human, he'd never been short of female company, even before receiving his dark powers.

He understood Alexandria Hart's anger. He wanted her home, and she didn't want to leave. They were at an impasse. But that didn't mean they couldn't have a nice evening out together.

How was he supposed to seduce her or bind her to him if he couldn't get her alone?

The blood from his feeding filled his face, turning his features a ruddy, angry Irish red. He was a hunter, one of the strongest, smartest predators roaming the world. And his chosen food was outwitting him. This couldn't be allowed. At this time even the slightest sign of weakness could be misconstrued. He could lose everything he'd fought so hard to gain.

And that wasn't going to happen.

Yes, he desired her. Yes, the image of Lexi's dark curls cascading around his bare flesh as she rode him sent his borrowed blood throbbing through his body. He wanted to nibble on her smart mouth, silence her taunts with his teeth. But he had a job to do, people depending on him. Lust could not control him or his actions.

Whatever method worked best, Lexi Hart would not be allowed to stand in his way.

Rafe stormed through the club, past Thane and Lennox as they began ticking off items necessary for opening. He grabbed his leather jacket from the

coatroom and shoved open the door without speaking
a word.

Chapter Five

Lexi sat behind the counter, kicking her feet and counting down the last hour until closing. She should've told Stella what happened that morning. She should've taken the day off, watched mindless court shows on TV. She shouldn't be sitting alone in her shop, wondering what happened to the young woman, wondering what her family was going through. Wondering if it was someone from out of town, or someone she knew but didn't recognize. The worst was wondering if the body really had been dumped there, or if her nice, open little town had secrets that wanted to be known.

Since Lexi didn't have a hot date waiting and didn't want to face her fears in her secluded beach house, she let Stella off early. Someone ought to get to enjoy her Friday night, and Stella jumped out the door the second that she realized she'd have time to catch her drummer's first set. According to her, he was hotter than the gates to hell and sweeter than cotton candy, a potent combination for Stella's danger-loving libido. They'd been seeing each other for a full month, starting the moment Stella clapped eyes on him. She spent every spare moment with the musician.

Not that Lexi didn't understand, but she would have liked a little commiseration and sympathy from her best and oldest friend. Which she would've had, if she'd told Stella anything. But how do you slip that into a conversation without sounding like a ghoul? Guess why I was late this morning? I had to talk to the cops. I found a dead woman. Want to hear about it?

Eww.

The tinkle of chimes drew Lexi's attention to the door. Her mouth dropped at the figure walking into her shop looking ready for a fight. She thanked God that Stella had already left. She knew her friend would've used her expression against her for weeks. But who'd have thought the man's gall would be strong enough to bring him into her place of business?

Well, he had the nerve to ask her out, even sending her flowers, as another way to try to finagle her name on the dotted line. She shouldn't be *that* amazed.

"So, I wondered how long it'd take you to get back to me," she said the moment she managed to find her voice. "You aren't one to take no for an answer. But I have to admit, I expected another certified letter or a telephone call. I didn't think you'd grace me with your presence."

"Ever the shrew, I see," Rafe growled in return, stalking towards the counter. "Here I come to your fine establishment for the first time, and already you go for my throat. It's amazing you keep your business afloat with that kind of customer relations."

Lexi snorted, pushing to her feet to face him down.

To hell with him. He was the capitalist scum, not her. "You aren't a customer. You're a pest. I don't know what you hoped to accomplish coming here, but it wasn't for a quick shopping spree. So why don't you get down to it and save us both the time and frustration? Make your offer, I'll turn it down, and we can get on with our evenings."

Rafe smiled, but the hunger reflected in the expression sent chills down Lexi's spine like a deer staring down the barrel of a hunter's gun. "That's why I'm here, our evening. I had a rather nice one planned. A little dinner, some dancing, perhaps a moonlight stroll, only to have my fantasy dashed when my assistant tells me of your rather abrupt reply. I thought I'd come and get the long version. I feel it's only good manners to turn down an invitation in person."

"Your assistant answers your home number? Pull the other one," Lexi sneered, her temper getting the better of her.

Rafe's brows wrinkled, bewilderment filling his features. "What does that have to do with anything? If you must know, until our homes are built, my associates and I all live in rooms built off of Nocturne. We'd have a normal home if we could get all the land necessary for the building, but we'll leave that subject alone for now. Patricia answered my office phone and took a message."

Heat filled Lexi's cheeks. "So that was your assistant? I want to be clear here, before I stick my foot in any further. She's not your girlfriend, significant other, or live-in?"

A slow smile spread across Rafe's face, making Lexi squirm. "That's what this was all about. And here I thought you saw me as the hand-rubbing villain of a silent picture, tying damsels-in-distress to railroad tracks in my spare time. Instead, I'm dealing with a simple case of female jealousy."

"Oh, don't get me wrong," Lexi was quick to defend her stance, anything to recover some measure of pride. "I question your motives for asking me out. I don't trust you. I barely know you, and what I do know I don't like. But you *are* becoming a permanent fixture in my community, so I should try to be civil."

"So you would go out with me in the spirit of civic duty?" Rafe laughed, leaning against her counter like he owned the place, a feudal lord surveying his domain. "I think I liked it better when you thought I stole candy from babies and stepped out on my lady-loves."

"What, you want me to wax poetic about your manly features?" she asked, staring at where his butt pressed against the glass. The sexual magnetism that fed his confidence surrounded him like a halo.

Rafe raised an eyebrow and smirked. "No, you could also consider my sizable...bank account."

Lexi shook her head, fighting not to glance down and check the accuracy of his innuendo, but stepped out from behind the counter to join him. "Don't worry. My employee filled me in on your financials. I'll be honest. I considered going out with you, before calling and having your assistant answer, getting the wrong idea about your relationship. I'm not good at holding grudges and was curious as to whether or not you were worth the energy."

"You'd best stop now. All this flattery will go to

my head." He shifted one hip against the counter, drawing her attention to his long, muscular legs.

Okay, he was hot, and she had a pulse. It didn't mean she had to fall panting at his feet.

Lexi tightened her hold on her convictions, a difficult task when faced with such temptation. "I'm sorry if it hurts your sensibilities. But that's where I stand. I don't know you."

"And you never will, if you don't go out with me." He reached out, running a finger over the back of her hand and sending chills through her body from that single touch. "So how about we try this again. No misunderstandings. Just two people getting to know each other."

Lexi clenched her jaw to kill her automatic, acerbic taunt. She would not fall under his seductive spell. She couldn't let herself trust the man. She had to stay immune to him.

Rafe watched her, lips narrowing with each passing second of silence. Then one edge of his lips curled. "I'll tell you what. I'll sweeten the deal. If you go out with me this one time, I'll leave you alone for a week. No letters from realtors, no phone calls, nothing. If I see you walking down the street, I'll ignore you. You can approach me, but I will not approach you."

Lexi looked into his deep, mesmerizing gaze and knew she fought a losing battle. When the tingling started in her stomach, she realized that the best she could hope for was damage control. "Just one week," she whispered.

He smiled, his perfect, white teeth flashing. "I'll make it two. And I won't mention realty and deeds tonight either. Since we missed the reservations I made for dinner, how about we get some drinks and take that moonlight stroll. No pressure."

Better than dinner and a movie. A stroll on the boardwalk would give them time to talk, air out their differences, maybe come to an understanding. "I'd like that. I have about thirty minutes until closing, and another twenty to thirty wrapping things up. Why don't you meet me out front in an hour?"

Rafe slid her hand into his, placing a soft kiss on her knuckles. The feeling of his hand wrapped around hers shot straight through her, leaving an achy, empty feeling. The quick burst of desire distracted her, nearly causing her to miss his reply. "That sounds perfect. I'll pull a few strings and make reservations for the patio at Sea Spray. We can have drinks, enjoy the music."

Lexi flinched as her nervous giggle bubbled through the room. Just when she felt in control, the damn thing had to bubble out. "Owning a club like Nocturne, I would've pegged you for a lover of hard, thumping, angry punk music, not sultry Southern jazz."

"Just goes to show how little you do know about me, doesn't it?" he teased, his dark voice deepening, pulling her in like a drug. "If I have anything to say about it, you'll know much more before this night is through."

With that closing remark, Rafe turned and walked out, leaving a reeling Lexi to recover her senses.

What was she getting herself into?

That evening at closing, Rafe helped Lexi pull the security gate down over her shop door and windows, protecting them from teenage vandals. Even this far from the city, the occasional tagger hit the boardwalk.

She couldn't help but shoot surreptitious looks at Rafe's tight ass and thighs as he stretched up to grab the bottom of the rolling metal. If he did turn out to be a decent human being beneath that ego, it wouldn't be fair. Someone that good looking had to have a fault. God wasn't supposed to create perfection. He was supposed to leave something for a person to strive for.

But that didn't mean she couldn't enjoy the view.

Lexi snapped the final lock in place, pushed her mass of hair back, and pulled her trench coat together to fight off the chill from the cool ocean breeze. A part of her wished she'd had time to dress up, but at least this way Rafe was getting to see the real Lexi, in all her retro-sixties glory.

He didn't seem to mind her funky, gypsy look, his intense gaze so strong she could swear it felt like a physical caress against her cheek. Without a word, he slid his hand into the bend of her elbow and led her down the boardwalk.

At eight-thirty, the nightly party was in full swing. Teenagers taking advantage of the eleven o'clock curfew gathered in knots around the cool hang outs, laughing and teasing each other. Arguments were few and far between.

Families hovered around the game areas. Fathers spent untold amounts of money to throw balls, darts, and coins in the perpetual effort to win cheap stuffed animals for their wide-eyed, begging children. Dotted among them were the boyfriends trying to impress their girls with their gaming skills, or the girls trying to outshine the boys.

Several couples walked arm in arm, snuggled close and kissed against the backdrop of the full moon and crashing waves. Lexi looked over at her companion, wondering what he thought as he watched the other couples.

The farther they walked, the thinner the crowd became, until only the romantic couples remained. A sprawling, two-story restaurant dominated this end of the pier. Colorful paper lanterns drew the eye, no cheap neon or blinking lights for Sea Spray, the premier dining experience in Santa del Sol.

But what really separated Sea Spray from the rest of the hoi polloi was the patio. Built on a jetting pier, the patio stretched over the ocean. The fresh ocean scent mixed with their haute cuisine. With patches of glass flooring and iron banisters, it gave the diners a view of churning water sparkling in the moonlight.

But for Lexi, it was the music that always drew her attention to Sea Spray. Soulful blues and sultry jazz poured out of the restaurant, permeating the surrounding area with an atmosphere of sex and romance. She loved to feel the wail of an alto sax pounding in her blood, or the melodious whine from a slide guitar.

Music, she thought, *should be felt with the emotions, the soul, not only with the body.*

Rafe guided her past the long line waiting at the door, earning a few heated looks from impatient patrons. When he gave his name to the hostess, she led him straight to one of the best tables in the patio section, far enough away from any other table to afford privacy, but well within the range of the music.

The waiter stood at their table, sliding the chair out for Lexi and helping her with her napkin.

"Do you have any preference for the wine," Rafe asked Lexi when the waiter handed him the list, "or would you rather I order?"

"I like dry reds, merlots, the best."

Rafe nodded and spoke to the waiter, who spun away. "I know you already ate, but would you like me to order an appetizer or two? It would be a shame to waste the reservation and not eat at all."

"And I'd rather not let the wine go to my head. Yes, a little something to eat would be nice. Maybe some bread and cheese to go with the wine?"

"Whatever you want. I ate a large meal before coming to confront you this evening, thinking I'd need my energy. So, I'll leave the food to you."

Lexi grinned at his attempt at teasing her. Despite his obvious Irish heritage, he didn't seem given to easy humor. She could tell he was working at it, that he wasn't as at ease as he'd like her to think. "Oh, sure, force me to make a pig of myself on our first date. Get all my secrets out in the open."

Rafe looked at her, in complete seriousness. "And is this our first date? You realize that suggests other dates to follow."

"Maybe, if you play your cards right," Lexi couldn't resist her flirtatious reply as she stared at him through lowered lashes. "I never start a date thinking of it as my last. Too defeatist for my taste."

She watched Rafe's entire body ease, as though until that moment he'd held himself braced against a blow. "I'd like that. I'd like to be honest with you. There's something about you that draws me. I'm not certain what it is exactly, but I'd like the chance to find out."

"That sounds nice."

For the next hour, Lexi relished sitting, drinking, and talking to Rafe. There was so much more to him than she realized. While she couldn't say she liked him yet, not with his heavy-handed tactics, she began to respect him for more than just his business acumen. He came from humble beginnings, a farmer's son in Ireland, to become a successful businessman in America. He risked everything to come to Santa del Sol and start anew, even bringing friends along, giving them a leg up while he was at it.

It was something Lexi could understand and admire.

By the time he took her arm and started walking her back down the boardwalk, she felt comfortable with him. She didn't feel like he was her enemy anymore. He'd be perfect if he wasn't so aggressive. Without him pressuring her about her land, she enjoyed his company. And heaven help her, she'd be willing to see where the relationship could go.

"Well, it looks like someone's having a good evening," a young woman teased as they walked by her.

"Shanna," Rafe said, stopping dead as a genuine smile spread across his face. "I didn't expect you back from your trip so soon."

"Things wrapped up quicker than I expected. The owners wanted to sell and move to Boca. So you could say everything ended up satisfactorily. To each his own, I guess," she answered, staring at Lexi. Something about the look in her jade-green eyes gave Lexi chills, like looking into an empty grave.

"Then I'll take it that all our business ended as well?"

"Of course. Did you have any doubt? I always work fast so I can come home and relax." The woman didn't take her eyes from Lexi, judging her and finding her wanting.

"Thane must have been happy to hear you're back," Rafe continued without noticing how Lexi crept closer to him. "I would have thought you'd still be with him."

The woman shrugged, her short, red bob bouncing around her oval face. "Things were getting too close at the club. I needed some air. Too many people packed in. I swear I could feel all the heat from their bodies building around me."

"Claustrophobic?" Lexi asked, trying to push away the aura of intimidation swirling around the redhead.

The woman smiled, staring through Lexi. "Something like that."

Rafe pulled Lexi close to his side, his arm surrounding her shoulder. "Shanna, this is Lexi Hart."

For the first time, Shanna looked *at* Lexi. Her eyes twinkled as she smiled and the tension surrounding her eased. "The woman who's been giving you fits. Thane said you'd asked her out, but Claudette told me she'd canceled on you."

"I talked her into reconsidering."

"I bet you did." She gave Lexi a conspiring wink, one Lexi didn't trust. "You have to watch out for this one. You know the phrase about a person being able to sell ice to Eskimos."

Lexi nodded, a touch of nostalgia calming her tight

nerves. "My aunt used it to describe just about any salesman who got the better of her."

"Well, he's the man they were talking about when they came up with it." Shanna grinned, but verbally backpedaled the second she got a good look at Rafe's dour expression. "Not that it's a bad thing. He's a vicious fighter when he's in your corner. You just better hope he's in your corner."

"Shanna, I thought you would be on my side in this," Rafe responded, a hint of warning in his voice.

"That all depends. I believe a person deserves forewarning. Don't you agree?" she asked Lexi.

Lexi grinned back, realizing that she was facing Rafe's version of Stella. "Forewarning is good, as long as you listen to the advice. It's been my experience that people seldom do."

Shanna laughed, the musical sound making the back of Lexi's neck tingle. "Oh, I like this one. We need to keep her. She'd be a breath of fresh air in the midst of all those living corpses at the club."

"Shanna," Rafe warned, drawing Lexi closer. He seemed worried about what his friend would say to her.

"Don't worry. I know what she means," Lexi reassured Rafe. It was nice to see this side of him, the long-suffering friend. "You don't need to sound offended. I'm blunt. It's a nice change for some people, while it gets me in trouble with other people, like yourself."

Shanna grinned and held out a hand, giving Lexi a clammy handshake. "It's been a pleasure meeting you, Lexi. No matter how things go with you and the boss, you'll always have a friend in me."

"Thank you, I think."

Rafe pulled her hand from Shanna's. "Now, if you're done trying to scare her off, why don't you leave us alone? We were enjoying a romantic interlude before you decided to butt in."

Shanna laughed again and saluted. "Aye, aye, sir. Far be it for me to interrupt a first date. Scurry along, children. Don't have too much fun."

Lexi shook her head as she watched the other woman strut down the boardwalk. "Remind me never to introduce her to Stella."

"Stella, your employee? Why not?" Rafe asked while he guided her in the opposite direction with a strong hand at the small of her back.

Lexi gave an exaggerated shiver. "It could get scary. They'd either fight like cats the first moment they met, or they'd be thick as thieves in seconds. I'm not certain which possibility scares me more."

"The fight," Rafe replied, his eyes going hard. "I've seen Shanna fight. It's not a pretty sight."

Lexi felt honor-bound to defend her friend's reputation. "Stella's no slouch in that department. She's been known to rip someone a new one when the situation called for it."

A dark look hovered on Rafe's face. "I don't think it could compare," he whispered, stopping to look out across the waves, the lights of the boardwalk dancing on the water.

Lexi stepped out of his embrace, turning to face him. "Are you all right?" she asked, unable to stop her hand from reaching out towards him and cupping his smooth cheek. There was so much pain in his eyes, empty desolation.

When he looked down at her, the lights of the boardwalk made his eyes seem to glow with pent-up emotion. He reached out for her, sliding his fingers through her dark curls. "For tonight, I am."

Without another word, he took her hand and led her back down the boardwalk, angling for one of the off-streets. He guided her to a black classic Mustang.

"This is nice," she commented, running her fingers along the smooth, cool lines before she slid into the passenger seat. "Did you fix it up yourself, or buy it like this?"

"It's been kept in shape," he replied, his pride obvious, "always owned by someone who loved it, the power of it. I've never had to do much work to it, just general up-keep."

Lexi nodded in understanding that only a fellow aficionado could manage. "I love this car. It was a classic when I was a kid, but I loved seeing them tearing up the road in old movies. This is the first time I've ridden in one."

"I hope it lives up to expectation," he said as he slid it into gear and eased it out of his spot. "It's lucky you live so far out of town. If you want, after we're on the main highway, I can cut it loose and let you really enjoy it."

Lexi felt her face light up, but didn't waste the time or energy it would take to be embarrassed over the kid-at-Christmas look she knew shined in her expression. She had a chance to live out a childhood dream. No way was she going to miss a single second of it, especially not over a little thing like self-respect.

They drove out of the city limits at a sedate pace, eyes out for police. When the lights faded behind them, Rafe let it rip. They tore up the twisting coastal highway. Lexi's fingers curled into the upholstery as her heart raced with fear and excitement. The man had amazing reflexes, keeping them on the pavement several times when she was certain they would lose control.

They reached her secluded beach-home in a quarter of the time it usually took her.

Lexi tossed her head back, laughter bubbling out her throat. Rafe watched her with shining eyes and a half-grin. "I'll take it that you enjoyed yourself."

"Immensely," she gasped between chuckles. "You're lucky you don't have a Porsche or a Lamborghini. The way you drive, you wouldn't last a week before you had yourself wrapped around a light-post."

"I don't remember hearing any complaining."

"Oh, I'm not complaining." Lexi grinned, brushing her curls out of her eyes. "Merely stating the obvious."

Rafe slid out of the driver's seat, walked around, and opened her door for her. When he reached in to help her out, he used a bit more strength than he needed. She fell into his arms with a gasp.

"You could enjoy yourself even more, if you give me the chance." He leaned forward, whispering against her lips. "I could give you new experiences you never dreamed of, take you places you've never been."

Lexi arched away from him, both palms braced on his chest. She fought the shiver of awareness that rippled through her. "I have to say, that's the smoothest delivery I've heard, but one of the cheesiest lines. What's scary is it's still tempting. You're tempting."

"Is temptation something to fear or to embrace?" he murmured as he placed gentle kisses against her neck, sending goose bumps up her arms. Her heart hammered as the manly scent of his skin drugged her senses.

"A little temptation is fun. It lets you know that you're still alive," she gasped, fighting against the moan that threatened to erupt from her passion-filled form. "The question becomes, how much temptation are you? What price will there be to pay? And there is always a price."

"Nothing too much, I promise. What price could be too much for the dark pleasures we would explore together?"

Lexi pulled back, that vile, nervous laugh lurking at the back of her throat. "Well, coming from the man who wants my home, we probably shouldn't be talking about price."

The smoldering flames lingering in Rafe's eyes startled her, but the corner of his mouth curled. "If this is your way of breaking the mood, it's working."

"I'm sorry. But you can't expect to go from the arch-villain of the piece to lover in one night."

"No, only hope. I tire of being the villain." His wide grin gave him a youthful appearance, like a playful child.

"Be happy. You've made headway tonight."

Rafe didn't disappoint her by leaving things unsettled. "But will you let me try for more tomorrow night?" he asked, holding her tighter. "I'd like the chance to try out that date I wanted, dinner and dancing. I'll even leave the choice of place up to you."

Lexi nodded. "You're on. But you can choose this one. Next one's on me."

"Oh?"

"If I have to go dancing with you, knowing what a rotten dancer I am, you'll have to do something for me that you won't be so comfortable with."

"Like what?"

Lexi twirled a single curl between the fingers of one hand while placing the other on an out-thrust hip. "You plan tomorrow night and let me worry about that."

Rafe smiled, his eyes roving up and down her form. "If I'm going to accept punishment from you, I should take my reward now."

He grabbed her by both arms, jerking her forward for a kiss. After his gentle, courteous treatment of her all night, his kiss came as a shock. He pressed hard against her lips, until they parted with a whimper.

One of his arms circled her shoulders, pulling her tight into his chest. His other hand slid through her curls, anchoring her in his embrace.

As his tongue slipped between her lips, Lexi felt her blood heat. Her heartbeat pounded in her ears as he devoured her mouth, leaving no spot free of his exploration, filling all her senses with him, the taste, touch, and smell of him.

She wrapped her arms around his back, flexing her fingers into his shoulder blades, struggling for an anchor in the maelstrom of feelings he set loose through her body. She never believed that a woman could be swept off her feet, but Rafe proved her wrong. In that moment, he could have done anything with her, and she wouldn't have thought twice about it.

When Rafe pulled back, Lexi almost cried, her body a mass of twisting hunger. She wobbled, holding his arms for support.

She could hate him for his knowing smile if she hadn't been so obvious. No wonder so many people were obsessed with sex. If she had ever experienced a feeling like this before, she would have been first in line for nympho school.

"Wow," she managed say, once she regained control over her throbbing tongue.

Rafe stared at her in amazement, a slow smile melting across his face. "Think about that tonight. I'm more than a businessman who's interested in buying your land. I won't allow you to relegate me to that role any longer. I have other, more interesting plans for you now."

"So, you'll stop harassing me to sell?" Lexi teased, her fingers pressing against her swollen lips.

"I didn't say that," he replied, tucking a raven-colored curl back behind her ear. "But you do have your reprieve. In the meantime, I plan on harassing you for other, more satisfying reasons."

With that, he held both her hands in his, the warmth flowing through her blood like aged scotch. Then he let her go, backing away, keeping her in sight until the last possible moment.

As he rounded the corner of the house, back towards his car, Lexi leaned against the wall. Her knees shook and her entire body tingled with desire. It would be hours before she came down enough to even think about sleep. What that man had should be bottled and sold for a hundred bucks a sip. No way could a sane woman resist him for long, not when he focused all his energy on her, making her the center of his sensual world. Lexi still had her reservations, her doubts. But Rafe was not going to make keeping her distance easy. For whatever reason, he'd targeted her for his attention.

She was in *so* much trouble.

Chapter Six

Lexi whistled an old surf rock tune horribly off-key as she wiped the glass counter, sweeping her cloth between the two vases sitting in prominent display. Now that they were no longer from her mortal enemy, she could enjoy the roses Rafe sent the day before. And the ones he had delivered this morning. Every time she inhaled their rich, dark scent, Lexi thought of her surprise in discovering how much she actually liked Rafe.

She'd never had a man show her this much attention. Even if it turned out in the end that he was in it for her land, she could bask in the Old World masculine attention in the meantime. American men didn't put out this much or this kind of effort when pursuing a woman, at least that had been her experience.

And instead of dreams filled with death, Rafe left her with dreams filled with sex and desire.

Stella waltzed in at eight o'clock sharp, slipping behind the counter and dumping her bag. She took one look at Lexi's shiny face and the new flowers, and cackled. "Oh, how the mighty have fallen. You didn't give him much trouble, did you?"

Lexi gave into the childish urge and stuck out her tongue, sending another peal of laughter from Stella. "Whoa. It must've been good. The man's rendered her speechless."

Lexi crossed her arms and glared. "Lay off, jerkette. Let a woman have a moment."

Stella fanned a hand in front of her face. "Ooh, he rates a moment. And after only *one* date. I think she likes him."

"I had a nice evening, which I admit surprised me." Lexi shook herself, wiping the silly grin off her face and hoping Stella didn't notice. "He's still a glorified claim-jumper, but I can have a civil relationship with him."

"Civil? That's no fun." Stella smirked, but couldn't keep up her playful expression. Her smile melted away, replaced by a look filled with worry. "But I have to admit, I'm glad to see that you were out with Rafe last night. After reading the newspaper this morning, I feel better knowing you weren't alone."

"Why?"

Stella reached into the humongous beach-bag she lugged around everyday and pulled out a copy of the paper, handing it over to Lexi. One look at the headline said it all.

"'Another Vicious Murder Shocks Small Beachfront Community'?" Lexi gasped, paling as she read the first paragraph. Icy fear formed over her heart. "Jesus. They can't even identify the body?"

"Police aren't giving out much info, and there are several rumors." Stella dragged a wingback chair in front of the counter and sat down. "One has it that animals got to her before anyone found her. Another is that it's some kind of Jack the Ripper copycat. Either way, she's dead. And according to the article, she's the second body found on the beach in the last two days."

Lexi tried to wrap her mind around it, the idea of her safe town hiding dark secrets. "I thought I left this kind of thing behind when I moved from Vegas."

"No," Stella replied, glaring at the paper. "I don't remember this kind of stuff in Vegas. All the rumors agree that she was in pretty bad shape."

"Oh?" Lexi asked, morbid curiosity getting the better of her.

"At the very least, her throat had been ripped out. Everyone I talked to agreed on that point. What other mutilations went along with that is up in the air."

"Jesus," Lexi whispered, sending up a prayer for the unknown woman.

"You can say that again," Stella agreed with fear in her voice. "I'm not going out anywhere at night without bringing a big, burly man along with me. I suggest you do the same, even if it means tagging closer to Rafe than you'd like this early in your relationship. Otherwise, do my heart a favor and stay at home. I mean, the first one was found on that beach you do your morning walks on."

"I know," Lexi whispered, trying not to picture that sand-covered leg. She tried not to imagine how the other woman looked, what animals could do to a human body.

"You know? What do you mean, you know?"

Lexi stared at her friend, eyes filled with the dark memory.

It didn't take Stella long to add things together.

"You were late for work yesterday for the first time I can remember. Shit. You were there. You saw the first body."

"No, I found the first body."

"What?" Stella shrieked loud enough that Lexi was surprised the crystals didn't shake. "You found something like that and didn't even tell me? You stayed at your place alone last night after finding something like that? I would've come over and stayed with you. You didn't need to be alone. Better yet, you should have come over and stayed with me. I live right around the block, for crying out loud. You're too secluded in your home, no neighbors or anything. Someone could come in, rape and murder you before anyone even knew you were in trouble."

Lexi stared at her friend, a wave of apprehension sweeping through her. "Hell, I'm more worried about you than me. I don't go for the high-risk shit anymore. I come home, lock the doors, and vegetate. I don't do the club scene and hang out with guys I don't know."

"And you think I do?" Stella crossed her arms and glared at Lexi, but her lower lip quivered.

"Not really, otherwise I wouldn't have hired you," Lexi was quick to assert, happy to watch Stella's pained look disappear. Yet she couldn't help but worry about her daring, adventurous friend. "But of the two of us, you're the most likely candidate to get snatched and hurt."

"Thanks, I've never been voted most-likely-to-be-found-in-a-ditch before," Stella sneered, her hands clenching the arms of the chair. "It's nice to know my friends have confidence in me."

Lexi let her friend's anger roll over her, while controlling her own instinctive desire to lash back. Anger helped no one, and it wasn't as if this was a new conversation between the two of them. They'd gone over this information a hundred times before in the course of their friendship, reassuring each other and pushing their limitations. Lexi thought of it as whistling in the dark. "Oh, I have the utmost confidence in you. But I also know you. You don't think about yourself. You charge into anything without thinking of the consequences."

"While you over-think things to death." Stella threw her hands in the air, brushing a display of wind chimes and sending up a chorus of jingles and clangs to punctuate her argument. "Why do you think I started hanging out with you? Without me and my impulsiveness, you'd never have tried anything new."

"Yes, and I remember how some of those 'new' things got me into loads of trouble."

Stella laughed and sat back with her ankle across her knee. "True, but it adds to your character. How many women your age know how to hot-wire a car or hack into even a minimum-security computer system? Without me, you would've missed out on a lot of fun, and you wouldn't have been sent up here. Admit it, no matter what the reason behind the decision, you're glad you got sent up here to your aunt."

Lexi couldn't say anything to that. Stella was right. Her friend had gotten her into a lot of trouble as a teenager, but that trouble landed her here. Her aunt taught her that a woman could be more than an extension of a man's will to be coddled and protected.

Without Stella, Lexi wouldn't have even *met* her aunt.
If anything, that alone taught her to believe in fate,
in a larger hand at work. You didn't always see why
things were happening the way they were, good or
bad, until much later in life, when you looked back.

But it didn't change the fact that someone took two
young women's lives away. A monster had invaded
her hometown, bringing big-city terror and blood
with him.

She hated to think that she'd be double-checking
the locks on her doors and windows tonight, wondering if anyone lurked in the bushes. Everyone in Santa
del Sol would be looking over their shoulders as the
inevitable paranoia set in.

Lost in thought, Lexi almost missed the tinkling
sound of chimes as two men swaggered into her shop.

They weren't her average customers, these tall and
lank men with hungry eyes. They both had shaggy
brown hair, worn almost identically except that one's
was longer than the other's by an inch. An aura of
danger cloaked them as completely as the long, black
dusters they wore.

Stella sat a bit straighter, her best come-hither smile
splitting her face.

The one with the longer hair smiled back. He
stepped behind her chair, bracing himself on the back.
"Told you we'd stop by, Starry Eyes. Check out where
you work for a change."

At the man's greeting, Lexi relaxed. Not shoplifters,
flirts. Stella attracted them like flies. Lexi could deal
with guys hitting on her employee. That was Stella's
business. She just hated chasing after kids with mer-

chandise shoved down their pants, especially this early in the morning.

"It's good to see you guys. I'd like you to meet my boss and best-friend, Lexi Hart." Stella leapt to her feet and grabbed the arm of the man who'd spoken first, tugging him forward. "This is Grant, the drummer I told you about, and his friend and lead guitarist, Victor."

"Oh, you play at Nocturne, don't you?" Lexi asked, eyeing the band members more closely, wondering about their relationship with Rafe.

"We just signed for five nights a week, three weeks a month, for the next six months," Grant answered, his pride obvious as he slung an arm around Stella's shoulders and hugged her close. "If things go well, the Alphas will be here for the long run."

Stella snuggled under his arm. "And we all want that."

"Are you playing there tonight?" Lexi asked.

"Yes, why?"

Lexi shrugged, but eyed the man embracing her friend. "I'm meeting my date at Nocturne tonight. I'd like the chance to hear you play. Stella's done nothing but rave about you since the first time she heard you. According to her, you're the next up-and-coming band. I want to hear you before you go big-time, so I can say that I knew you when." *And check out the guy my friend's falling for.*

Grant gave his first honest smile since he entered the store, taking years off his age and making Lexi wonder if Stella was robbing the cradle. "It's nice to know we have such supportive fans. Stella's our most loyal, but we need a good, strong fan base before we start thinking about going beyond a steady gig. We've got bigger dreams than just being a headliner, even at as hot a club as Nocturne."

Victor grinned in agreement, but remained silent. He kept sniffing the air with a puzzled look on his face.

"I hope the patchouli isn't bothering your friend," Lexi commented, turning to put out the incense stick burning on the shelf behind her. "It's given people with allergies a bad time, and I've been thinking of toning it down a bit."

Grant cast a questioning look at his friend and sniffed the air as well before looking at Lexi with a playful grin. "No, Vic doesn't have allergies. He likes different scents. He's probably trying to pin down the mixture."

Lexi raised her eyebrows. "This may be a dumb question, but what's with his Silent Bob routine?"

Grant rolled his eyes and smirked. "He's superstitious. He has to do lead vocals tonight, since Trevon's come down with something. Vic tries not to overuse his voice before he has to sing. Don't take it personal."

Victor smiled and nodded, reaching out to take Lexi's hand. He held it tightly, taking more deep breaths before letting her go. He jabbed his elbow into Grant's side.

Grant shrugged, but turned back to Lexi. "Okay, it's none of my business, but this is a small town and maybe the whole gossip thing is rubbing off on me. Who are you meeting tonight?"

Lexi blinked. Whatever she'd expected him to ask, it wasn't about her dating life. "The owner, Rafferty O'Neill."

Victor snorted and Grant's face split into a wide grin. "That explains it. I wondered why the big guy came in so late last night and smiling, too. He doesn't usually even *leave* the club, much less come back happy. Now I see the reason why. Good for him."

Lexi blushed, flustered. "Thanks for the vote of confidence."

"Oh, it's definitely good for him," Grant replied, his eyes roving her body in a way that made Lexi worry about Stella and his amount of commitment to her. "Just be sure it's good for you. His kind can be over-powering for the ladies. But don't worry. Any friend of Stella's is a friend of ours. The Alphas will keep an eye out for you. If the big guy gives you any trouble, let us know. We'll take care of the rest."

Lexi let his words sink in, not certain whether to be honored or insulted. "Thanks, I'll be sure to remember that, I guess."

Victor's voice rumbled in a low growl, sending the hair on the back of Lexi's neck dancing. "It's not a promise given lightly."

Chapter Seven

Rafe paced in front of his desk, thankful for the soundproofing that prevented the customers from hearing his irritated shouts. He had neither the time nor the energy for this mess. He'd woken with the image of Lexi laughing, her dark eyes flashing as her curls cascaded down her back, making his fingers itch, only to be confronted with a situation that could be the end of his entire nest.

"You're certain the dead woman found this morning is the same woman Jordan played with, fed from?" he asked, wishing for a moment that he still prayed. He yearned for the time when he could ask for celestial aid.

"Yes, Rafe," Thane answered, darkness filling his voice. He didn't like what was happening any more than Rafe did. "I caught but a glimpse of her before they zipped up the bag, but it was enough to recognize her."

"And when I asked you to check on her before, she was well?"

Shanna nodded this time, supporting her mate. "Yes, Rafe. Thane and I went to her home again before I saw you last night and added our powers to Jordan's, making certain she'd remember nothing. She lived when we left her."

"No one saw you?"

Both Thane and Shanna shook their heads in unison. "We were careful. We aren't fledglings who can't cover their tracks. No one but an elder or ancient vampire would have sensed our presence in the woman's home."

"You'll have to excuse me if I don't find that to be a comforting thought," Rafe replied, staring at a painting of a bright dawn that hung beside his door. If another elder or ancient was involved, they were all screwed. "Jordan is still restrained?"

"As ordered, he hasn't left his room and has been fed only enough to keep him alive and sane." Thane's expression said that he wished it weren't true. They would all love a simple answer, that a hunger-crazed fledgling was responsible.

"Then who did this?!" Rafe yelled, sweeping his arm across his desk. He took dark pleasure at the sound of smashing glass. It was better than shattered bone. He was losing his tenuous control as his carefully laid plans threatened to explode around his ears.

Thane and Shanna both rocked back, and it was Shanna who answered. "We don't even know *what* did this yet."

"From all descriptions, it wasn't human," Rafe replied, striving to stay in control as his fangs sprang out and the fire behind his eyes began to spark. A glacial chill traced the edge of his words. "I want to know if it was one of our resident werewolves or if it was one of us."

"And if it was one of us?" Thane asked softly.

Rafe felt his face empty of all emotion, the skin pulling tight to the bones. He gave a nasty chuckle. "Then there will be one *less* of us to worry about. We will find out who did this. I don't care what we have to do to get answers, or how many of our people we must terrorize to obtain the information. We will find out who dared take such an action in my territory, without my consent, and he or she will be made an example of, a bloody, graphic example."

"You sound like Eldora," Shanna whispered, stepping closer to Thane.

Rafe faced his two most trusted followers, willing their support if not their agreement. "Right now, I don't care. If I have to use her tactics to keep my people safe, then I will. We are in a precarious situation, our survival at stake. If Edmund gives Eldora a good enough reason, she will pull us back into her fold and under his command. Risking our kind's exposure to the mortal world would be more than enough excuse for Edmund. After all we gambled in order to break free, do any of you want to be back under his control? Because if you thought he was vicious before, I guarantee he'll make us all think of the past with nostalgia."

"Of course not." Thane said, taking his mate's hand, lacing their fingers. Rafe didn't blame him. If he had a woman, he would die before letting Edmund near her.

Rafe wrapped the mantle of leadership around himself, the weight bearing down on his shoulders. "Then do what you have to, whatever it takes, to get the information we need. I give you my permission to use whatever means necessary."

"And when we find the culprit?" Shanna asked, staring up at Thane.

Rafe's smile, fangs gleaming, held pure, arctic ice. "We make an example of him or her that none will soon forget."

Thane kissed Shanna's knuckles before releasing her hand. "What do you plan to do in the meantime?"

"I leave this up to you two," Rafe replied, his brain struggling to switch gears. "Miss Hart, Lexi, is coming to the club."

"So, your seduction is going well?" Shanna teased, a tired attempt to break the tension.

Rafe speared his fingers through his hair and willed his fangs to retreat back into his gum-line. "She's seeing me tonight, if that's any indication. I plan on showing her what I'm building here, at least as much as a mortal should see. Win more of her trust. She's protective of her town as much as she is of her property. That is the angle I'm playing for now."

"I don't know, Rafe," Shanna repeated. "Sex always worked for me. It's my favorite angle, my favorite position. Are you certain that isn't the approach you should take? I mean, I know you haven't had much to do with human women in several decades beyond feeding, but surely you aren't *that* out of practice."

Rafe narrowed his eyes and glared at her, not comfortable with her playful teasing. It caused him to feel protective of Lexi last evening, not wanting Shanna to say something that would hurt his chances. Shanna had brought light and happiness to his somber friend, but Rafe was unsure how to handle that same warmth being directed at him. "If Lexi ends up in my bed, it won't be for her land."

Shanna smiled, knowledge of his internal response apparent. "No, it will be for her pleasure and yours. But why not kill two birds with one stone? A woman in lust is easily led."

Rafe looked at Thane, searching for his reaction to his mate's words, but meeting carefully blank eyes. "Because I don't want her in my bed for any other reason than she wants to be there and I want her there."

Thane's lips twitched. "And you do want her there, don't you? A woman you can't control, can't bend to your will. It's quite a lure."

"Shut up," Rafe snapped, done with letting these two direct the conversation. He might be unsure of his leadership abilities, but of particular strengths he was certain. "You've made your feelings known on the matter. I won't turn her. I'm not ready to turn anyone. I won't risk creating a ghoul. All we need is a soulless eating machine wandering around the town. The authorities might be convinced for now that a serial killer is using Santa del Sol as a dumping ground, but when faced with a man-eating, walking corpse, I doubt they'll remain clueless for long."

"You're strong enough to make a true vampire and not a mindless ghoul," Shanna replied without doubt. "If you want the woman, and she wants you, take her. We will stand by you. We will help guide her through the transition."

Rafe glared, letting his eyes glow again. The nest couldn't take the risk right now. "It will not happen, and that is my final word on the subject. There shall be no new fledglings, not until we understand what is happening in our town. We don't need a new fledgling to care for under these circumstances. Now go and find out what you can about these murders. Take one of the younger wolves with you. They have as much at risk as we do, and they have a better nose. Maybe they can smell something that we can't."

Thane and Shanna stood in unison, and gave a quick bow. There was a flurry of motion that a human eye wouldn't have been able to catch, and the two were gone.

The moment the door closed, Rafe collapsed into his chair, leaned both elbows on his desk, and rubbed his temples. He felt drained, hollow. If his heart could still beat, his head would have throbbed from the pounding pressure. As it was, the ghost of a headache lingered behind his eyes as all his muscles tightened.

They had come so far. His people were close to solidifying their freedom, to making their own way in this new land. Who would be stupid enough to put everything at risk? And for what?

Or worse yet, who would want to jeopardize everything on purpose, to consciously destroy all that had been gained?

The buzz of his intercom pulled Rafe out of his dark thoughts. Patricia's voice could barely be heard over the din of activity from the club. "Sir, Miss Hart has arrived. Claudette is seating her in the reserved section next to the stage."

Rafe detected an element of stress behind the words. "What's wrong? Is there a problem?"

"I couldn't say for certain, sir," she replied. He could hear her measuring each word. "Claudette didn't seem in the best of moods when she left with Miss Hart. I would suggest you step in quickly."

Just what I need—a jealous, viper-tongued vamp targeting my date. Claudette won't get it through her head that she's safe here without having to sleep with me. "I'll be right there. In the meantime make certain Gemma or Matthew picks up her table. Keep Claudette as far from Lexi as possible."

"It's already done," came Patricia's clipped reply. "I was simply concerned about any damage Claudette may have wrought already. I know you're at a delicate stage with Miss Hart. I wouldn't want anything to interfere with your plans and thought you should be made aware of the situation."

"Thank you for your diligence, Patricia. Let Lexi know I'll be there momentarily and provide her with a complimentary drink."

"Don't worry, sir. I'll do what I can to smooth out any ruffled feathers."

Rafe knew that Patricia took great pride in her skills. "I trust that you will. I'll only be a moment."

Rafe spun in his chair and reached for a closed cabinet by his desk. He pulled out a decanter of blood, swirling it in his hand before yanking out the stopper. Without bothering with a glass, he took a gulp straight from the bottle. The werewolf blood, a gift from when he first opened the club, burned through his veins. The intense, life-giving flavor mixed with something magical, making him as close to tipsy as he'd been since leaving behind his mortal life.

The heavy, punk beat joined the were-blood throbbing through his body as he walked out of his soundproofed office. He took a moment to get his bearings, letting the noise flow over him as he sighted his prey, his date.

Lexi looked particularly beautiful this night, sitting by the stage at an intimate table for two. She'd allowed her raven curls to tumble and flow freely past her shoulders, framing her delicate, classic features. Her tight, vest-like red top and flowing black skirt brought to mind nights sitting by a gypsy fire, listening to the music and dancing into forgetfulness.

Her eyes sparkled with pleasure as she watched the young werewolves romping and howling on stage, never suspecting the truth behind their wild antics. She felt the energy in the music, the abandon. He could hear the musical rhythm of her heart beating even at this distance. Though he'd fed for the night, the lure of her taste drew him across the floor.

"Enjoying the show?" he asked, surprising himself with his ability to keep hidden the jealousy beneath his words. The werewolves were an attractive, sexual race. He didn't like the thought of Lexi enjoying their presence.

Lexi looked up, her lush lips curled into a wide smile that hit him like a punch to the gut. "Yes. You've found quite a talent there. Stella's been raving about them for weeks, but I haven't heard them play before."

"The women flock to their sides in droves," Rafe couldn't help saying, watching her reaction. "I hope you won't fall prey to their musical spell."

Rafe's chest tightened as Lexi tossed her head back and laughed, exposing the long, pale line of her neck. "While I think their music has something to do with it, I'd bet that isn't their biggest appeal. I met Grant and Victor this afternoon."

"Really?" Rafe croaked, before clearing his throat. "While I have great respect for your business, it doesn't seem to me to be the type of place those two would frequent." *Sniffing around for a new bitch*, Rafe fumed, *they'd better be keeping their noses to themselves.*

"Stella's going out with Grant. They've been together for about a month now, a regular record for her."

"I hope she knows what she's getting into," he muttered, turning to look at the stage where Victor leaned down to woo a group of twenty-something girls, his husky voice crooning suggestive lyrics.

Lexi shrugged and took a sip from the fruity, frothy concoction sitting on the table in front of her. "She's used to the type. She's run with tougher crowds before and always seems to come out on top."

"I doubt there are many crowds tougher than those young men. And I doubt she'll be the one on top," Rafe commented, mindless of the double entendre.

Lexi smirked, a daring, teasing spark dancing across her face. "Well, with a name like The Alphas, I didn't think they were the shy, retiring type. But Stella will give them a run for their money if any one of them thinks he can control her. Whoever ends up on top, they'll both be satisfied with the situation."

Rafe leaned forward, towering over Lexi's chair. "And what about you? Do you want to try your luck with the hoodlums on stage?"

Lexi's eyes darkened with passion, and she licked her lips. "No, I prefer the brooding type, not the angry, young rebel. Care to try your luck?"

Never one to back down from a dare, even one he

suspected to be alcohol-induced, Rafe swooped forward, jerking Lexi out of her seat and into his arms. "Why don't we start with a dance," he whispered in her ear, delighting in her body's shivery response.

They flowed out onto the dance floor, people stepping out of their way without comment. The Alphas eased out of their perpetual punk slam-fest into a soft, soulful song, heartache filling every note. Rafe pulled Lexi into his embrace, thanking the new era for a more intimate mode of dance while cursing the years as well. He could hold Lexi against his body, feel her heat warming his cold existence. He heard the blood flowing through her veins, smelled the salty-sweet temptation lying just beneath her skin. It was an enticement he didn't know if he had the power or strength to resist. He didn't hunger, didn't need sustenance, but he wanted to know her taste. Would she be sweet? Would she be spicy? What would her life-force feel like sliding against his tongue? The slightest bit of pressure to break through and the ambrosia would flow freely into his sensation-starved body.

He throbbed in response to her nearness. His gums ached with the desire to sink his fangs deep into her delicate throat and feast on the bounty pooling just beneath the surface. His lower body ached for a different kind of piercing, but one that would join them even closer.

He settled for leaning down and covering the first area of temptation with feathery kisses. The sound of her moan as he lapped at her jugular undid him.

He felt his fangs pushing out, the need for a connection to her so great he could already taste her blood tingling against his tongue.

Suddenly, the music changed, no longer a sweet, aching seduction. Jarring tempo and a growling voice pulled Rafe back from the brink, saving Lexi from his dark kiss.

He looked up at the lead guitarist, the singer for tonight as the Alpha's usual lead vocalists voice was far from human sounding this close to the full moon. Victor had better control than Trevon. But that control didn't reflect in the heated glare Rafe received when their eyes connected.

It seemed he and the wolves needed to have a discussion about who ran things in this town. But all other reasons aside, Victor was right to interrupt Rafe. This was much too public a place to even consider what he'd been close to doing. Not to mention he had no business biting a mortal while standing in the heart of his nest. Jordan had been blocks away when feeding on a human, and Rafe nearly ripped out his throat. What kind of a leader couldn't obey his own laws?

Later that evening, Rafe drove Lexi home. Knowing that someone, human or inhuman, stalked the streets of the small town, Rafe wouldn't hear of Lexi going home alone.

"I had a wonderful evening," she said as they pulled to a stop in front of her quaint, Victorian-styled beach house. "You have a nice club, not at all what I'd imagined."

"Not the den of iniquity you'd pictured?" he teased as he walked her up the creaky steps to her front porch. He enjoyed feeling her shudder as his hand caressed the dip in her lower back.

Lexi turned to face him, leaning against her door with her hands grasping the doorknob behind her. "I already told you that you weren't the evil, blood-sucking, conglomerate money-grubber I first thought you to be. What do you want, a full-page ad in the paper declaring you not to be a bad guy?"

"That would be a nice start. But I'd rather get a more hands-on apology." He bent forward, bracing his hands on either side of her head, trapping her. His lips caressed hers for a moment before sliding down her cheek to nibble at her earlobe.

God, how her flavor called to him.

"How about I invite you in for coffee instead," she whispered, turning the knob and ducking inside.

Rafe took a step forward, crossing her threshold before pulling back. Staying with her tonight would be too much of a temptation, more than even an elder vampire would be expected to resist. The fact that she'd invited him in was enough of a victory for one night. He would always have access to her home, until she withdrew her invitation. He would enjoy that victory first.

"I'd better not."

Lexi tilted her head, a look of puzzlement tinged with hurt pride filling her bright features. He knew it wasn't an offer she often made to a man, and it had to hurt her to be turned down. He couldn't leave her thinking that he didn't want her.

Rafe reached forward, taking her by the elbows and drawing her to him. He might have to resist the siren call of Lexi's blood, but he didn't have to deny himself a taste of her sweet lips. He twisted her on her feet, catching her gasp with his mouth as he bowed her over one arm. She stiffened in his grasp, her hands clinging to his shoulders for support. She needn't have bothered. He possessed strength beyond her imaginings. Holding a grown woman in a dip was child's play.

His mouth devoured hers, unleashing every ounce of yearning he'd kept under control for so many hours near her. His tongue swept through her mouth, memorizing her taste and feel as he destroyed her senses. Small, animal whimpers rose from her throat as she dug her fingers into his hair, the pleasure/pain sending spasms through his body.

Dear God, when had it ever felt this good?

When he lifted her back to her feet, he held her a moment longer, pressing his forehead against hers. "If I stayed here tonight, even for a moment longer, I don't think I could fight temptation. Do you understand what I'm saying?"

Lexi stared, blinking at him for several moments before finding her voice. "I understand. I don't agree, but I understand."

Rafe guided her through her doorway and waited on her stoop until he heard her locks engage.

As he left, he felt eyes following his departure, burning into his back. He turned to wave to Lexi, but she wasn't there.

Rafe ignored the pit that opened in his stomach.

Chapter Eight

Amusement bubbled through Lexi at the shocked look on Stella's face. Her friend had a flair for the melodramatic. When she heard Lexi say she was taking the rest of the day off to go shopping, Stella gasped, throwing her hands in the air before declaring with an emphatic, prophetic air, "It's the second sign of the apocalypse! Hide the women and children! Run for the bomb shelters! Stock up on bottled water and canned goods! The world is about to end!"

Lexi laughed, gave a little wave, and skipped out the door to the sound of Stella's ravings.

It hadn't been *that* long since she'd shown interest in dating. Had it?

Lexi shook off her momentary doubts. It wasn't as if it were a real date. He could still be after her land, not her. And if she really believed that, she wouldn't be on her way to her favorite retro clothing store, Now and Again, on the lookout for a stunning dress to wow Rafe with.

The man made her hormones throb. She had no intention of selling out to him, but she was beginning to consider doing other things to him; naughty, nasty, wonderful things that could take all night and last into the next morning. She didn't move so fast normally, but something about him drew her.

His kiss last night left a fire burning in her veins, a dark temptation she wanted to explore. So what if his reasons were suspect? That was true of any guy, though most wanted an easy lay, not real estate. It didn't mean she couldn't enjoy the ride.

Lexi had to keep her head straight and her wits about her, enjoying him for what he was and not expecting too much. Her heart could stay out of things and let her hormones have some fun without complications.

Hell, she was in her mid-twenties and had never had a meaningless fling. This was the twenty-first century and she could do whatever the hell she wanted to.

So why was she having this internal debate?

Lexi stood with her hand on the door to Now and Again, her throat closing as her heart took a sudden leap. Dear God. Her emotions *were* involved. She liked Rafe O'Neill. If she wasn't careful, she'd be in over her head before she knew what hit her.

Was a little fun worth the possible pain? Was she over-thinking things like Stella always accused her of?

Did she really know what she was getting herself into?

Lexi gritted her teeth and pulled the door open. Her mother hadn't raised a coward. If there was risk involved, then so be it. Lexi would see things through to the end, come what may. Otherwise, she'd always wonder about what might have been. Long ago, before ever coming to Santa del Sol, she'd sworn to herself that she'd never regret things she *didn't* do. She might live to regret her actions, but not her inactions.

She'd made that decision sitting in the police department waiting for her parents to pick her up. At sixteen years old, seeing one of her friends killed in a knife fight changed her life. She wasn't as tough as she thought. She didn't want to be that tough. She never wanted to watch someone she cared for die.

From that moment on, Lexi Hart took hold of her own destiny.

With that thought firmly in place, Lexi set about plotting her own seduction. Nothing like starting with the perfect outfit.

She hummed to herself as she picked through the racks. Silks and satins of every imaginable color fluttered together in no discernable order. That was what she liked about the store. She had to hunt for what she wanted, but it was always there, hiding in plain sight.

She pulled out a black, beaded flapper dress, imagining what the woman who owned it had been like, what she'd experienced in her life. She pictured herself standing in a speakeasy, sipping bathtub gin and dancing the Charleston with a sharp dressed young man who bore a remarkable resemblance to Rafe.

Lexi chuckled and put the dress back on the rack. Daring, but not quite the look she was going for.

Next, she pulled out a multicolored gauze-and-mesh creation of the sixties. With go-go boots and her hair ironed flat, she could see herself boogieing away in a smoke-filled club. The wild abandon of an era imbued with testing and breaking boundaries filled her, enticed her.

But still, not what she wanted for her next date with Rafe.

Her fingertips tingled as they brushed a satin and gauze-covered hanger. She pulled it free and gasped. She had found *it*, the perfect dress for the perfect evening. The gown spoke of the late forties or early fifties, a gown belonging on the red carpet or in a movie filled with the opulence of old money, a dress fit for a queen.

Shimmering with the red of a stormy sunset, the long satin under-sheath cinched tight at the chest and waist to loosen into a flowing fall to the floor. The back was cut dangerously low, leaving her bare to the dip right above her bottom. Gauze over-laid the entire creation, a swirl of yellow with silver and gold thread worked in to add to the shimmering illusion of fading light.

All in all, the dress was to die for. While it was more daring and dressy than she thought her next date would be, she had to have it. A man like Rafe would eventually take her out somewhere that would do justice to the gown. And when he did, she'd knock his eyes out.

She couldn't wait and she couldn't believe what she was thinking.

It took another half-hour of picking through the shop to find the perfect shoes and handbag for the ensemble, a strappy pair of gold, high-heeled sandals and an embroidered clutch purse. But the final result was well worth the effort.

As the young girl at the counter rang up her purchase, Lexi didn't even flinch. She never spent much money on herself, so one splurge, even a huge one, wouldn't kill her. It wasn't like she'd have to live on ramen noodles for the next month to be able to afford it. Those days were long gone.

With her glorious new outfit tucked safely in a dress-bag slung over her arm and two small boxes hanging from taped-on handles looped over her wrist, Lexi began her walk to the other side of the board-walk. She didn't worry about walking alone for such a long distance to get to her car. She did it every day, and it was two hours until sunset. People crowded the beach and boardwalk. There was no way she could be in any type of danger.

Lexi carefully folded her dress into the trunk of her battered green VW bug, placing the boxes next to it. She slid behind the wheel, blowing curls out of her eyes before revving up the engine. Not as nice a ride as Rafe had, but she loved her little friend.

So it was without the slightest fear that she pulled up next to her home, juggled her purchases, and unlocked her front door. She tossed her keys on the small Victorian table placed by the door and walked straight to her bedroom. She unpacked her dress, hanging it up and smoothing it out in the same motion. She put the boxes with her shoes and purse on the floor below the dress.

She rummaged around until she came up with an old pair of sweats and some comfy slippers. She changed and went to her small, cheery yellow kitchen to make some hot tea while looking out the window at the dancing colors shimmering above the lowering sun.

As the sun sank closer to the surging waves, the sight pulled her out of her warm, peaceful home and out into the cool evening. Sipping her jasmine tea, she stepped out onto her porch to watch the waves ebb and flow until the setting sun finished its descent. She'd surprise Rafe by meeting him at the club later, but now was her time. Time to relax and enjoy life.

But something caught her attention, a strange smell that didn't fit. She put her tea down on the railing of her porch and took a deep whiff, fighting her gag reflex. It smelled rancid, curdling at the back of her throat. It smelled like something dead washed up on the beach.

What was it with her, dead things, and the beach?

She followed her nose and stepped off her porch. She started walking towards the shore, but the scent lessened with each step she took away from her home. She turned back, sniffing around her porch. Damn, something must have crawled under and died. Just what she wanted to deal with before getting ready to surprise a guy, but if she left it, that smell would ooze into her house. She hoped the smell didn't seep into her skin. *Eau d'road kill* didn't seem very seductive.

She went to the small shed where she kept her tools and grabbed a rake. That way she wouldn't have to touch rotting house cat or whatever the creature turned out to be. She shoved it under the porch, sweeping it around and hoping to snag something before pulling it back out. With any luck, she'd get it in one try and be done with it. Tugging on the handle, it felt like she had something.

When Lexi yanked the rake out from under her porch, she stared at the dirt-caked object she'd managed to drag out. For a moment, her mind refused to grasp the significance of it, the horror.

A single hand curled at her feet. A single, severed, manicured hand.

Lexi dropped the rake and gagged, stumbling back. Terror, stark and vivid, swept through her like a crashing wave. Clapping a hand over her mouth, she darted inside for her phone.

Her fingers trembled as she dialed, mentally thanking whoever had come up with the idea of making the emergency number only three digits long. She couldn't have managed punching more.

Again, the police arrived within minutes. Lexi's hands shook as she pulled back the bolt-lock to let them in, her fragile control hanging by a thread. Her voice quivered as she told the officers where the hand was. Two went out to take a look, while another took her by the shoulders and led her to her couch.

The officer that sat with her, a young woman who'd stopped by Lexi's shop a few times, asked her questions. Where had she been that day? How long had she been away from her house? Who'd seen her? Had she used her card for her purchases or had she paid cash?

Lexi answered, her voice monotone and her face numb. The chill settling inside her grew to a tight, pulsing knot of fear. How could something like this happen to her, in her home, her sanctuary from the stress of daily life? Out on a public beach was one thing, but her home?

The other officers came back, gesturing for the woman questioning Lexi to join them. Lexi sat, shivering and watching as the officers whispered amongst themselves and looked at her every so often.

When she came back, the officer took Lexi by the shoulder. "We're going to close your house off. You need to pack what you can't live without for a few days and come with us to the station. You'll need to answer some more questions, and you can call someone to pick you up from there."

Lexi nodded, not even noticing that the officer followed her as she packed a couple of outfits and her toiletry. She felt cold, shocked, disconnected.

At the police station, she was questioned thoroughly, but time began to blur. She had to account for every minute of her last week, as well as she could remember. Lexi thanked her lucky stars for her sudden increase in a social life. She'd always been with other people except for the time she was asleep.

After what seemed an endless interrogation, the police finally let her go and make some calls.

Stella answered her cell on the first ring. Lexi could barely make her out over the sound of music, chatter, and laughter. "Hello," she shouted.

"Stella, it's Lexi. I need you to pick me up at the police station."

Stella laughed, clearly not grasping the seriousness of Lexi's situation. "Yeah right, pull the other one."

Lexi didn't have the time or the energy for her friend's disbelief. "Yeah right. Pick me up at the police station. And I need a place to stay for a few nights, if the offer's still good and you don't mind the company."

Her tone must've gotten through to Stella. Her friend dropped the laughter. "What's going on? Why are you at the police station? What did you do? What do they think you did? Whatever it is, we'll get you the best lawyer credit cards can buy."

Lexi looked around her, at anxious, shell-shocked victims and both snide and terrified criminals walking by in cuffs. "I don't want to talk about it over the phone. I'm not under arrest and haven't been accused of anything. But I'm stuck here, and I can't go back to my place. Please, Stella, I'm hanging on by a thread. Ask me about it later. I'm sick to death of answering questions. You answer mine for a change. How soon can you be here?"

"Five minutes, ten tops," Stella dropped her voice as low as she could and still be heard of the din. "Are you all right?"

"I'm as good as could be expected. Just get here."

Stella must have heard the tears in Lexi's voice, because she didn't argue.

Lexi hung up the phone, then dialed again, a new number she already knew by heart. When a woman answered the phone this time, Lexi didn't feel a jab of jealousy, only disappointment. "Hello, Nocturne."

"Hello, am I speaking to Patricia?" she asked, to be certain.

"Yes," the woman's clip voice answered.

"This is Lexi Hart. I need to leave a message for Rafe."

"I can get him if you'd like," Patricia was quick to offer, making Lexi wonder what Rafe had told her. "He's in a meeting, but I'm certain he wouldn't mind the interruption."

"No, no. That isn't necessary," Lexi jumped in. "I'd planned on stopping by tonight, but something's come up. Would you let him know that if he needs to contact me that he can reach me on my cell. I'll be staying with a friend for a few nights."

"I'll let him know. Is there anything else?"

Lexi sighed. Telling Patricia that she was at the police station wasn't high on her to-do list. She didn't want to talk to a complete stranger about what happened, but Rafe deserved a heads up in case they check on her alibi. "You might want to tell him the police will be asking him some questions about my whereabouts for the last few days."

Patricia's immediate reaction didn't surprise Lexi. "Is everything all right? Are you certain you don't want me to get Mr. O'Neill?"

"I'm fine, and I'd rather talk to him later when I'm more collected," Lexi reassured Rafe's assistant, downplaying the fear stalking her in an effort to banish it. "Something happened at my house while I wasn't home. The police will be checking it out. Everything is fine."

"If you say so, Miss," Patricia's voice echoed with disbelief. "But I can guarantee that Mr. O'Neill will be calling this evening to hear that from you."

Lexi grimaced, watching as another shift of officers marched out of the station. "That's fine. Tell him I'll be staying with Stella."

"I will." For a moment, Patricia's voice lost the efficient secretary tone, flowing into that of a comforting friend. "And watch out for yourself. You heard about what happened yesterday? No woman should be alone right now."

"You don't know the half of it."

Chapter Nine

"You should have forwarded her call immediately," Rafe snarled at Patricia while Thane scurried out of the room to call his contact with the police department and find out what was happening with Lexi Hart. Alarm and anger sent Rafe stalking across the room to glare down at his most trusted servant.

Patricia stood her ground, even if she didn't meet his gaze. "Miss Hart didn't want me to disturb you."

"And her desires outweigh mine? You serve me, not her." The growl coming from Rafe had been known to send grown warriors to their knees, terror holding them prisoner.

Again, Patricia surprised Rafe with her trust or her courage by holding still before the force of his fury. "Of course not, sir. But she was adamant that her position wasn't urgent. And she sounded on the edge, sir. I remember that sound in my own voice. She needed time to herself, with her own thoughts. And she left a number for you to contact her as well as where she would be staying. I felt that was enough to ask of her at the moment."

Rafe trembled with restrained rage, no suitable

outlet available. Until he knew what had happened, he couldn't strike back. Lexi was his, until he said otherwise. Any who thought to threaten her must deal with him first.

Someone was going behind his back, and he would have none of it.

Thane rushed back into the room, startling Patricia who saw nothing until he appeared beside her.

"Well?" Rafe asked, staring at his second-in-command with a single arched brow.

Thane ticked off the facts, emotionless. "A body was dumped at Alexandria Hart's house, under it to be precise. The body is that of a female, age twenty to thirty. She'd been completely dismembered: hands, feet, head, legs, arms, and torso. My source tells me that she died sometime yesterday evening, the precise time to be determined. Lexi was attracted by the smell and found the woman's right hand. She's been questioned and the police are in the process of eliminating her as a suspect. No one believes she could be capable of doing such a thing, but, under the circumstances, they're following strict procedures."

The lack of information about the investigation left Rafe unsatisfied. And an unsatisfied Rafe was something to be feared. "Human or inhuman?"

Thane's voice remained expressionless. "My source couldn't say for certain. One of us will have to go to the morgue to see. But I find it hard to believe that this murder isn't connected to the others, all three coming so quickly and being so vicious in nature."

"Someone or something is sending a message." Rafe stepped out from behind his desk, his anger filling the room and spiking the temperature. No one else had the bravery or stupidity to move. "I want a meeting with every non-human in the club, immediately. Let the mortals take care of things their way. We need to talk."

"What about the Alphas?" Thane asked.

"Tell them to end their first set. I need to speak to them as well. Have everyone meet in the center chamber."

Rafe dismissed his most trusted followers with a wave of his hand. They would do as he asked, no questions and without delay, or pay the penalty.

Dim lamps lit the circular chamber hidden deep beneath Nocturne, a room not listed in the blueprints registered with City Hall. Located deeper than the panic rooms the vampires used for their temporary homes, this single hall had better security than most government facilities. Lined first with a steel alloy, then layered with brick and stone, the only way in was the single, guarded, coded, and locked door to the surface. Only one other door existed in the chamber, leading to a huge pantry filled with a separate generator and refrigerators and freezers filled with raw meat and bags and bottles of blood.

Rafe called it his siege room.

In the middle of the center chamber, a small, eclectic crowd gathered. Werewolves and vampires stood shoulder to shoulder, waiting to hear what the owner of the only sanctuary in Northern California had to say. It was the first time since his arrival that the Master had called such an interracial meeting. Curiosity and fear ran high.

Rafe glared out at the crowd, letting each member

feel the extent of his anger as the temperature in the room rose one degree at a time.

"There is one among us who endangers us all," he shouted without preamble over the din of chatter. "I charge each and every one of you to find this renegade and bring him to me."

"What has this one done that is so heinous as to put all of us at risk?" a voice answered from the back of the crowd. Others muttered in agreement.

"Three women have been murdered, in a fashion violent enough to attract unwanted attention," Rafe answered, his voice booming over the babble of the doubtful. "All three victims were torn to pieces. All three victims were found missing both flesh and blood. A member of the supernatural community killed all three women. To bring that kind of death to our doorstep risks this safe haven for us all."

Rafe swept forward, the crowd parting for him as he walked to the center of the room. He stopped, staring out at the masses surrounding him. "When my people and I came here, came to you, we all made a pact. This community, especially this club, became a neutral zone. Here there would be no hunting. Here, we would all be safe. Someone has broken the pact. I charge you all to find this creature and bring him to justice."

"Whose justice?" a low voice growled. "Your justice? We are not your fledglings to keep in line. We are the Wolf. We answer to no man and no vampire."

Several members of the group howled and nodded in agreement. Rafe couldn't let this get out of hand. The danger to all could not be overshadowed by petty ethnic differences. "This has nothing to do with who is the stronger. This creature has broken your laws and your pact as well as those of my people. He or she will face us all. We will decide his or her fate together. But we must find the culprit, and quickly. With such sensational murders, the media will be attracted to the carnage, and then there will be no hiding for any of us."

"You fear being brought back to your own creator as a failure," the older, gray-haired werewolf snapped, challenging as he stepped forward. He led many of the wolves in the room, and would make a formidable enemy for Rafe should he mishandle the situation. "You do not care what happens to any of us. As long as your daytime hiding place is safe and you don't have to face your Dark Lady, nothing else matters."

"If my nest is called back, as you suggest, we all lose," Rafe responded, stressing their common goals as he walked towards his challenger. "The treaty will be broken and no safe harbor will exist for any creature, mortal or immortal. Is this what you want? Before we came, before we all banded together, your pack was hunted to near oblivion. My nest took care of the hunters, bent their minds and removed all evidence of your existence. Do you want to risk becoming prey again, losing your women and children to the hunters?"

"No," another wolf called out from deep within the crowd, silencing the first. "We don't wish for that."

Grant stepped forward, a hush falling as the wolves in the group stepped back to let him through. "Share your information with the wolves. We will hunt for you. We give you our word that the oath-breaker will be found and brought to our collective judgment."

"And who says you speak for all the wolves here?" the first wolf asked, bristling with authority and dominance. "You may be an alpha, but you haven't proven yourself to be leader of every wolf here, only your own pack."

Grant's body shivered. Had he been in his fur, Rafe knew Grant would've puffed up. His voice fell down into a snarl. "Do you challenge me?"

The other werewolf tore off his shirt, muscles already rippling and contorting. "Yes," he sneered, the word barely able to make it out of his lengthening snout.

Grant wasted no time, falling to all fours and letting the change rip him out of his clothes. Rafe respected the werewolf as a cool-headed leader, but had never had the occasion to see him in battle.

It looked like tonight was the night to settle many issues. Not only was it the first time the Master Vampire called out to all creatures to support their treaty, it looked as though an overall leader of the werewolf population would be decided as well. After months of diplomacy, of trying to forge an alliance with all the fractured packs in the area, it came down to this. If Grant won the challenge, sanctuary would stand. If he lost, Rafe and his people would fight alone, no one else guarding their backs.

Howls filled the hall as the wolves crowded round, marking off the space for this battle over supremacy.

Grant tossed his head up, growling and snapping at his opponent even as his legs gained their last bit of extra muscles and snapped violently into a more canine shape. The other wolf leapt forward, swiping with massive claws and snapping his powerful jaws. He aimed for Grant's neck, trying for a quick, decisive end.

But Grant flew into motion, mid-aid when the other wolf landed. He grabbed the older wolf by the hair, pulling his head back and forcing him to the ground at the same instant. He used one of the wolf's arms to leverage him back, opening him further for attack.

The other wolves stamped and howled, jostling each other for a better view.

The older wolf spun and snapped, letting his shoulder be forced out of socket with a stomach turning crunch of cartilage. He rolled back, distancing himself from Grant to gain recovery time.

Grant gave him no quarter. The wolf barely had time to pop his shoulder back into place before Grant raked his claws down his back then snaked around to find purchase in the soft stomach tissue.

The other wolf lashed out, catching the side of Grant's face. Skin split like a ripe melon, laying open his cheek and slicing into his left eye. Grant stumbled back, but remained silent save for a deep growl that echoed through the hall and sent chills down Rafe's spine.

He wouldn't want to take on Grant if it could be helped. Win or lose, the cost in blood would be too dear.

But the lupine crowd went wild, yipping and howling as the smell of blood from both combatants filled the air. The entire room smelled of warm bodies, deep night, blood, and rage.

Grant stepped back, circling his prey, head tracing his every movement. His opponent might be older, but he was a tough, experienced fighter. Grant would do well to remember that and not get too cocky.

The other wolf held his arm close to his chest, clenching and unclenching his fingers. It would heal quickly, but not quickly enough to do him much good in this fight. It was a disadvantage. Of course, with his now limited vision, Grant also had a handicap, one that would heal as he changed back to human but not before.

So the two circled each other, looking for an opening, the first sign of weakness. Grant growled and snapped, feinting with both hands reaching for his opponent's midriff.

That movement triggered the other wolf's downfall. He leaned forward, protecting his belly while preparing to launch forward in attack. But Grant was ready. He didn't move his arms back, instead twisting them upwards to slice across the other wolf's neck.

Blood sprayed through the room as the artery spewed forth. Even Rafe couldn't help reacting to the warm, metallic scent permeating the air. It was a testament to his control over his nest that his vampires didn't dive into the fray and feast.

Grant leapt forward, locking his teeth across the wound and ripping it wider, deeper. The other wolf had only a moment to gurgle, bubbles and blood filling his throat, before the loss sent him, lifeless, to his knees.

Grant stood, hurled back his head, and howled in triumph. Other members of his pack, now the highest ranking of all packs present, joined their voices in the celebration.

Bones cracked and muscles pulsed once more as Grant regained his human aspect, healing his wounds. He bent down, grabbed the dead wolf, and dragged the body to Rafe.

"This one would have broken our treaty, the word of every werewolf in this room. I offer you his blood as recompense. My apologies for any insult to you and yours. We wolves hold ourselves to our bonds. We will help find the one who threatens all our safety."

Rafe nodded, his shoulders relaxing. If he had Grant's support, the rest of the wolves would fall into line. Rafe won a small battle in this war by gaining Grant's cooperation.

"Pick who you wish to represent you and send them to my office. Thane will give you all the information we have." Rafe turned back to the crowd. "As for the rest of you, seek out this creature in your own way. If it is discovered that you are aiding him or her, you will share the same fate." He looked down at the body, nudging it with a foot. "And I believe we can all imagine what form of punishment we as a group will come up with. I promise you, it will not be quick, and it will be excruciating."

Rafe watched as all the people left, muttering to themselves and looking back at him. He didn't want to be a ruler, but every time he turned around, the role was thrust upon him. Someone had to keep order, keep the monsters of the world from creating chaos and anarchy. If that someone had to be him, well then so be it.

But it was a lonely place to stand.

Stella's home was a small, loft apartment above a bakery. Rafe supposed, in his human life, he would have enjoyed the smell of fresh baked bread greeting him every morning. As it was, the scent only held a faint sense of nostalgia, of a distant home and hearth. He hoped it gave Lexi some comfort after her terrifying evening.

Seeing your first body shook a person to the core. This he remembered with perfect, bloody clarity from his vicious, uncontrollable fledgling days.

It was several moments after his knock that he heard the locks disengage. He knew someone stood looking out before letting him in. Her heartbeat raced, the loud pounding audible even through the two inches of wood.

But he stood patient, concentrating on portraying the picture of understanding and sympathy, a man waiting to comfort his woman. He felt none of it. Overwhelming anger and protectiveness flooded him, filling him with the urge to drag Lexi away and lock her in one of his panic rooms, where he could keep close watch and protect her from any threat.

But it wasn't Lexi who opened the door. Stella, her jagged, multi-colored hair pulled up in a ponytail on the crown of her head, gave Rafe a weak smile. "I wondered how long it would take you to get down here. Two and a half hours. Lexi owes me a twenty. I bet her it would take at least two or three to break away."

"Some things are more important than business,"

he replied, staring at her arm blocking the door. "How is she?"

"Shaken, but better than when I first picked her up. I guess finding a dead chick tucked in under your house would freak anyone out, and the police questioning didn't help any. Hell, that makes two this week, since she was the one to spot the first girl," Stella answered as she stepped back and gestured for Rafe to follow her inside.

Rafe took that as an invitation and stepped inside, taking in the bright colors and open spaces of Stella's loft. Then her words registered. "Lexi found two of the three bodies? I didn't know, hadn't heard. Surely she's not a suspect because of that," he replied, as it seemed like the thing to say if he hadn't already investigated the incident.

Stella walked to the middle of the large room, where several wood-panel screens and sheer curtains divided the living area from where she had a dining table set up. She pushed back a yellow curtain before answering. "Well, they didn't arrest her or anything. But it is her property, and she did find two of the bodies."

"And now isn't the time to tell me how none of this would have happened if I'd sold to you when I had a chance," Lexi finished for Stella, looking up from the over-stuffed couch she stretched across.

Rafe took a moment to look his fill. She wore an old, gray sweatsuit and had her bare feet propped on the coffee table. Her toenails bore a fresh coat of strawberry-colored paint. A bowl of half-eaten popcorn sat perched in her lap, and her beautiful, black curls lay in two long plaits on either side of her head.

Rafe had never seen a more beautiful sight.

He glanced at Stella and gave her a mental push. She mumbled something about drinks and scurried for the kitchen.

Rafe sat down next to Lexi, taking the bowl from her lap and setting it on the table. He took both her hands in his and kissed her knuckles, holding tight to her warmth. "I'm so glad that you're unharmed. When I received your message, and having read about the other murder, I was certain you'd been attacked. Next time, please demand to talk to me. I don't ever want to feel that way again, unknowing and powerless."

Lexi gave a weak smile, but gripped his hands as though he was the last solid thing in her crumbling world. "I didn't mean to worry you. I wasn't thinking too clearly. Hell, if I had been, I would've called my lawyer as soon as they brought me to the station."

"You had every reason to be off-balance." He let go of one hand to reach up and cup her cheek, the silky smooth feel of her skin caressing his palm. "I can only imagine how frightening that must have been for you."

"I keep wondering, keep thinking, how long was she under there?" she whispered, leaning into his touch with closed eyes. "Was she there while I slept last night? Did we stand on top of her when you kissed me goodnight? How long does it take a body to smell like that?"

"Not as long as you would think," he muttered under his breath. At her questioning look, he continued. "If it makes you feel any better, she may have been dead long before she was dumped there. It might have happened this afternoon for all you know. Obviously, she didn't die under your porch. I know it sounds cold, but there's no telling how long she was dead before she ended up under your porch."

"Then why put her there?" Lexi asked, her eyes bright with pain. "What purpose did it serve? Did they want me to find her? Do they want to scare me? Am I next?"

That was the question weighing heaviest on Rafe's mind, the why. Was Lexi the next intended victim? Had she been targeted because of his interest in her? Was this a warning or a threat?

Was he going to get Lexi killed?

"Listen, pack up your things and come with me," He said, his hand sliding from her cheek to grab her shoulder. "You'll stay in one of the guest rooms at the club. We have top-notch security. You'll be safe there."

Lexi blinked. "You want me to stay with you?"

Rafe ignored the incredulity in her voice, pushing for her to obey. "Just for the duration. I want to know you're safe."

Lexi shook her head, trying to pull out of his embrace. "I'm safe here. I'm in the middle of town. The police have already arranged for round the clock surveillance of Stella's place, my house, and the shop. I don't need to stay with you to be safe."

Rafe stared at her, willing her compliance with every ounce of his power, his grip tightening on her shoulder and hand. "Then do it for my peace of mind."

Lexi showed no sign of relenting. "It's my peace of mind that's important right now, not yours. I know this place. I know Stella. I feel safe here, not in a club that's going to be raging all night, keeping me awake, filled with people I don't know and don't trust."

Rafe eased his grip on her hand, not wanting to hurt her, but wanting to hurt something. He could hear her heart pounding with the rhythm of her anger, the color of blood rushing to her face. He ran his tongue over and over his top teeth, feeling the tingling of the flesh above his canines where his fangs lay sheathed.

He hadn't fed since right before the meeting. While it kept his hunger at bay then, faced with Lexi, Rafe found it harder and harder to resist. His desire for her blood went beyond a bodily need. His craving tore at him now that he had such a tender, warm specimen within easy striking distance.

As much as he hated leaving Lexi, he had to get away from her before *he* became the threat.

He dropped his hands from her, leaping to his feet. Lexi looked startled, but he didn't have time to explain his behavior, not now. If he didn't get out of here soon, there would be hell to pay, for both of them.

But he couldn't resist looking back at her again. She was dangerous to him, a weakness, but one he couldn't rid himself of, even as it grew. "I can't stay, but I had to see that you were safe. We'll continue this discussion later."

With those words, he spun and left the loft as quickly as he could without seeming inhuman. Outside in a darkened alley, he met with Thane.

"Keep watch over her," Rafe snarled, his fangs flashing in the dim light. "I charge you with her protection. Make certain no others approach her. Do you understand?"

Thane said nothing, only nodded.

Rafe grimaced. "I trust you, Thane. I only trust you and Shanna. I can't watch over Lexi, as much as I might want. I'm going to the morgue to start the hunt myself."

"I understand, Rafe. Maybe better than you do," Thane replied, clasping Rafe's shoulder. "I'd kill anyone who tried to harm Shanna, and I'll protect your woman with the same ferocity."

"She's not my woman," Rafe snarled before racing in the opposite direction.

"Not yet," Thane whispered at the retreating form, knowing Rafe could still hear him. "But she will be."

Chapter Ten

Lexi stared at the door in stunned disbelief. He hadn't actually said all that. He couldn't be as primitive, chest-poundingly male as he sounded.

Could he?

And how dare he leave in the middle of an argument! He stops by for a couple of minutes to check on her, and then leaves? He expected her to believe he was romantically interested in her, but pulls this kind of crap? Did he think she was an idiot?

Stella walked around the curtain, carrying a pot of hot tea and three cups.

"Dump the tea," Lexi pouted, crossing her arms. "Chamomile isn't going to cut it this time. This just became a quart of cookie-dough ice-cream situation."

"Are we talking diet soda and corn chips, too?" Stella asked, putting the tea and cups down on the table and sitting beside Lexi.

Lexi rubbed her stomach, contemplating her choices of dietary sins. So many calories, so little room. "No, call the pizza place. I'm thinking pepperoni and Canadian bacon."

"Whoa, you're suffering from something way beyond shock," Stella replied. "We're moving into guy problem territory."

"You said it. Now be a good best friend and gather the supplies while I mope. By the time you're done, I'll be switching into vent mode."

Stella snorted, casting her eyes towards the heavens for divine inspiration. "Well, he might not have done it in a way I would've enjoyed hearing about, but you've got to give Rafe credit."

"For what?" Lexi sulked.

"He's got your mind off today."

Lexi stared at the ceiling and counted the cracks before glaring at her friend. "I'd be careful what I said if I were you. You *are* the one who talked me into going out with Rafe in the first place. Any jerky behavior I have to put up with now, I can land squarely in your corner."

Stella smirked. "Like you wouldn't find someone else to blame if I hadn't."

"Are you saying I don't take responsibility for my own actions?" Lexi asked, a dangerous warning lurking in her voice. With anger already riding her hard, it wouldn't be difficult to redirect it.

"I think you take too much responsibility. You think too much, you over-analyze, and you cast blame. But somehow you manage to be blind and loyal at the same time, which is the only reason I put up with you. Now shut up, turn off your head, and relax. We'll commiserate when I finish ordering the feast."

Lexi smiled, tension easing. Stella's words worked, as she had planned, pulling Lexi out of the self-defeating doldrums that threatened her peace of mind. Staying with Stella after everything that had happened was the best thing she could've done. Stella would force her to find her balance, taking each hurdle as though it was situation normal. Stella never had anything strange happen to her, because as far as she was concerned, everything that happened in life had to be normal.

And Lexi appreciated that attitude.

She tilted her head back and closed her eyes, her yoga mantra rolling through her mind and anchoring her in the moment. She could hear Stella's voice in the distance, but concentrated on clearing her thoughts. She didn't have the strength to deal with Rafe's attitude right now. She needed to shove it aside, into a back corner of her mind until she could pull it out and examine it. In the meantime, focusing on dealing with the corpses that kept popping up when she hit the beach took priority.

The police couldn't think she had anything to do with it. She'd lived in the town for years and had a solid reputation. Any misdeeds of her past were sealed in juvenile records and were nowhere near this magnitude, a little shoplifting and vandalism while traveling with a pack of young thugs. Rebellious youth getting back at an over-protective male family. That old history wouldn't work against her now, after she'd worked so hard to make something of herself.

Why was this happening? Why now? What had she done to bring this on herself? Lexi was a great believer in nothing happening without a reason, if you looked hard enough. But what reason was there in this kind of violent insanity?

Lexi felt like she was in the center of a hurricane, no way out to be seen in any direction.

She hated being at the mercy of fate and the actions of others. She lived by her logical mind, having total control over her life and her environment. Someone had taken that control away from her. She had to figure out who, and why.

Otherwise, she wouldn't be able to kick his ass for putting her through this emotional upheaval.

And until she settled this, she couldn't concentrate on Rafe. And it didn't matter how she shoved him and his macho attitude into that box in the back of her head, he kept coming out and teasing her. Damn it, how much was one woman supposed to take before going insane?

Over-thinking, over-thinking, over-thinking. She had to shut down her mind or go mad from over-thinking.

Stella hopped back over to the couch, a huge grin splitting her face.

"What?" Lexi asked, her voice filled with suspicion.

"We're going to have company," she replied in a singsong voice, eyeing Lexi in a way that brought to mind her misspent youth.

"You're getting me into trouble. I just know you're getting me in trouble."

Stella's look of practiced innocence caused the hair on the back of Lexi's neck to stand on end. "No way. You're imagining things again. You need cheering up, and we both need to feel safe tonight. So I called in the reinforcements."

"I thought you were calling for pizza," Lexi replied, eyes narrowing.

"That too. I ordered extra, because the guys can pack away the food."

"The guys?" Lexi asked, although she had a pretty good idea who Stella meant.

"The Alphas," her friend replied with a dreamy grin. "They had an early set tonight and are off now, so I asked Grant if he'd mind coming over and keeping an eye on two lonely, frightened females. He's bringing a couple of his friends for backup."

Lexi couldn't believe her friend's lack of priorities. "I find a body under my house, and your solution is to set up an orgy?"

"No, silly. I'm lining up bodyguards; sexy, mouth-watering bodyguards. Grant's bringing sleeping bags, and they'll be crashing out by the door. That way, anyone trying to get to the two of us will have to fight their way through the guys first." Stella picked up a chenille blanket and tucked it around Lexi. "Think of them as a warm, hunky early-warning system."

Lexi smirked as her mind shot to the real reason for Stella's invitation. "Plus, you spend more time with Grant while getting back at Rafe for hurting me. He *is* the owner of Nocturne. He *will* find out where his band is, won't he?"

"I wouldn't be surprised if Grant mentioned staying over at my place, playing the protector," Stella said, her musical voice shaking with suppressed glee. "I mean, why shouldn't he watch over me? I'm a woman living alone, with a mad killer on the loose. It makes perfect sense that Grant would come and spend the night."

"Right, perfect Stella-sense." Lexi snuggled in, letting the warmth of the blanket settle deep in her bones. "You should write a book about your pearls of wisdom. It would make the American Psychological Foundation proud."

"Yeah, yeah, keep laughing," Stella griped, sitting down on the floor on a pink pillow with the word 'Diva' embroidered on it. "Just you wait and see. I'm right. This way we're safe, and we get to make Rafe jealous at the same time. What more could you want?"

"Right now, I doubt Rafe will get jealous over me," Lexi grumbled, her lower lip sticking out as she thought of how the man practically ran out of Stella's apartment.

"Are we talking about the same man who rushed over here, just to see if you were all right?"

Lexi glared at Stella, not willing to let her friend cheer her up. She was headed for a good, old-fashioned pity party and didn't want to be distracted. "Yes, he's the same one who rushed out before saying more than three sentences to me."

Stella surprised Lexi by defending Rafe, something unheard of from the normally hormone-driven, Uber-feminist. "I'm sure he had his reasons, and until you know them, you can't make any judgments. Sheesh, as the thinker in the group, you should've put that together for yourself without my help."

"Then why try to make him jealous? If he had his reasons, shouldn't I take him on faith, trust him?" Lexi taunted, while deep inside wanting an honest answer.

"To hell with that," Stella snapped, not giving Lexi her sought after soft words of condolence. "Just because he had his reasons doesn't mean he was right. He deserves to face the consequences of his actions,

119

especially if it means I get to invite several hot guys over to my house for a sleep-over."

Lexi rolled her eyes and threw a pillow at Stella. Her friend ducked, laughing. "The truth comes out at last," Lexi said with a dramatic sigh. "I'm the excuse you need to live out some prurient fantasy of your own. At least be honest with yourself about your motives."

The Cheshire cat grin on Stella's face sent shivers down Lexi's spine. "Who says I'm not honest with myself? I'm talking to you."

Lexi giggled. She couldn't help it. Stella put the absurd back into life.

Just then, a knock sounded at the door. Stella scurried to answer it, careful to look out the peephole before disengaging the bolt-lock. Three men stood in the doorway, identical wolfish grins on their faces. Grant and Victor, Lexi recognized as she leaned over on the couch and peered around the curtain. The third man, dressed in the same casual clothes as the other members, she'd seen only on stage. He was the bass guitarist if she remembered correctly.

Stella shooed them in.

After the other two passed him, Grant bent down and kissed Stella. "Hey, Starry Eyes. I'm sorry you had to run out like that. How's your friend doing?"

"Why does everyone keep asking her that when I'm right here?" Lexi called out from her spot on the couch.

"After the evening you've had, I expected you to be conked out already," Grant answered, swaggering over to her. "Since you're still awake, I'll ask you. How are you holding up?"

Lexi shrugged, but pulled the blanket tighter, finding comfort in her cocoon. "Well as can be expected, I guess. I'll feel better when the police tell me I'm not a suspect. But I don't know how I'm going to face my home after this. I wonder if I should fumigate or have an exorcism? What do you think?"

"When in doubt, do both," came Grant's quick answer. "It can't hurt anything and, contrary to popular belief, peace of mind *can* be bought."

Lexi stared at him, his teasing features serious. "I was joking."

Grant smiled, flipping a piece of shaggy hair out of his eyes. "Maybe, but it might help."

"The fumigation, maybe, but an exorcist?" Lexi shook her head. "I don't think so. I live in California, not the Twilight Zone."

"Life *is* an episode of the Twilight Zone. And the sooner you realize that, the better off you'll be," the third man said as he walked to the other side of the room to look out the window.

"Quinton," Grant growled, warning in his voice.

"Hey, don't get mad at the guy," Lexi rose to the defensive. "I found a body stuck under my house today. You don't get much more Twilight Zone than that."

The other man turned and gave her a surprised smile. "You're right, Grant. I do like her." He walked back to Lexi, his eyes roaming over her from head to toe, a seductive appraisal. "Too bad about Rafe, though. He got to her first, but I don't think he's worthy of her. She'd be safer with one of us."

"She has a name, you know. And she doesn't like

being talked about like she's an inanimate object," Lexi replied, glaring up at the man.

He smiled, bowing to her. "I apologize, Miss Hart. You're right, and my mother would rip me for my bad manners. My name is Quinton, and it is an honor to meet you, even under such unpleasant circumstances."

For some reason, the man's touch neither attracted nor repelled her. It simply was, giving her strength and solace. "That's better. And call me Lexi. Miss Hart makes me sound like somebody's maiden aunt, like I should own a dozen cats or something."

Quinton released her hand as a child-like smile spread across her face. "Okay, Lexi it is. You don't look like a cat person to me, more a fan of canines."

"Sorry, no pets at all. I had a fish that lasted six months, and he was a survivor. I can't even keep plants alive."

"Dogs are self-sufficient. They let you know when they need something. And as a single woman, a big, vicious-looking canine might be a good friend to have around."

Lexi considered it, thought of the comfort to be found in a mass of fangs and muscles under a coat of fur ready to defend her at a moments notice out of unconditional love. "Well, all things considered, you might be right in that."

Grant moved in between them, plopping down beside Lexi on the couch. "Be a bud and grab us something to drink."

Quinton rolled his eyes, but ducked behind the curtain in the direction of the kitchen. Victor sat down on the floor, leaning against the wall and facing the couch. Stella pulled her large pink pillow out and sat on the floor in front of Grant.

"Do you feel safer with us here, or would you rather we left?" Grant asked Lexi, his expression gentle, filled with sympathy.

Lexi shrugged, but couldn't meet his gaze, afraid he'd see how needy she felt. "It sounds silly, but I do feel better with you guys here. Stella's great company. She can keep my mind off what happened and keep me laughing, but she wouldn't be much good if some psycho broke in."

Grant looked down at Stella, a warm, endearing smile covering his face. "I don't know about that. I think Stella can handle anything life throws at her. She's been handling me well enough these last few weeks."

"Yeah, but it takes brawn and testosterone to make a girl feel safe. I don't rank high on either count," Stella replied, stacking her hands on his knee and resting her chin on top.

He reached down to cup her cheek. "And the moment you said you needed me, I came."

Lexi felt her skin heat as she watched her friend light up beneath Grant's soft touch. Maybe, for once, Stella had found the real thing. Maybe Grant wouldn't be the flavor of the month.

It gave a girl hope, but that didn't mean Lexi wanted a ringside seat for the festivities.

"Thank you for staying with us," she said, trying to break the rapidly heating sexual tension or at least tone it down. "Even if you are doing it as a favor for Stella."

Grant looked up, his hand still cupped around

Stella's cheek. "I'm glad she asked us to help. I like you, Lexi. And as much as we joke about him, we all like Rafe. He's fair and considerate, if stuffy and laced too tight. Staying the night and making you feel safe is the least we can do."

Quinton stepped around the curtain with a tray full of drinks. He passed them out, and then pulled up a piece of floor near Lexi. "Now, don't you start feeling guilty about bothering us or any nonsense like that. You're a friend, even if it's through Stella. If it weren't for Stella and Rafe, maybe you'd be more than a friend, but that's out of the question. So you're a friend, and we watch out for our friends. Drink your soda, pig out on pizza when it gets here, and sleep well."

Lexi nodded, snuggling back on the couch and listening to the three men and Stella laugh and joke, almost like a family, a real family.

Chapter Eleven

Rafe glided past the people milling about the morgue without pause. He cloaked their thoughts with ease, slipping through the shadows of their minds. The smell of antiseptic death filled the air, blocking any other scents he might pick up, partially blinding him as well. Sometimes Rafe forgot how much his sense of smell helped guide him to his prey. It disturbed him to think about being dependent on anything.

He flipped through the minds and memories of passers-by, seeking directions to where bodies were stored, particularly the ones so recently murdered. It wasn't difficult to find, murder of any kind being a rarity in the small community and on everyone's minds, close to the surface. Most inhabitants of this small morgue were the elderly or younger accident victims, nothing as spectacular as the gruesome murder victims of the past week.

He walked passed the autopsy rooms, glancing in long enough to check for the ones he searched for, but not long enough to trigger his hunger. He fed before coming, wanting to be at full strength, but while he couldn't smell the blood, the sight was enough to have his fangs elongating.

It was difficult to resist a buffet already prepared, weighed, and measured.

Finally, he came to a closed and locked door. It was easy enough to use his powers to slide back the bolt. Luckily, this was a public facility, not a private residence. As such, he could enter and leave as he wished with nothing to prevent him. He had to have an invitation before entering a home; otherwise his powers would not aid him once inside. Under those circumstances, it was better to wait to be invited. After one invitation, it took stronger measures to keep a vampire out.

In his earlier, human life, the grizzly sight that greeted him would have turned even his hardened stomach. The fact that the corpse was a woman became secondary to the brutal image she presented.

One of the bodies had been laid out, piecemeal, on a metal table. Considering the jigsaw puzzle of meaty parts, some missing, Rafe decided it must be the remains of the woman found under Lexi's home. Either that, or autopsies had changed a great deal since the years he fed off John Doe's in morgues. Little else had been available after Eldora forbid him feeding from the living as punishment for involving himself with mortal conflicts during WWII. It seemed she didn't care about the atrocities humans acted out upon other humans, beyond how easy it made for her own feeding. Helping the cows only led to unwanted attention which led to severe punishments.

Rafe shook his head, forcing himself back to the

present. Reliving old wounds would do nothing, help no one. He needed to focus on the now.

But something kept pulling him back to the past, something faint and elusive. A familiar presence lurked at the edge of his awareness, teasing him, tormenting him.

"You don't disappoint," a dark voice muttered from the corner, sending Rafe's fangs down to their full length as a shiver of panic racked his form. "You came to investigate more quickly than I expected."

Rafe's body tightened, every muscle preparing for the inevitable attack, waiting to be bloodied but refusing to go down without a fight. He scanned the room, looking for the man he knew to be lurking in the shadows but seeing nothing.

No one saw Edmund unless he wanted to be seen. It was an ancient's trick.

Then suddenly, he was there, leaning against the wall two feet away with a grin curling over his lips. Not intimidating to look at for one who didn't know him, with his slight stature and ropey muscles, but this creature could tear a human in half with his bare hands to bathe in his blood. It was one of his favorite tricks.

"Hello, Rafferty."

Rafe flinched as the other vampire's voice coated the air, filling it with harsh memories and bitter promises. An ancient's voice was a physical thing, a weapon in its own rights. It took centuries upon centuries to master such a skill and Rafe wasn't nearly old enough. He wasn't even an elder, much less an ancient, a creature of living myth.

Edmund's dark eyes sparkled as he watched various

emotions dance across Rafe's face. "You can't tell me you did not expect to find me, young one. You knew in your black heart that I was here."

"I can't say that I didn't suspect," Rafe acknowledged, standing firm while a part of him trembled, broken, in a dark, cold corner. Any sign of weakness or retreat, and Edmund would pounce. He couldn't give Edmund a reason.

He'd learned that lesson well and early in his existence.

Edmund kept his grin, sliding forward without touching the ground, another of his favorite tricks. "Eldora wanted me to check up on our little fledgling enclave at the edge of the New World. She wants to be certain she chose right when she decided to let you lead this radical experiment. She doesn't trust the other supernaturals and wants to know that you're holding a tight rein."

The ancient's eyes flicked down to the dismembered body lying on the cold, metal table. "I would say her concerns seem to be well-founded if you are allowing such vicious attacks to be discovered so near your nest. Haven't you taught your fledglings to clean up after themselves? An action like this deserves immediate discipline."

Rafe's eyes narrowed, locked on Edmunds thin, rat-like face. "Now that would depend on whether or not one of *my* people did this."

Edmund laughed, the sound causing every piece of glass and some of the metal to tremble throughout the room. "You doubt this is our work? You don't honestly expect me to believe that a *human* managed such beautiful viciousness. You give them too much credit."

"I don't doubt the killer was supernatural," Rafe replied, keeping his voice calm, even, and devoid of emotion. "I doubt any in my nest would be stupid enough to do this. There are others here."

"The wolves?"

Rafe stared at Edmund as long as he dared. "Perhaps."

Knowledge shined in Edmund's dark, dead eyes. "You need to dispense some tender care, a little of what the modern age calls tough love. It's best to find someone in your house to blame and punish them quickly, brutally. It keeps the rest of the young ones in line. Surely you remember this lesson?"

The skin on Rafe's back rippled, itching with remembered pain of the whip burning and the knife stripping the flesh. Though no scars marred him, thanks to his superior healing abilities, the memory of the agony he suffered under Edmund's tender care scarred more deeply than any whip or blade the other vampire used. No one escaped Edmund's tender care unharmed the type of damage alone changed, not the degree, terror, or pain of it.

"I never forget an example, Edmund," Rafe answered, schooling his emotions, knowing the ancient could easily pick apart his mind if the mood took him. "But I would take greater satisfaction in having the true culprit in my hands than a scapegoat."

"I'm certain you would, but I doubt you have the strength or cunning to achieve your goals."

In a fraction of the time it would take a human to blink an eye, Edmund crossed the small distance between them to grab Rafe by the neck. Rafe held himself perfectly still, not giving the ancient a hint of the turmoil seething inside him.

Keep your mind blank, blank, blank.

Edmund's smile faded, his own fangs dropping, two inches of pure menace. "You had best watch your step, child," he hissed, his spittle dotting Rafe's face. "I will have you and all your traitors in my grasp again. And when I do you will regret every moment of displeasure you've caused me. Thane and Shanna will serve at my feet, crawling to grant my every whim, while you lay strapped to a table for me to feast upon at my leisure."

Rafe arched an eyebrow, face impassive. When facing a rabid dog, show no fear. "And does Eldora know you intend to do whatever you feel necessary to take us back, even risking our exposure to the humans? Do you really want to start another Inquisition in this era? They may be weaker, lesser beings, but they've managed to hunt us to the brink of extinction time and time again. With their new technologies, humans might succeed in eradicating us this time. Do you want to take that risk?"

Edmund's fingers tightened, threatening to crush Rafe's throat. "I don't know what you're talking about. I'm here to watch you and pull you back after you fail, nothing more."

Rafe smirked, thankful he had no need to breath. "After so many centuries, I'd have expected you to be a better liar."

Edmund heaved and threw Rafe across the room. Rafe winced as his shoulder connected with the wall, feeling the bone fracture against the concrete.

"Watch your step, leech," Edmund sneered, walking to put a foot on Rafe's prone body. "I was there when you crossed over. I remember the weak, illiterate brute you were. I remember the mindless, bloodthirsty thing you became. I know of every sin you've committed, every promise you've broken. You are nothing to me, boy. A mere insect, a pest to be crushed under my heel. The only possible worth you have in this world is to serve as entertainment. If you can't manage that, you are insignificant. I have been Our Dark Lady's right hand for over five hundred years. I was her first fledgling. Never think to threaten me with her wrath."

Edmund lashed out with his foot, catching Rafe across the ribs. Rafe grimaced, but pulled himself back to his feet, using the wall for support. He rubbed his neck and sneered at Edmund. "Seems I hit a nerve. My deepest apologies. But I find your reaction interesting for an innocent. No denial, only a promise of retribution."

"Don't imagine yourself to be smarter than I. When this is over, this town will be bathed in blood while you lay starving at my feet. All you hold dear will be left in ruin. You will rue the day you thought to rise up against me, embarrass me in the face of Our Dark Lady. Your time has come, young one."

Chapter Twelve

Lexi was disoriented when she woke the next morning. She felt fuzzy around the edges, not quite connected to reality. The fact that several snoring bodies littered the ground surrounding her place on the couch had nothing to do with it. The bright light blazing through the wide-open space from a row of windows taking up one entire wall of Stella's studio didn't shock Lexi's morning sensitive system.

Yeah, right.

Lexi dragged her fingers through her sleep-mussed hair then stretched her arms high above her head. The guys barely twitched a muscle as she stood to weave her way through them to the bathroom at the opposite end of the room. Even Stella opted for a sleeping bag on the floor, whether for Lexi's peace of mind or the chance to sleep next to Grant, Lexi wasn't sure.

In her morning-dulled condition, it took Lexi a full half-hour to make herself presentable, even without putting on any make-up. When she stumbled back into the main room, the blessed smell of caffeine embraced her.

"Thank God," she muttered, sagging into a folding chair sitting next to a Formica table.

"I've been called a lot of things in my life, but God's a new one." Stella dropped a full cup in front of Lexi, and then brought a box of artificial sweetener packets and a plastic container of non-dairy creamer. "I've known you long enough to know that you're not worthy of being considered human until after your second cup."

"Ha, ha," Lexi grumbled as she dumped enough creamer in her cup to turn the coffee a nice caramel color.

Stella sat across from her with a smirk on her face, giving Lexi the greatest urge to smack her upside the head.

Cheerful morning people sucked.

Lexi didn't say anything until the last drop had been drained from her cup. She stood to pour another. "You want one?"

"No," Stella replied, her grin growing. "I pride myself on my non-addictive personality. Chemicals don't rule me."

Lexi snorted. "Holier than thou this morning, aren't you?"

"Hey, you're the one who called me God, remember?"

"Is she always this snippy in the morning?" Grant's rough voice asked as he stumbled to the table, shirtless, with his low-slung jeans giving Lexi naughty thoughts.

"Yes," Lexi and Stella both answered. Lexi glared at Stella while her friend burst out laughing.

Grant rolled his eyes and scratched his chest. "And I thought the guys were bad."

Lexi couldn't help but laugh at the expression on Grant's face. It was nice to feel normal after what had happened. "I want to thank you guys for staying with me last night," she said as she came back to the table, careful not to slosh the steaming liquid as she sat her cup down. "It was nice of you, especially since you barely know me."

"At the risk of sounding like a chauvinist, I'd think less of any man who wouldn't help a woman in distress." Grant pulled up a chair, flipping it around so he could lean forward against the back. "It may be old-fashioned, but I was raised to step up for those weaker than me."

Lexi raised an eyebrow, waiting for Stella's explosion. When it didn't come, she had to ask, "Weaker?"

Grant didn't flinch or even blink an eye. "Physically, yes. Any other way, you're probably superior, but with a few noted exceptions, men are physically stronger than women. Not to mention, you are a friend of a friend."

"Nice recovery," Stella teased.

Grant grinned down at Stella, the obvious attraction blazing in his eyes heating the kitchen area. Lexi sighed, wondering what it would be like to have someone feel like that about her. At times, she thought maybe Rafe did, but then he'd do something bone-headed like he did last night and make her think it was all about her property after all.

"Well, as much as I'm not looking forward to it, I need to get to work. The shop won't open itself."

Grant reached across the table, laying his hand on hers. "Wait for a little bit, and we'll come with you."

Lexi pulled away and scooted her chair back to stand. "Thanks, but you don't have to do that. I've taken enough of your time."

"It's no trouble," Grant told her, standing in unison with her. "It'll give me a chance hang out with Stella and check out your shop."

Lexi shook her head with a grin. "You've seen my shop, and you can hang out with Stella anytime."

"True, but it's a nice place to spend an afternoon." Grant walked over to her and smiled down at Lexi, but his eyes filled with determination. "And, besides, you can't keep us out. It's a place of business. Would you rather have our company as we walk you to work, or do you want us to just turn up and haunt the place?"

Lexi faced him, spine straight. But there was no staring the man down. He just raised an eyebrow and crossed his arms against his chest. Lexi sighed. "Losing battle, huh?"

Grant's lips twitched as he fought a smile. "Lost battle's more like it."

Shaking her head, Lexi sat back down. Grant nodded, and then went to get the others.

"He's great, isn't he?" Stella said, stars in her eyes.

Lexi couldn't help but agree. He was different than she'd assumed when she first met him. "He's something, I'll say that much. Definitely easy on the eyes, but you've always had a way of attracting good eye-candy."

"I think he might be a keeper," Stella said, emotion coloring each word. "He's understanding of my friends, he's fun to be around, and, as an added bonus, he's incredibly hot."

Lexi stared at her friend, her eyes wide in amazement. "You're serious about a guy? Really serious?" she asked in a whisper.

Stella closed her eyes and nodded. "Maybe. You have to admit, I could and have done a lot worse."

"True, but does he feel the same way about you? I mean, he's in a rock band. It may be a stereotype, but guys in bands are notorious for sleeping around with groupies. Is he serious about you, or is he playing with you?" Lexi knew what Stella's answer would be well before she opened her mouth, but had to hear Stella say it.

"He and his friends all came to help you with one phone call from me. What do you think?"

Lexi's shoulders sagged, her forehead wrinkling. "I think that you're my best friend. He could be a candidate for sainthood, and I'd still worry about you."

Stella dismissed Lexi's concerns with the wave of a hand. "Worry away. But in the meantime, I'm going to enjoy myself."

There was nothing else Lexi could say. All she could do was hope for the best. "Just be careful. And I wish you luck. I hope he *is* everything you think. You deserve a guy like that. My only concern is that he's too good to be true."

Stella grinned, watching as Grant bent over to nudge the lump that was Victor in his sleeping bag. "Well, I can tell you this much. He's definitely too good. Hell, I haven't even managed to get him in my bed yet. I thought that kind of honorable guy died with the advent of the birth control pill."

Before Lexi could comment on Stella's revelation, Grant rejoined them, this time with a dark t-shirt covering his wide chest. "Don't worry. I told the guys to hurry, since you have to leave soon. It'll only take a few minutes. We're used to getting ready in a hurry."

"Always on the run, huh," Lexi needled, still perplexed by her friend's admittance.

Grant took it as a playful jab, returning in kind. "What can I say? I haven't had anything to stay still for until we came here. It's nice to have a chance to put down some roots for a change."

This sentiment struck a cord. Lexi nodded. "I understand. That's how I felt when I moved here."

"Right. It's a great little town for settling down. I hope things work out so we can stay here. This would be a nice place to call home." Grant kept looking over at Stella, who actually blushed. Lexi had never seen her friend blush, ever. Not even the first time Stella had worn heels, got one stuck in a patch of mushy ground and ended up lying in the wet grass with her mini-skirt hiked around her waist.

"You're a little young to be using words like 'settling down.' Are you sure that's what you want?"

"First, I'm older than I look. And second, it only takes a few years out on the road to have a guy longing for a place to call home. The band's the only family I have, so wherever we stop will be home."

Lexi didn't realize how somber her expression was until Grant tipped his chair back and grinned. "Hey now, none of that. There will be no more serious talk. It's too early in the morning. Now that you're awake, you need to cheer up. If you don't, I'll tell Rafe. He'll drag you out tonight and keep you up all hours trying to entertain you. You don't want that, now do you? You'd much rather stay hanging with us."

Lexi felt her own blush rising across her face. "Well, I do like your company, but having Rafe entertain me is pretty tempting. Let me think about it and get back to you."

Grant shook his head, eyes rolling and a grimace on his lips. "It's the Irish accent. Girls go gaga for the accents. Even rock star status can't compare with a good, sexy accent."

"You keep right on thinking that," Lexi tossed back.

Victor walked in on the conversation, thankfully fully dressed. "I don't know what the big deal is with us coming to work with you. Think of us as a new attraction, a draw for the young, female crowd. We won't be under your feet. We'll be luring in any number of prospective customers. Then Stella will swoop in and make the sale. Everyone goes home happy."

Lexi watched as the third man stumbled in, looking as groggy as she did first thing in the morning. Light stubble covered his chin, and his hair stuck up in several different directions. With his shirt off, a thick patch of hair pointed like an arrow towards more interesting territory. Even half asleep, Quinton exuded sex from his pores. If she'd been in the market, Lexi would've been tempted. He made a woman want to throw him back down and have her wicked way with him. Thankfully, Rafe had cured her of the desire for an easy fling. Too much emotional turmoil to deal with.

But not a bad thing to have hovering around her

shop. And it wasn't as if she could reason with their testosterone-poisoned brains.

"Grab your stuff. We may only be a few minutes walk from Afterthoughts, but I have some stock to move from the back and I want to change the window display before opening. I might as well make use of you if you're going to be following me around all day like guard dogs. You are hereby impressed into service as manual laborers and glorified pack mules."

"We are at your service, Milady," Quinton murmured, his voice several octaves lower and sleep-roughened, sending chills through Lexi. He clapped his hand over his heart and bowed.

Grant glared. "Rafe," was all he said.

Quinton smiled, but stepped back. Lexi felt the blood rush to her cheeks. Grant was warning his friend off, because of Rafe. While she could understand the sentiment—he was their boss and flirting with a woman he was dating couldn't be considered smart—the thought that they believed she was somehow taken ticked her off. She'd been seeing the man for a couple of days, not even half a week. Before that, he'd been her nemesis. It boggled the mind that she could be connected to him so quickly.

But it made her wonder. "Why are you warning him off? Surely Rafe has several women he takes out. You can't tell me you steer clear of all of them."

"You're the first, and I'd rather not lose my new gig because one of my friends hit on the owner's girl. Might as well play it safe, until I find out otherwise," Grant replied with a wink.

Lexi didn't bother trying to disabuse them of their

notion. It wasn't worth the energy it'd take her to argue. Rafe had made it clear, she wasn't his anything.

Instead Lexi sighed, stood, and gathered her things. She felt like a teen idol surrounded by her people and bodyguards. All that was missing was a mass of paparazzi snapping shots as they strolled down the street. They had the audience, people craning their necks to watch the group stroll down the boardwalk.

There wasn't a moment that she didn't feel other people's eyes on her.

She couldn't say she didn't appreciate the help once they got to the shop. For once, she didn't strain her back pulling open the rolling chain gate over her door. She set the men to work moving furniture around the store that she'd been putting off for weeks. It surprised her how amiable they were. No complaints greeted any of her requests, no grunting or groaning as they moved couches and chairs. They even lugged in boxes from the back room for Stella to restock.

All in all, it made Lexi wish she could afford to pay some high school kids to help out on a regular basis. For the time being, she'd rather save the money and be that much closer to expansion and worry about extra employees later.

But it didn't stop the wishful thinking.

And Lexi was glad for the men's presence in other ways as well. The gossipmongers managed to get wind of what happened to Lexi the night before. People started stumbling in, looking for fresh juicy news. She heard all kinds of theories on who the killer was.

The people who posed the nutty-out-of-towner

theory kept their eyes glued on every move the men made.

The new resident theory was followed by questions about Rafe and the couple of dates he'd been on with Lexi. They seemed to think the bodies had been left for her like dead presents dropped on her doorstep by a pet cat.

There was the shut-in theory with rumors of insane children kept in attics and basements.

But Lexi's personal favorite was the alien/monster theory brought in by a few of the town's more colorful residents. Butchered cows and crop circles mixed with ghouls, what a combination.

Without Grant, Victor, and Quinton providing distraction, she would've been stuck listening and nodding and thinking about her back porch. At least the majority didn't ask questions about what happened at her house. They just gave her curious looks and the occasional sympathathetic pat on the back.

The whole situation amused the men. Grant took great pleasure in schmoozing the customers, flirting with young and old women alike. He played the role of lure to the hilt. Lexi couldn't believe how many times she heard the register ring.

Who knew that personal horror and a trio of cute guys could be such a draw for business?

As darkness fell, Stella and the guys started pressuring Lexi to close up early. They needed to stop at Nocturne and didn't want to leave her completely alone in the dark. They didn't have to perform until the next night, but needed to sign some papers. Afterthoughts had done good business, and Lexi could barely keep her eyes open. Lexi couldn't resist the temptation of a few extra minutes of privacy and sleep.

Grant invited her to come to Nocturne with them, have a nightcap, but Lexi declined. She wanted the time alone to take a nice, hot, relaxing bath. A long soak is good for the soul, especially followed by a long, heavy, deep sleep.

Grant and Stella escorted her into Stella's loft and did a walk through, checking every room and closet. Lexi wanted to tease them for being over-protective, but was too thankful to belittle the gesture. As they left, she locked the door and threw the bolt-lock. She hummed to herself as she walked to the bathroom and started the water. When the temperature was just short of scalding, she put in the plug.

She lay, soaking up the heat and letting her muscles relax for a half hour before dragging herself out. She didn't want to turn into a prune, but it was hard not to fall back in. Not to mention, if she fell asleep and drowned, she'd feel the embarrassment beyond the grave of being found dead in the tub, naked, by her best friend and a rock band.

Dressed in her sweats again, she straightened the comforter on the couch and fluffed the pillow. She'd be fast asleep before anyone got back, but that was good. She needed the rest.

She didn't turn off the lights, though. She didn't feel *that* comfortable.

Sleep dragged her into its comforting embrace, dreams following close on its heels.

In dreams, Lexi stood in front of the huge wall of windows in Stella's apartment. The clouds covered the night sky, blocking the nearly full moon from sight. No one walked on the street below. The noise from downstairs seemed muted, distant.

A man stood, mid-air, hovering in front of the window. He was of average height, maybe shorter, with dark-brown hair and midnight eyes. His lips were tilted upward in a parody of a smile, but there was no pleasure in the rest of his sharp-faced expression. The cold, bleak features sent chills through Lexi, causing her to take a step back.

The man reached forward, tapping on the glass and beckoning for her to open it. A part of her, a part hidden deep in her mind, struggled not to step forward, not to reach for the latch.

As Lexi took a step back, away from the dark temptation, the man glared and hissed, the light from the signs dotting the boardwalk reflecting off his long, pointed teeth.

A sound came from him that her conscious mind couldn't deal with, couldn't wrap itself around. The glass quivered.

Lexi clapped her hands over her ears, closed her eyes, and fell to her knees.

The feeling of her flesh bruising against the hard tile brought Lexi crashing into consciousness. She lay kneeling on the floor in front of the windows, her hands clasped to her ears and tears flowing down her cheeks. She looked out the window, her dream seeming so real, but she was greeted only by the cloud-covered night sky.

Chapter Thirteen

Rafe sat in his office debating how much he should tell Thane about what had happened. All the vampires needed to be alert and on guard with Edmund in town, but he knew the amount of terror the vampire's name alone would engender in some of the fledglings. It didn't take a genius to figure out Edmund was behind the rash of murders, but how to prove it without everyone working on it was the bigger problem.

A pounding at the door jerked Rafe out of his thoughts. What now?

Without waiting for an answer, Grant surged into the office. But one look at the other man's face kept Rafe from saying anything. Had he possessed blood in his face, it would have drained from the sight of panic in Grant.

"One of my people has been killed," the werewolf growled without preamble, his lips peeled back in a snarl, canines elongated past the point of human teeth.

"What happened?"

"I don't know, but I left one of my people to stand

guard on Lexi. He and your fledgling, Matthew, were to contact me at the slightest need. Now my wolf is dead and your vampire is catatonic."

Rafe leapt to his feet, knocking his chair back as terror filled him. "Lexi? Is Lexi all right?"

Grant took a step back, sensing the rage and fear of the vampire, but was quick to reassure. "She's fine. Stella's with her. I left Shanna inside with them. Lexi recognized her and seemed comfortable with her being there. Only Shanna knows what happened. Stella didn't see anything on the way in and shouldn't be able to tell Lexi."

Rafe nodded, the fear ebbing, but the deep pit it left behind lingering in his chest. "Matthew is catatonic and your wolf is dead. How?"

Grant closed his eyes and took several deep breaths. Rafe watched his teeth and jaw reform as he regained control. "We just got back to the apartment. Shanna and Thane offered to walk us there. I smelled the blood as we approached, so I sent the women up and went to check on the guards with Thane. My wolf was ripped apart. It will take some time for my people to find all the pieces. Your fledgling isn't responding to anyone. He sits on the ground rocking back and forth, babbling. Thane stayed with him and sent me for you."

Rafe trembled with rage. He allowed this to happen by letting Edmund run free over his land. Had he stopped the other vampire at the morgue, it would be over and Grant's wolf would be alive.

Of course, with Edmund having several centuries on him, Rafe wouldn't stand much of a chance against him, not in a fair fight.

"We need to investigate. I'll want you and another wolf to help comb the area, but no heroes. You see something, you run, not fight."

Grant snorted. "I saw what was left of Erik. I'm not ready to die, not like that. Victor's waiting to come back with me to Stella's place. He'll be my second."

Rafe barely listened as he headed for the door. Too much was at stake. With luck, Edmund left something of himself behind to connect to the crime. If he could connect them, Rafe could request aid from Eldora herself. Without it, he would have to justify or hide his actions from her.

Traveling with the wolves slowed him down slightly, but he still made it to Stella's apartment in a fraction of the time it would've taken a human to run. He found Thane sitting on a bench on the opposite side of the boardwalk trying to comfort a hysterical Matthew. The flickering boardwalk lights didn't quite reach the shadowed corner, but the sounds of carousel music, squeals, and chatter mixed with the roar of the waves to drown out Matthews senseless babbling.

"Has he said anything coherent?" Rafe asked, kneeling in front of the damaged vampire. He whimpered, but otherwise showed no sign of acknowledging Rafe's presence.

"No," Thane whispered, worry etched in his face. They'd both known Matthew since he'd been brought over. To see him in this condition brought back too many memories of their own early years with Eldora and Edmund.

"It was a mental attack," Thane said, filling in the silence.

"Yes," replied Rafe, hating what his next words would be and how his friend would react, "but can we connect it to Edmund?"

Thane's attention swung from Matthew to Rafe, eyes widening and fangs sliding free. "Edmund?"

"He's here." Rafe watched his friend absorb the news like a blow to the face. "I saw him last night at the morgue. He says he's here to check up on us for Eldora, but you know as well as I that he wants us to fail."

"He was never given his own territory," Thane murmured as he separated himself from his fears. Rafe could feel the other vampire stomping down his emotions. "To have those he feels to be underlings in a position he himself has coveted must sting. He would do anything to get us back under his control."

Rafe met his friend's eyes, not willing to lie to him and give pithy words of comfort. "Yes, anything. But can we prove it? If I am to declare war on an ancient, I would like all support I can muster. Evidence that he killed the humans and the wolf would go a long way. We could cement werewolf support and possibly get Eldora's blessing."

Thane smirked. "Get the Dark Lady's blessing to destroy her favorite? You don't ask for much, do you?"

"Hope springs eternal, and we are eternal."

Thane tried to laugh, but the sound came out more of a weak croak. "You realize it's a pipe-dream, don't you?"

Rafe closed his eyes. "Yes, I know I will have to face him. I don't relish it, and I doubt I will survive without help."

"Then we will make certain you have that help," Thane leapt in to reassure. "You have to tell the others about Edmund. They need to be on their guard."

"I know. There will be panic. I am depending on you and Shanna to help the others in coping with the news." Rafe looked down at Matthew still wrapped in a nightmare of his mind's own creation. Every vampire Edmund eliminated was a new weakness for Rafe to deal with.

Thane didn't give any false encouragement. Goal oriented, Rafe's second started planning. "We will do whatever necessary. It's our lives at stake too. Claudette will need the most help. I'll have Shanna break the news to her privately."

No sound of movement alerted them to another's presence, but the pounding heartbeat of a werewolf pulled their attention to the present. Grant walked up to them. "I have bad news."

Rafe gave a humorless laugh, looking away from Matthew and Thane. "There was good news and I missed it?"

Grant didn't crack a smile, his concern obvious. "We aren't dealing with one person. Victor and I both detect multiple scents, three that we can definitely connect with the crime. I think that qualifies as bad news."

Rafe exchanged a look with Thane. The information wasn't entirely unexpected, but it wasn't good. If Edmund had brought some of his elite guard with him, they would need all the help they could get. This wasn't a battle to keep their independence, a small skirmish. It was a war.

"Your people are handling clean-up?" Rafe asked

Grant, concentrating on handling one mess at a time and not to drop any balls.

"Yes," Grant replied with an incredulous look. "We have no intention of allowing human doctors to poke around the body of one of our dead. We don't want exposure anymore than you do."

Rafe chose to ignore the snappy tone in Grant's voice. There was too much to do without dealing with hurt feelings and in-fighting. "Good. Afterwards, get your people to gather at Nocturne. We need to have another meeting. There is information that has come up that needs to be shared."

"Do you know who did this?" Grant asked, a snarl held in check with each syllable.

Rafe stared at the young alpha, leader of the pack and worthy ally. "Not that I can prove, but yes, I know who we're up against, who to hold responsible."

"Is it one of your kind?" Grant faced Rafe, body held still but alert, restrained power visible in every quiver of his muscles. "I smelled the undead, but the scent of wolves mixed in as well."

Rafe decided on the truthful approach. "A vampire is involved, most likely several. He might have brought in wolves as backup. It isn't beyond the realm of possibility."

Grant nodded, giving his support without hesitation. "We'll be there. He's hurt my pack. We take care of our own. He did damage to us. We do damage to him."

"I will hold you to that," Rafe replied, giving Thane a curt nod as he stood and turned to cross the street.

"Where will you be?"

Rafe looked up at the window of Stella's apartment,

straining for a glimpse of movement. "I want to speak to Lexi, find out if she saw anything."

"Is that all?" Grant chuckled, his expression softening.

Rafe turned at the amusement in the wolf's voice. "Is there something you have to say?"

"Nothing," Grant replied, flipping his hair out of his eyes. "I like her. She's been a good friend to Stella."

Rafe felt his fangs lengthen. Grant was a strong ally, someone Rafe couldn't afford to lose. But Lexi belonged to him. Grant and his pack better be happy with Stella, because they weren't getting Lexi. "You will stay away from her," he growled.

Grant laughed, holding up both hands, palms out in surrender. "Don't worry. I don't poach. But Stella cares for her and, as such, so do I. I wouldn't want her to be harmed."

Rafe's eyes narrowed in distrust of the handsome young wolf. "What I do with Lexi Hart is my business. No one will hurt her. No one will touch her."

"That's all I wanted to know." Grant grinned wider, showing that his teeth had returned to normal. "She had a lot to say about you last night, not all of it good. I'd say you have some making up to do before you're going to get her to answer any of your questions."

Rafe's mouth dropped open. "You stayed with her last night?"

"What, your sentry didn't tell you?" Grant smirked, clearly enjoying his moment of one-upmanship.

Rafe said nothing, looking over at Matthew and back to Grant.

"Oh," Grant replied, mollified when he realized who that sentry had been. "Stella thought Lexi would feel better with company last night. Three of us came over and crashed on the floor, helped her feel safe. I mean, after what happened, how safe is she going to feel with only another woman and a few locks to protect her? It's not like she had a boyfriend there to help guard her."

Rafe resisted the urge to growl. He didn't have time to get into a playful pissing contest. But he didn't like the thought of Lexi being surrounded all night by what she had to consider prime examples of manhood.

He settled for an all-purpose threat. "Don't push your luck, wolf. I don't think either one of us wants to know who's the stronger leader, not when we have a common foe to face."

"Is he that strong?"

Rafe felt the shudder building. "Stronger than you could imagine," he muttered as he turned his back on Grant and headed towards the apartment.

Shanna answered the door before the first knock, her expression grim. "Be happy she has such a strong mind," she whispered too low for mortal ears to hear.

"What happened?"

Shanna stepped out of the way, ushering Rafe inside. "I don't know. She won't say. Whatever happened, I don't think she believes it to be real. Whoever came could cloud her mind that much. But I know someone was at her window. I can feel the lingering affects of magic there."

"Vampire?" he asked, already knowing the answer.

Shanna shook her head, but fear etched her face. "I'm not certain. I can't see it clearly, but I think so."

Rafe peeked in the direction of Stella's living area. He didn't have much time, but Shanna needed to be made aware. "Edmund is here, in Santa del Sol. I've seen him. We're meeting at the club as soon as I'm done checking on Lexi. I want you to talk to Claudette before the meeting."

Shanna hissed, glancing over her shoulder. "He must have seen you with Lexi. If he knows of your interest in her, he will hunt her, play with her, and leave her body at our doorstep."

"I realize that," Rafe grumbled, hating the fact that he'd brought Edmund down on Lexi, not knowing if he could protect her. "The body at her home was a warning. I thought someone was watching me when I left her there the night before. He must have taken the body from his previous dumping place and left it there for her to find."

"What are you going to do about it?"

Rafe listened to the steady beat of Lexi's heart coming from behind the curtains. "Whatever I have to in order to protect her."

"Will you turn her?" Shanna asked, putting voice to the dark thoughts tormenting him.

Rafe closed his eyes, but forced himself to be honest. "I don't want to. I don't want to take her life from her, but if I have to, I will. I won't let Edmund have her. As a human, she's much too fragile."

Shanna smiled. "It's about time."

Rafe's eyes flashed, not pleased with Shanna's automatic support. "I don't like the risks involved, and I don't like that I'm taking so much away from her. But I feel the connection to her, the draw. I won't let that be destroyed before I have a chance to investigate it to the fullest."

"That's what having a mate is all about, having someone you can depend on, someone with whom to share all the years stretching out ahead of us." Shanna stopped, reaching out to touch Rafe's shoulder. "This isn't the best way to start. You're right about that. But I like her and I'm happy for you. We just have to make certain that we all survive to see what happens between the two of you."

At that moment, Stella stepped through the curtained divider. "Oh, you're back," she said, crossing her arms and smirking at him. Rafe couldn't remember the last time a human other than Lexi had the gall to smirk at him. "Boy, do you have some shoveling to do."

"Shoveling?" he asked, stepping around Shanna to face the termagant.

"Yeah, shoveling. After your last visit, do you think Lexi's going to let you waltz in here without some groveling?" Stella made tsking sounds. "You're going to have to dig yourself out of the hole you made last night."

"What hole? What did I do?"

"God, men are stupid," Stella muttered under her breath, looking to Shanna for support. Rafe watched his vampire roll her eyes. "You came over here for all of five minutes and then ran out without so much as an attempt at an explanation. Do you think Lexi let that roll off her?"

"I hurt Lexi?" Rafe asked, still not entirely clear on what the problem was. He left to save Lexi from his blood lust and that somehow hurt her. What did they think would have happened if he'd stayed? "Are you saying she's angry that I left?"

"Let me see," Stella answered, tapping one finger against her lips. "She goes through a traumatic experience. The guy she's been seeing stays with her for a few minutes, while three guys she barely knows but are my friends crash out here to make her feel safe. Now, why would she be unhappy with you?"

"There were reasons, things I had to take care of." *Like Lexi.*

"Then you'd better explain yourself to her, because if you hurt her again, I'm not sticking up for you. I'm going to beat the crap out of you, understand?" Stella glared at him, reminding Rafe of a small, spitting kitten.

"I understand," Rafe answered, though it was a lie. But if she said Lexi's feelings had been hurt, he needed to correct it. If he was to keep her safe, he needed her trust. He looked over at Shanna, willing her help.

Shanna's lips twitched as she fought back a giggle. "Hey Stella, why don't we give the man some privacy? I'm sure he doesn't want an audience while he pleads for forgiveness. As his friend, I think we should leave him some pride."

Stella shrugged, "It's his funeral."

"No, but if Lexi has half the gumption I think she does, he's going to wish it was." Shanna patted Rafe on the back.

Rafe swept past the two women, ignoring the giggles as they left, locking the door behind them.

Lexi sat on the couch again, her knees drawn up

to her chest as she stared blindly at the T.V. Without a word, Rafe sat down beside her.

Lexi inched away.

Rafe grimaced, not liking his lack of control in this situation. He kept flying blind when dealing with her. That a mortal woman could twist him into knots bothered him more than he could say. "I'm told that I owe you an apology."

"I don't want your apology," she replied without glancing up.

Why did women have to make things so difficult? In over three hundred years, that was the only thing that hadn't changed. Women were a mystery, one men would never solve. Any who attempted to went mad.

"I'm sorry I had to leave you so abruptly last night," Rafe said, deciding to give her what she thought she wanted, even if it was a blatant falsehood. "I didn't want to. I would much rather have spent my time with you."

"Uh-huh, right." She still didn't look up.

Rafe felt his temper rising. He never apologized. He learned early that it made you appear weak, and any weakness shown could lead to a quick, decisive demise. He'd seen too many of his brethren staked and burned by humans and other supernatural beings alike. So an apology did not come easily.

He didn't appreciate it being thrown back in his face.

But Lexi had been through much in the last twenty-four hours. First finding a body lodged under her home and then being threatened by an ancient vampire. She deserved some room for tantrums.

Not that the realization made his position any easier.

So he swallowed a bit more of his pride, trying to ignore how it lodged in his throat, and tried again. "Lexi, I am deeply sorry. Had I known how much it meant to you, I would have done what I could to stay with you."

"Why?" she whispered, finally turning to look at him. "Why would it make any difference to you? I keep telling myself that we barely know each other. I shouldn't take it as hard as I have that you left, so why should you be sorry?"

Surprise shot through Rafe as he realized how much her words hurt. "We haven't had much time together, but I wouldn't say that we barely know each other. I thought we were getting to know each other very well."

"Well, I think you're wrong."

Rafe stiffened in shock. No one told him that he was wrong, not even Thane or Shanna said it outright. Only an ancient would dare challenge a vampire of his age and strength. That this woman dared challenge him sent amazement colliding through his body.

His anger propelled him forward to strike. At the last minute, he changed his target from her jugular to her lips. His mouth slammed across hers, forcing her lips open for his invasion. His tongue thrust inside, possessing every inch of her warm flesh.

Lexi whimpered and stiffened at first under the assault, but melted under Rafe's skillful touch. Rafe heard the throb of her pulse increase as her heart raced. Her arms wrapped around his shoulders, her fingers raking through his hair, the slight sting bringing a growl to his throat.

The thunder of her blood flowing beneath her skin sent the monster within him clawing to escape, to sink its teeth deep into a vein and drink. He wanted a connection with her, needed to connect with her. As far as the monster was concerned, she was his mate. She existed only to provide for him whatever he needed: blood, sex, comfort, warmth, love, anything.

He dragged his hands down her sides, rejoicing in every quiver, every quake and moan. He slid beneath her sweatshirt, heating his cold hands against her warm, living flesh. Her breasts were warm, pulsing weights cupped in his hands, her nipples peaking between his fingers.

But that wasn't enough. He needed more.

Breaking away from her mouth just long enough, he pulled the shirt over her head. She gasped and started to pull away. He growled as she shrank back, jerking her into his embrace. He had to touch her, needed the feeling of flesh and skin.

He felt his fangs slipping, but didn't care. Nothing mattered but the feel of her skin against his, her mouth against his, her body against his. He had to warm himself in the circle of her living flesh.

The small whimpers coming from Lexi set his body aflame. She was so helpless, so willing, so *his*. He didn't care about all the reasons he shouldn't be with her. He didn't care that to most of his kind, she amounted to little more than a quick meal. Lexi meant something to him. She was intelligent and spunky. She was attractive, and he couldn't control her. Every response he pulled from her body was for him alone; no vampiric powers worked on her. Her response came from him, what he did to her, what she felt for him.

With her body fused so close to his own, he had no doubt where she belonged, with him for all eternity. Even the smallest whimper falling from her lips burrowed into his cold heart, filling it with heated emotions.

She was his.

He pulled away, staring deep into her eyes. A fine trembling filled his body. In his heart of hearts, he recognized her as his other half, the one being in the world who could make him whole. She had all the power, the ability to thrust him back into his previous cold, purposeless existence. With her, he was whole. Without her, he was a fractured being.

He bent over to nuzzle her breasts, pulling moans from her lips with each caress on her tight flesh.

He could do this. He could make love to Lexi without biting her. He had control of his hunger and he would not harm her. His hunger didn't control him.

Rafe nipped at her breasts, careful to apply steady pressure and not to break the skin. Lexi shuddered in reaction to the tiny prick of pain, causing Rafe to wonder how she would react to his bite. Would she wallow in the feeling of his teeth sinking into her flesh? Would it send her to a higher plane of pleasure, taking her body to a place she'd never dreamed possible?

Oh, the temptation.

He guided her down across the couch, determined

to lose himself in her body, to take away both his fear and her own. She arched her back, her neck vulnerable, a pale temptation, the jugular and carotid arteries pounding below the thin layer of milky skin.

A small nibble, a taste. What harm could there be? Without an exchange, no compulsion would be laid upon her. Lexi wouldn't miss a few precious drops. So it might give him a peek into her emotions, create the tiniest, one-way bond between them. The rich flavor of her blood flowing across his tongue would be worth the risk.

Rafe ducked his head as his fangs slid out to full extension, hiding his action by holding his cheek to her chest. He couldn't feed off her. Lexi was warmth and passion, not food. She was beauty and temptation, not food. She was love and lust, not food.

His hands struggled with her clothes and his, fighting to leave them both bare. If he could be inside her, any other way possible, he could fight off his darker desires. He slipped his hand down, cupping her wet, needy flesh. The want and passion of her entire existence packaged in that small bit of ecstasy.

She tossed her head back and forth, rubbing against him in desperate need for contact. He couldn't hold back, couldn't resist.

He reared back, his head dipping to her neck while he slid home, his body delving within her.

As he bit, that part of him that remembered being human prayed that she would forgive him.

"Rafe," she gasped, her voice frantic. "Don't stop. Whatever you're doing, don't stop."

Her body convulsed. She clawed his arms. She murmured incoherent words of carnal pleasure.

Rafe shivered with each movement as Lexi squeezed him. The bite of pain as her nails broke his skin sent his senses further into overload. The taste of her blood surged into his mouth, filling his body with her essence. Emotions not his own, but matching them, pushed at the walls of his mind.

An aching emptiness filled. A wild abandon swelled. He felt Lexi's desire to curl into him and bask in his strength, bathe in the feel of his body locked with hers. Panic didn't permeate her. She shook with the yearning to reach that one pinnacle which only another person could push her over.

Rafe felt her body gathering, knotting. His own body tightened, trembled. He pulled back at the last moment, licking the punctures on her neck. His voice joined her cries of completion as he pumped some of himself into her. His one lucid thought as their two pleasures combined in his mind was the wish that he shared more than just his seed with her.

He wished his blood poured down her throat, joining them for all eternity.

Chapter Fourteen

Lexi woke with sun streaming into her tired eyes. She stretched, reaching out to feel the warm comfort that held her throughout the night, keeping her personal demons at bay. Nothing greeted her grasp but the edge of the couch and the crunch of a small scrap of paper.

She squinted as she opened her eyes, her fingers convulsing over the paper. Moving her arm took more effort than she could believe. She felt like an accident victim. Her tongue stuck to the top of her mouth, and she ached all over, even in places that hadn't had a reason to ache in years.

Hell, even her neck hurt.

Looking at the paper clutched in her hand, she dragged herself into a sitting position. She couldn't believe what she read. She'd opened herself up to the man. She'd been wrong.

Rafe had left.

Of course, he wasn't a complete jerk about it. He wrote that he had business to attend to, that he couldn't stay. He said that he didn't want to leave her side and wanted to see her again. He said she looked so comfortable and slept so deeply that he almost felt guilty for keeping her up so late. He couldn't bring himself to wake her. He'd call in the evening and set up a time to pick her up, so they could have dinner and spend time together.

Blah, blah, blah.

He didn't say anything about having feelings for her, not even signing with love, just writing a large, scrawling Rafe. He didn't say what she wanted to hear. Worse yet, he wasn't lying next to her on the cramped couch, holding her close.

Yeah, right, he'd call. She'd believe it when she heard it.

Lexi tried not to let his desertion bother her too much. It hurt. She couldn't say that it didn't. But in the *tiniest* corner of her heart, hope lived. She remembered how gentle he'd been with her, how his cool hands felt sliding over her body. She remembered his muttered words of praise and the way he held her close throughout the night, chasing away her fears and dark dreams. He had to care for her. But what was with the quick escape? Was it second thoughts?

Had she done something wrong?

Lexi sat pondering Rafe's behavior, trying to put reason to it, when a delicious aroma tickled her senses and the sheer curtain parted for Stella.

"I come bearing your elixir of the gods," her smirking friend said, sitting a tray loaded with coffee and cheese Danishes in front of Lexi.

Lexi forced a smile, putting the note down on the table and shoving it from her thoughts. She wrapped her blanket around her naked body, toga-style. "Bless you, my child. Keep this up, and you'll be getting one heck of a Christmas bonus."

Stella ran her fingers through her bangs, fluffing the colorful fringe. "And here I was trying for a raise. Oh well, be thankful for what you get." Stella's smirk grew and her eyes twinkled as she stared at a disheveled Lexi. "Speaking of which, I take it you got something pretty good last night. Want to talk about it?"

"What's to tell?" Lexi pouted, sagging back and staring at the pastries not certain if her stomach could handle it. The way she felt, it'd sit like a stone. "He's not here now, is he? How good could it have been?"

Stella said nothing for a moment, and then shook her head. "It didn't look all that bad to me. When I came in, after three in the morning I might add, you two were curled up so tight, I couldn't tell where you ended and he began."

Lexi took a cup and sipped the coffee, testing her stomach's endurance. "Yeah, well that was last night."

"That bad, huh? Well, shoot. I was hoping he was as good as he looked. I'm disappointed in the male species again."

"I wouldn't say that," Lexi replied, blushing at the memory of Rafe's mouth and tongue caressing every inch of her body. "It was great. He was great, fantastic even. I'm just feeling let down that he wasn't here when I woke up."

"I caught him sneaking out this morning, before dawn," Stella said, watching Lexi closely. "He didn't look too happy about leaving either. Said he had a few meetings he had to get out of the way so he could clear this evening to stay with you. He hated that you had to depend on Grant and his friends instead of on him. I'd say you have nothing to feel bad about."

Lexi hated the needy, achy pit chewing away at her heart, but she had to know. "Are you sure that's how he felt?"

Stella beamed and shoved a Danish at her. "Positive. I know guys, and he's all over you. What does the note he left say?"

"That he wants to see me tonight," Lexi whispered, staring at the mass of gooey sweetness in her hand.

"There you go. That doesn't sound like a man who's had enough of you. That sounds like one who wants a second helping."

Lexi nibbled at the edge of the pastry, letting the sugar and buttery taste melt on her tongue. Her stomach clenched for a moment, but didn't revolt. "Stella, he said he wanted to take me out to dinner, not make me his dinner."

"You say that like it's a bad thing. You can't say you wouldn't enjoy having him eat you all up."

Lexi closed her eyes and flashed back again the feeling of Rafe's lips gliding across her entire body, his tongue flicking her sensitive flesh, the shivers that traveled through her as any part of their bodies connected. "True, but I deserve a dinner first."

Stella threw her head back, laughter bouncing off the walls of her studio. "That's my girl," she managed to gasp between bouts of guffaws, "keep your priorities straight. No more nookie before getting something in return. Even a dumb, hormone-driven teenager knows that much."

Lexi didn't giggle, but it was a close thing. Instead, she licked the last sugary crumbs of Danish from her fingers and pried herself off the couch. "I have to get ready for work. The shop won't open itself, and you're obviously not there doing it."

"Is that a hint to get my butt in gear?" Stella asked, sighing as she sat her cup down. "So much for my bonus."

"Yeah, yeah, I'm the driver, you're the slave. I'll pick up a whip and chains on the way."

"Oh, you better not tell Rafe about that." Stella teased, her eyes dancing as she jumped out of smacking range. "He might think you're into that kinky stuff."

Lexi started to throw a Danish at her, but that would be a wasted of a perfectly good pastry. Stella wasn't worth it. "Cut it out, you freak, or I'll start grilling you on your relationship with Grant. Do you honestly want to tell me all the juicy little tidbits about what you two do while you're alone?" Lexi asked, making her way to the curtain, intent on the bathroom and a quick shower before work.

Stella smirked again, raising her hands and batting her eyes. "Hey, to hear about you and Rafe in conjunction with whips and chains, I'll tell you anything you want. But unlike you, for once, I'm not that far yet."

That stopped Lexi dead. She turned back to face her friend, shocked at what she thought Stella was telling her. "You've got to be kidding. Isn't that a record for you or something? You've never gone this long dating one guy and not doing the mattress mambo."

"Hey now, watch it. You're making me sound like a complete slut. I don't sleep around *that* much."

Lexi winced at the obvious pain in her friend's face.

"I'm not saying you do, but it *is* a part of the regular progression in your relationship history. And I've never seen you so gone over a guy before. All that without, how do I say this without sounding completely vulgar, giving him a test drive?"

Stella crossed her arms and leaned against the far wall. "He's not like that."

Lexi snorted. That wasn't the Stella she knew talking. "I may not have the track record you have, but even I know that there isn't a man alive who isn't like that. You offer a man sex, unless he has a really good reason, he's not going to turn you down. So what's his reason?"

Stella's face went serious. She started pacing, rubbing her arms and pacing. "I don't know. He tells me that he wants to take things slow, that he doesn't want to rush me."

Lexi felt like she was watching a tennis match as her friend wore a path in her floor. "But you don't buy it."

Stella's voice held equal measures of hope and despair. "I'm not certain what to think. He believes what he says. I just can't help thinking there's more to it than that."

"Is it the whole rock star mystique, not wanting to be tied down?" Lexi asked, trying to find a reason for the man not to jump her best friend's bones. So her head might look like an Easter egg barfed on it. So she dressed like Elvira one minute and Tank Girl the next. It never once stopped a guy from tumbling her friend Stella before.

Stella thought about it for a split second before shrugging it off. "That's stupid. Sleeping with me *is* the rock star mystique and has nothing to do with commitment."

"Is there someone else?"

"I hope not," Stella whispered, her eyes turning liquid.

"But you suspect something."

"I don't know. I think he's keeping something from me." Stella stared at Lexi, her gaze begging for aid, an explanation. "I don't think it's another woman, but I don't know what it is. I can tell he and his friends have something that they know and they're keeping from me."

Lexi thought of Rafe and his own air of mystery and had to know. "How? How do you know that Grant has a secret?"

Stella threw up her hands, frustration apparent. "I couldn't tell you for certain. It's a feeling I have. It's in the way he looks at me sometimes, like he wants to devour me, and then turns away. It's in the way he and the others will be talking then go silent when I walk up to them. I know Grant cares about me, but what does that mean in the long run? Will we stay together? Will our relationship make it another day, week, or month? Who knows?"

"But you're willing to risk it?" Lexi asked, thinking of her night with Rafe, her doubts, hope, and attraction.

"Life is a risk, love a gamble. I'm not willing to forego playing the game because there's a chance that I'll get hurt. There's a chance that I'll be struck by lightning tomorrow or be hit by a bus crossing the street. That doesn't mean I'm going to lock myself in here and refuse to come out. And let's face it, Grant is worth it."

But how do you know when the man is worth it? Lexi asked herself. No matter how different this morning was compared to what she expected, after last night she had no doubt that Rafe found her attractive, and not for the deed to her sliver of property in the midst of his planned compound. Like Stella with Grant, she suspected Rafe of something. She couldn't put her finger on what it was, but there were many things that didn't add up.

First, there was his habit of running out on her at a moment's notice, not something she appreciated, but not worrisome in and of itself. Then there was the reaction of the various Alpha members to him. Grant seemed to respect Rafe as a boss, but there was an underlying feeling of challenge there as well.

But Lexi also recognized the fact that she had an innate distrust of men in general, after growing up in a family over-populated with the testosterone-poisoned. How her mother survived her father and four older brothers without committing suicide or murder, Lexi would never understand. She simply thanked God she'd gotten into enough trouble to get dumped on her aunt.

She glanced up to see Stella watching her with a smirk. "I'm over-analyzing again, aren't I?"

Stella plopped back down in a chair and grabbed another Danish. "With a stress on the anal part, yes."

Lexi swallowed, trying to wet her dry mouth. "Throw caution to the wind?"

The teasing twinkle in Stella's eyes rivaled the sparkle of her extra-strong hold, silver-glitter hair gel.

"I was thinking sanity and clothing myself, but then, I'm the risk-taker."

Lexi rolled her shoulders, easing the stress and tension as she stood. "Enough of this. We could babble incessantly for the next four years and never figure out what the guys were really thinking. I don't have the time to waste trying to figure out the inner workings of the male psyche."

Stella groaned, standing amid a creaking of joints. "Work, work, work. Everything is work with you. Wait a couple of minutes, already, and I'll come in with you. Might as well, seeing as I'm up and all. After the late night, I should still be asleep."

"Then why aren't you?"

"Are you kidding?" Stella snickered, tilting her head to give Lexi her patented teasing stare. "After seeing tall, rich, and mysterious slipping out this morning, do you honestly think I could go back to sleep? I wanted details, graphic erotic details. Instead, I get a woe-is-me speech from a woman who thinks she's being dumped now that she's put out. I expected more from you. Be prepared to spill over lunch, or I'll start the torture and harassment."

"Deal."

Lexi sat back down and sipped on her coffee as she waited for her friend. Stella was true to her word, getting ready in record time, though why it should take that long to look so not-dressy, Lexi couldn't understand. But her black-encased friend held open the door for her, then carefully locked it, slipping the key and chain back around her neck, where it served a double purpose as a necklace.

The two were quiet on the walk to Afterthoughts,

both lost in their own little worlds, wrapping their minds around the questions of the risks involved in including someone in their lives and hearts. But those thoughts evaporated at the sight that greeted them at the shop.

"Son of a bitch," Stella whispered, filling in the silence coming from Lexi. Lexi stared at her shop, her pride and joy, with horror and tears. Her prized possession looked like a riot had hit it; broken glass and paint leading the way to the security gate that Lexi now thanked, despite the hassle it represented every morning and evening.

Red paint covered the area with strange designs and symbols along with words. Every horrid thing a man could call a woman decorated her shop, 'bitch' being the nicest represented. A small crowd had already gathered, murmuring and giving her looks of pity. The man who ran the churros cart at the end of the block stepped forward, putting his arm around Lexi's shoulder and leading her away.

"You don't need to see this, Lexi. I called the cops as soon as I saw it and they're on their way. You just step over here and sit down. We'll get some people together to clean things up when the police are finished. Don't worry about a thing. We take care of our own around here. No scum will be allowed to terrorize a part of our family, not with all of us around."

Lexi stared in the direction of her shop, but sank down onto the bench he led her to. Her face glazed with despair. "Thanks, Frank," she said, her voice vague, emotionless. "I appreciate it."

The man gave a weak smile and looked to Stella

for guidance. For once, the other woman seemed at a loss for words, sitting by Lexi and taking her hand.

"Lexi," Stella whispered as she rubbed Lexi's hand.

"What?" Lexi replied, despondent as she listened to the sirens as the police cars pulled up in the alleyway.

"Maybe you should take Rafe up on his offer."

Lexi blinked several times, clearing her mind of inappropriate, Kama Sutra-type images his name brought up. "What are you talking about?"

Stella looked uncomfortable, but determined. "Staying with him." Lexi stared to interrupt, but Stella held up a multi-ringed hand, postponing any argument. "I've talked to Grant and the club has heavy-duty security, not to mention there's always somebody around, day or night. Maybe you should stay with him."

Lexi stopped. She put Stella in jeopardy. Her friend, who never worried about anything, was worried. "Are you scared? Have I put you in danger? Some psycho's fixated on me. Are you afraid of getting caught in the fallout?"

Stella refused to meet Lexi's gaze. "I don't know. But I hate feeling helpless and afraid, for you and myself. I'll come with you. You won't have to be there with him all alone, if you're worried about that. But we'd both be idiots if we wait for this maniac to get around to coming after us."

Lexi's throat tightened and her eyes filled with tears. She clenched her hands, pounding them against her thighs. "I hate this. I wish I could joke with you and accuse you of wanting to be closer to Grant, to pretend this isn't serious. But it *is* serious. I'm in over my head and I'm dragging you down with me."

Stella laid her hands over Lexi's, pressing down until Lexi released her fist. "Hey, you forget, if you get to the point of branching out, you promised to make me a partner," she teased. "With that and the fact that we've been friends for more years than I'll confess to living for fear of someone guessing my real age, no way am I bailing on you. So get used to it."

Lexi didn't think long. She wanted to be near Rafe, just not when she was still angry with him. But Stella's life, her life, weren't worth the risk if it was only jealous cowardice standing in her way. "Do you have your cell on you?"

"Always. You calling Rafe?"

"Before I lose my nerve."

Chapter Fifteen

Rafe woke to Beethoven, the warmth of his room seeping into his flesh. The memory of Lexi's sweet body heaving beneath his own teased the edge of his consciousness, sending erotic pictures, real and imagined, through his mind and straight to his groin. Sliding his tongue across his lower lip, he could almost taste the salty nectar that was her blood slipping down his throat. The sexual surge coupled with the surge of strength and power from that one, tiny sip left him aching for more, the beast within growling for satisfaction.

It was only a matter of time until he brought her over. No matter how much he wished things were different, he wasn't fool enough to deny the truth. He wanted her, needed her, had to have her. It was inevitable. Lexi Hart would be his. The only question became, how much time could he give her to adjust? Would he tell her first, or take her and work out the details later?

Was it easier to beg forgiveness than to ask permission?

Rafe sat up, smiling. He hadn't smiled spontaneously in centuries. His cheeks almost hurt form the action. Yet he smiled.

Danger lay ahead, but he had Lexi by his side. Thane and Shanna were right. Having someone to share eternity with made all the difference in the world. It gave purpose to a meaningless existence.

He couldn't wait to show Lexi everything eternal life had to offer, the dark beauty and sights no mortal eye could comprehend. He knew she would have fears to overcome. Superstitions and horror lurked in her future. But Lexi was strong and caring. She would see past the myth to the advantages of the life he offered her.

All he had to do was defeat Edmund while he had a chance. Now he had more to fight for. Not only was he protecting his life and that of his nest, he had a mate to care for, a woman to guard.

The thought alone warmed his unbeating heart.

He pulled on the first matching outfit he found, not bothering with taking the time to choose a perfect ensemble. He needed to get out there, finish things, and take his woman again. He wanted her where she belonged, naked and beneath him, or naked and over him, or naked and beside him. He had a couple of hours to get the bulk of his work done before Lexi closed her shop. By then, he wanted to be with her and only her.

He yanked open the door without taking his usual moment to check the security screens.

Patricia surprised him, standing in front of his door with his evening meal ready for him on his silver platter.

"You read my mind this time," he said, scooping

up a bottle and gulping it down without any of his usual finesse.

Patricia eyed the disappearing blood with raised brows. "I have news for you, both good and bad."

Rafe froze. While Edmund shouldn't have been able to harm Lexi in the daytime, he might have other followers who could, especially the werewolves Grant detected. Visions of the piecemeal bodies of the dead women flooded his head. He dropped the bottle on the tray and grabbed his servant by the shoulders. "What has happened?"

Never attempting to break his grip, Patricia answered. "Miss Hart's establishment has been vandalized. The culprit used both human and vampire scripts in their graffiti. While the human writing included crude insults directed at Miss Hart, I'm told that the vampire writings were a blatant challenge to you and your authority."

Vampire politics. It always came down to vampire politics. Rafe couldn't face another sunset if Lexi were butchered due to vampire politics. "Has Lexi been harmed?"

Patricia's lips curled slightly. She reached forward for an instant, as if to give comfort, before jerking her hand back. "No, sir. That's the good news. The incident pushed Miss Hart and Miss Jones into action. Both women are presently sleeping in the adjoining rooms to the back of Nocturne's third floor. They've been told that the rooms are the guest quarters."

Rafe stared at Patricia, speechless. His fondest wish was a reality. Lexi was here, living under his roof. She slept in his bed, within easy reach. He didn't care how it happened, but Lexi was here.

She would stay here, forever.

A predatory smile spread across his face, his fangs, fully extended, framing his lips. "She's here."

Patricia nodded, a needless gesture that Rafe barely registered as he flew past her and up the stairway. He had to see for himself. He had to see Lexi in his home, her things hanging in his closet. Her personal effects scattered across his sink and the warm smell of her skin perfuming the air.

As he skidded to a halt by the door of the room Patricia had indicated, he made a disturbing discovery.

His woman's room was directly across from the suite occupied by the Alphas.

A growl rumbled deep in his chest. His logical mind understood the reason Patricia would have placed his woman so close to the other males. Lexi was in danger. Here, she had aid close by if she needed it, creatures of supernatural strength rivaling most vampires.

But the men were so close to her. Rafe knew they searched for women to bring into their pack. They needed mates desperately, as a hunter stalking their previous pack grounds had decimated a large portion of their female population. Without women to mate with, their pack would die.

And Rafe's woman would be sleeping fifty feet from some of the strongest members of their pack, completely unaware of the dark forces surrounding her. He didn't know if he could tolerate it.

He stood in front of Lexi's door, his hands clenching and unclenching as he fought the demon within him for control. She wouldn't get a calm, gentle man, but Lexi deserved a considerate lover, one who didn't horrify her. Rafe refused to face Lexi with glowing red eyes or glistening fangs. He would not frighten her, not now, not after deciding to bring her over. It would complicate the situation, make it more difficult for her to adjust to life as a member of the undead.

Now if his primitive side would agree with him.

It didn't help that he could smell the werewolves' presence surrounding him. They'd marked most of the upper levels of Nocturne as their territory after Rafe had granted them the area. It was their home, and they claimed every inch as thoroughly as his vampires had claimed the lower levels. But it made it harder for him to regain control with their scent surrounding him, silently challenging his authority.

He forced back the demon snarling and clawing to break free. His hands shook. He needed to pull together his courage and take the next step.

He reached out and knocked on her door.

His inhuman hearing caught the sounds of her feet rushing across the deep, plush carpet before the door swung inward, soft light framing her lush body wrapped in a short silk robe. She flicked a wet, silky curl behind her shoulder with a self-conscious smile.

"I was just stepping out of the shower," she mumbled, a blush coloring her delicate, creamy cheeks.

Rafe grinned at her modesty. He'd worshipped every inch of her body with his tongue the night before, but she somehow managed to feel insecure being in his presence in her present state of undress.

He dropped his gaze from her smooth face, down to her shoulders and breasts, then back up again.

"Don't dress on my account. That looks fine to me. More than fine."

Lexi's blush spread farther up her cheeks, but she didn't drop her gaze. Instead, her lips pursed, and she stood straight. "I found it in one of the closets. I hope it's all right."

Rafe's lips twitched as he realized what she was really asking. "I think it belongs to Shanna. She chose this room to be her 'Thane's done something stupid and I refuse to sleep with him' room. She doesn't use it often, so probably doesn't even remember she left anything here."

Lexi's musical laughter brightened the dark corners of the room. "Thane doesn't stick his foot in it that often?" she asked between snickers.

"Oh, he does, believe me. But now, Shanna's more likely to kick him out than retreat herself."

Lexi tossed her head back and laughed again, the purity of the sound sending chills up Rafe's spine. "I can understand that. If he messed up, why should she have to leave her room?"

"Exactly her words." Rafe stared at Lexi's hand, still clutching the doorjamb. "Is it all right for me to come in, or do you want to stand here for the rest of my work crew to pass by and see?"

Lexi's eyes widened and she stuck her head out into the hallway, checking left and right. When she saw no one, she reached out and pulled Rafe into her room and slammed the door shut behind him.

"You make me forget myself," she said as her fingers played with the sash holding her robe together. "I don't normally stand around waiting to flash whoever passes by."

Rafe gave in to the unfamiliar urge to tease, wanting to see Lexi's blood rush up to flush her cheeks with crimson color. "I didn't think you did, but I can't say I don't appreciate the view."

Lexi made a strangled sound, but hurried across the clean, white room to scoop some clothes off the red and black oriental-styled bed. "Make yourself at home, as it *is* your home. I'll be out in a second."

"Take all the time you need," Rafe answered, looking around at the various signs of her inhabitation. "I'm not going anywhere."

She nodded and scurried into the adjoining bathroom, shared with the next room where Stella slept. Rafe grinned at Lexi's obvious discomfort. He'd never seen her at such a loss before. He played with the idea of undressing, stretching out on the king-sized bed, and soaking up the warmth her body had left in the blood-red satin sheets, if only to see her reaction. But he feared that might be pushing things a bit too far, settling instead on the small, white love seat under the large, sealed, and bullet-proof window, framed by wrought-iron bars.

Safety first.

The bathroom door squeaked open, revealing Lexi in her customary flowing skirt and top. Rafe took a moment to bask in her presence, inhaling her floral scent. "Amazing, a woman of her word."

Lexi stood above him, hands on her hips. "What do you mean by that?"

Rafe's lips twitched. "You said you'd be a few minutes, and it only took you a few minutes. I've never met a woman who was honest about how long it would take her to get ready. I'd come to the conclu-

179

sion that there was some type of problem in the
female genetic code that prevented proper judgment
of time once they entered the bathroom."

"Did anyone ever tell you that you were a complete
chauvinist?" Lexi asked, glaring down at him. But she
couldn't hide the smirk that lingered on the edges of
her mouth.

Thinking back over the years, past bra-burnings
and suffrage movements and into days of arranged
marriages and the belief that women were chattel,
Rafe laughed. "I believe it's been mentioned a time
or two before."

"Somehow, I'm not surprised." Lexi plopped down
on the seat beside him, making up for her lack of grace
in the warmth of her presence beside him. They both
stared out the window at the deepening night, dotted
by the lights of the boardwalk and the shimmer of
the moon rippling on the waves. "Be honest. You're
trying to distract me."

"Distract you?" Rafe asked, struggling to put a look
of innocence on his face that hadn't existed within
him for centuries.

"From the fiasco that is my life." Lexi replied, staring
at the night sky.

Rafe turned to face her, his hands cupping her chin
to force her to look at him. "My dear woman, I'm not
trying to distract you. If I were trying to distract you,
I'd do something like this." With that warning alone,
Rafe pounced.

His mouth slammed against Lexi's as he pushed
her down across the love seat, using it as its name
intended. He couldn't stand another second without

tasting her, if only the warm, sweet nectar of her mouth and not the salty spice of her precious blood.

Lexi whimpered, but didn't struggle. She melted into his passionate embrace, wrapping her arms around him, opening for his demanding tongue, and sliding against him in a rhythm as old as time, older than any vampire alive.

Rafe groaned, thrusting against her in a parody of the sexual act, aching to get closer, to feel more of her. He knew he couldn't. The timing was atrocious.

But it felt so good, so close to being alive.

Lexi agreed, if her nails digging into his shoulders were any indication. She wanted him closer, arching against his chest and moaning into his mouth. Her hard little nipples begged for attention as she struggled to pull him into her.

Rafe forced himself to pull away. She needed to be comforted, made to feel safe. She might want to escape her problems by drowning her senses in him, but he had other plans for her, for them. She didn't need a lust-filled vampire screwing her on her love seat the second he has five minutes alone with her.

He moved away from her lips, placing soft kisses across her face, murmuring words of comfort and endearments under his breath as he pulled her arms from around his neck, sitting back up and dragging her across his lap. He held her against his chest, rubbing circles against her back and rocking her ever so slightly.

Lexi shook in his arms, her heart pounding a tempting, delicious beat. Rafe kissed her temples.

"You know, I might not want a gentleman," she said, a drop of pain coating her words.

Rafe raised an eyebrow, looking down into her dewy eyes. "Excuse me?"

"I might not want a gentleman." She repeated, determination setting her lips into a firm line. "I know what you're up to. You want me, but you don't want to push a poor, emotionally-distraught woman. Didn't you ever think that I might want to be pushed, that I might want to forget?"

Her needy face looked up at him, full of beseeching desire. Rafe ached at the fear and pain at the foundation of her longing, but he couldn't allow himself to be moved. "And maybe I want to be more to you than a way to forget your troubles."

Lexi blinked, as though the thought that he might feel like that had never occurred to her. "You slipped out without saying anything to me."

"That doesn't mean that I want you for sex alone, that I don't care for you." Rafe cuddled her on his lap, petting her arms and placing soft kisses along her jaw. "This club is filled nightly with attractive young women, women more than willing to share a bed with a wealthy entrepreneur in hopes of more, or maybe for a quick tumble and nothing else. But I don't want any woman, Alexandria Hart. I want you."

"Why?" Lexi asked, her own insecurities out in the open for him to read even without his ability to search a human mind.

"Why not?" he shot back. He pushed her away from him, to look at her and force her to see herself as he did. "You warm my nights. You bring me laughter and understanding. Your body sends shivers of heat through my flesh. I can't be in the same room with you and not become aroused. But you are more than that."

He ran his fingers through her hair, watching as she arched into the caress with a soft moan. So responsive. So giving. But how to convince her of her own worth? How could he make her see herself as he saw her? "You're fun and understanding. You're intelligent, kind, and loyal. You make me look at things differently and give me a reason to smile when I wake up. And you have the gall to say that I want you for sex alone? For someone with such a low sense of worth, you think very highly of your ability to incite blind lust."

Lexi looked everywhere but at him, an amazing feat considering her face was only inches away from his. "You realize it's way too early for you to feel that way about me. We've only known each other a few days. Before that, we never said more than a few words, and most of those weren't exactly nice words. Most of the time you pissed me off."

Rafe closed his eyes and kissed her forehead, as he would a child in need of comfort. "I know everything that I need to know. For now that is enough. I won't tell you that I think I'm in love with you or that I want to spend eternity with you in my arms." *At least, not yet.* "But I think I deserve a chance, especially seeing as you're staying here with me."

Lexi shrugged, twisting her hands together and stiffening on his lap. "Stella says it's the safest place for us to be right now. You heard about what happened to the shop."

"Yes. I'm sorry this is happening to you. You have friends here, not only me, who will be more than happy to help you set up once you are able to return. But for now, Stella's right. At Nocturne, you'll never be alone. Here, we would all guard you." *With our very lives.* "No one can hurt you."

"I hate thinking that I'm inconveniencing you."

"You're not."

But Lexi wasn't having any of his sympathy. She shoved herself off his lap to sit next to him, hands folded. "Let me finish. I don't know how much anyone told you about what happened to my shop. There were threats, some nasty language. A part of me feels violated. And for some reason, the thought of being here with you made me feel safe, even for an instant. I had to come. I needed that feeling."

As do I. "I understand. Never feel sorry for feeling safe in my presence." Rafe felt a strange bubbling in his chest and realized he was about to chuckle. Safety with a vampire. Who'd have guessed such a thing was possible? "Not everyone can say that. Hell, very few people have ever told me that they feel safe near me. But you will always be safe with me. I would never hurt you on purpose. Anything I do will only be with your best interests in mind."

Lexi threw her hands in the air. "I know that. It sounds silly thinking about how badly I thought of you only a week ago, but I know now that you wouldn't hurt me. You might do something stupid and piss me off, like your disappearing act, but someone out there wants to hurt me. I know it's not you, so I feel safe."

But it *is* because of me, he thought to himself, but told her, "I'll do whatever's in my power to help you. I have investigators on my payroll. I understand that you have trust in your hometown police department, but it would make me feel better to know that there are more people out there looking for whoever is responsible for this. I'm going to do this, with or without your agreement, but I'd prefer with."

"When you put it that way, I guess I'll have to say with. I'll reimburse you for it somehow." She held up her hand when Rafe started to disagree. "Even if it's just redecorating a room without charge, I need to do something. It's one thing to take you up on your offer for a free place to stay. It's another to take your money to hire a private detective, even one already on retainer. If you agree to that, I'll agree to let you butt in on my private nightmare without argument. Deal?"

Rafe stared at her outstretched hand, not believing the ease of her agreement. But he couldn't leave it at a handshake. "Deal," he replied, grabbing her hand and pulling her, giggling, into another scorching kiss.

If this was how mates made up, Rafe could understand why Thane and Shanna argued as often as they did. Lexi's skin was chilled from the shower and her hair still damp, but she warmed his cold body. He rolled her beneath him again, his hands sliding across her skin. Being here, with her writhing in his arms, made him believe that maybe God hadn't forsaken him after all.

But now was not the time to bury himself in desire. He had an army of supernatural beings to muster and give orders to. He pulled away from her mouth and sat up. But he tucked her under his chin, holding her against his chest and taking comfort in the pounding beat of her heart. "Don't worry about anything. You'll be safe here. I'll make certain of it."

Lexi shoved her hair back with trembling fingers. "I don't see how I couldn't be, but thank you for the sentiment."

Rafe brush her hands aside. He straightened her shirt and smoothed her hair. It felt good to have someone to care for. "Now why don't you stay here and relax until opening. I'll bring you up some dinner, as I'm certain Grant has already done for your friend. I have a few things to deal with while you eat, and then I'll come escort you down for an evening of music and dancing. Would you enjoy that?"

Lexi stared up at him, desire and thankfulness filling her eyes, making him want to pull her even closer. She could be so prickly and independent that when she gave over even the tiniest bit of control, it made him feel like a god.

"I'd like that."

"Any special requests?" Rafe asked, standing and putting distance between them before he felt the urge to pull her down and taste her again.

Lexi's face took on that charming flush again, as though she knew exactly what he was thinking. He could only hope it was in her mind as well. "Stella keeps raving about this pasta dish you have."

"I know the one you mean. Diana, our head chef, brought that with her when Thane brought her in. She's only been with us for a few months, but her Italian recipes have earned rave reviews for Nocturne's dining. I'll bring you her special."

"And garlic bread? I love garlic bread."

Rafe thought it was a good thing that the myth

about garlic was just that, a myth. "Okay, but I would hope you'd feel more social than that."

Lexi stood on her toes, wrapping her arms around his neck. She kissed his cheek, working her way up his jaw to his ear. "Don't worry," she whispered. "I packed a toothbrush."

Rafe laughed at her weak attempt at humor, recognizing it for what it was—whistling in the dark.

He kissed her on the forehead and backed out of the room, reluctant to leave her side for even a moment. But if he wanted to ensure her safety, he had to leave, to set up security and check on the investigation.

Thane met him at the foot of the stairs. "I hear we have some visitors."

"From this moment, no one but the Alphas, you, and Shanna are allowed upstairs. I won't take any chances with Lexi's safety."

"You trust the wolves?"

Rafe understood Thane's confusion. Relations between werewolves and vampires were strained at times, downright bloody at others. But Grant had the same goals as Rafe, of that there was no question. And if Grant made Stella his mate, as Rafe planned for Lexi, the connection between his pack and Rafe's nest would be unbreakable. "I do not trust all of the wolves, but the Alphas are connected to Stella and will protect Lexi for her sake. I trust Grant to keep them in line."

"But you don't trust your own people?"

"Not beyond you and Shanna." Rafe frowned as he searched for the right words to express his fear for Lexi. "You know Edmund as well as I. Terror can make anyone do something stupid. I don't want Lexi to be the victim of stupidity."

Thane nodded, tilting his head. "Anything for me to do?"

"I want you to see your contact with the police and get a copy of the pictures taken at Lexi's store." Rafe began making his way to the kitchen as he spoke, his mind already flipping through all the things he needed to take care of before the dawn. "I want to know exactly what kind of threats, in human and vampire tongues, were made against her."

"That's no problem."

"Not yet at any rate." Rafe watched his friend's reactions to his next words, gauging his understanding of the severity of the situation. "This means war, Thane. Edmund must know of my connection to Lexi and plans to use her against me. I can't allow that. I won't allow that."

To his credit, Thane didn't blink. "Quick and clean or slow and messy?"

"I prefer quick and clean, but with Edmund, I make no promises."

"What do you think his next move will be?"

Rafe stopped before reaching the door. The human servants didn't need to know all his concerns, not as Thane did. "I can't predict the ancient. If I could, I would have left a hundred years ago. Instead, I almost waited too long. We should prepare for anything."

For the first time, Thane let his own horror show. He too had spent decades serving Edmund. He knew first-hand what punishments Edmund's sick mind could produce. "Should I send Shanna away?"

Rafe turned to look over his empty club. So much

time and effort. So much blood and terror. Yet, here was his dream, everything his undead heart ever hoped to accomplish. He mastered his own area. People listened to him and feared him, not the other way around. And he was loved. He had so much at stake. "If I could send Lexi somewhere I trusted her to be safe, I would. As it is, I don't know if my woman would be more at risk out of my sight. The same applies for any of my people. They are safer where we can protect them."

"Not to mention, Shanna would never leave. Not in the middle of a fight."

"No, she's too much like you in that."

Thane smiled. "We're a matching set, like you and Lexi will be. We make each other stronger, pull from one another. The longer we live together, the closer we become. You realize Lexi would be safer if she wasn't mortal."

"I know. It's only a matter of time. But I want her to have the chance to become comfortable with the idea, break things to her gently. I don't want to rip open her throat and thrust her into a world she has no concept of." Rafe looked at the only person in this world he could truly call friend. "I haven't been able to say anything to her about my life yet, much less what I want her to become. I don't want her to hate me."

Thane put a hand on Rafe's shoulder. "I understand the feeling. I don't know how I would've handled having to bring Shanna over. I was lucky she was already one of us when I found her. I don't know if I could kill her, even planning to bring her over. I don't envy you, my friend."

189

"I don't either."

Rafe turned without another word, retreating to the kitchens where the majority of his human staff worked, well away from the inhuman and easily tempted clientele. If anything went wrong in his great experiment, Rafe had no intention of letting one of his human servants become a casualty.

Rafe watched Diana's face light up with pride as he gave his woman's request to her. Everyone at the club knew who Lexi was, and who she would become. Even without knowing it, his little gypsy was a queen of the undead, and was honored as such.

Lexi made Rafe happy for the first time in more years than he wanted to contemplate.

Yes, Lexi was where she belonged, in his home, in her home. She might not realize it yet, but she wouldn't leave. When the time came, he'd have some people go out to her house and bring her belongings here. He wouldn't raze the beach house, as was the original plan. It meant too much to Lexi. But he'd find a way to incorporate it. That wouldn't be too difficult. It was only when a human would own property so close to his enclave that Rafe worried over security.

Now that wasn't a problem.

His days as a lone creature of the night no longer stretched out in eternal service to the needs of his nest. Now he had a personal reason to continue; a beautiful, vibrant armful of a reason.

Chapter Sixteen

Rafe should have known better. Even with Shanna taking her aside to speak with her, he should have known that Claudette could not be trusted to leave things at that. She lurked outside Lexi's door, waiting for him. She sneered at the tray he carried, tossing her wavy blond locks over her shoulder.

Rafe felt his muscles tense as he faced the woman whose expression filled with contempt.

"You've brought the mortal woman here? Are you insane?" she shrieked, flourishing her hands towards Lexi's door. "Edmund wants her. He's marked her as his prey. Housing her under our roof will bring his vengeance down upon us. Do you wish to meet death in truth?"

Rafe pulled himself up to his full height. He wrapped an aura of intimidation around himself that would have done Eldora proud as he sat the tray of food down on a small table. Looking up, his felt humanity bleed from his eyes, revealing the monster within.

Claudette blanched and started to step back, but not quickly enough. With a speed that no mortal eye could follow, Rafe lashed out, striking Claudette across the face and flinging her to the floor.

Snarling, he pounced on her, his hands forcing her shoulders down onto the cold tile as he rubbed his face against her neck. "Don't think to challenge me, woman," he snarled. "I have been more than lenient with your behavior up until this point, understanding what you suffered beneath Edmund. But Alexandria Hart is mine. I claim her. Edmund will not have anything that I claim as mine. Not you, not Lexi, not Nocturne, and not even Santa del Sol. If you want my protection to continue to shield you, I suggest you learn your place in the order of things. Lexi will not be my thrall, my servant. One day she will stand beside me as my queen, as your queen. Think of that and what the future will hold for you before you let your viper tongue loose again."

He pulled her head up far enough to slam it down again. "My patience is gone, your leniency over. I will tolerate no more disrespect."

But Claudette had never known when to quit. Instead of backing down, she laughed, a desperate, high-pitched cackle. "You think you can bring someone over without creating a ghoul? You think you can stand up to, much less defeat, Edmund? You're more insane than people think I am."

Rafe let the nail on his ring finger curve out to a talon. He raked it against her cheek as he answered. "I stood up to Edmund before. I lost flesh and blood, but I survived the challenge. I have Eldora's blessing to be here in America and to bring over any I wish to join me. I chose those who were already of us, but I have permission to claim any human who can survive the transformation. I will drive Edmund from my land if I have to drag every other supernatural being within calling distance into the fray."

"You fought Edmund in an honest challenge and survived, I'll grant you that. But you didn't win." Rafe watched as Claudette's eyes filled with blood-tinted tears. "If the sun had not risen, ending the contest without a kill, you would have lost. But your sacrifice saved me, freed me from Edmund. For that I owe you my loyalty and support. That is why I question your judgment. Not because I think you incapable or too weak to rule, but because I want you to win. Edmund doesn't fight fair, not if Eldora isn't right there standing over his shoulder. You can't expect him to."

Rafe rolled back on his heels, looking down at the pale, drawn female lying shivering on the ground. "And what makes you think I expect a fair fight from Edmund? He comes from a time before chivalry, before honor in battle. He lives only for the fight and the kill. He has no rules, and I expect nothing but treachery from him. That is why I want those under my protection to be beneath my roof, where I can keep an eye on them. He will do whatever he can to draw me out. If he kills me, Eldora takes back her support, and he can claim this place for his own."

Claudette sat up, wrapping her arms around her knees. Her fierce voice trembled. "I don't know what I fear the most, living under his control again or facing death. With Edmund, there is a living hell. In death, I might have a vague chance that I am not damned, merely changed."

Rafe shook his head, feeling pity again for this woman who'd once attracted so much of Edmund's attention. "Popular culture believes that vampires aren't monsters, only misunderstood, tragic figures forced to exist of the blood of others, but never truly enjoying a half-life. Claudette, we *are* all monsters; Edmund, Eldora, you, and I. Every non-human who steps through the doors to Nocturne is a monster. The only difference between any of us is our levels of power and our personal capacity for evil."

Claudette chuckled again, but Rafe wouldn't let her off that easily, not this time. "I kill without remorse. What separates me from Edmund is that I'm more logical and I despise waste. I want a reason to destroy; otherwise, I'm taking out a human I could use again for food later or another supernatural creature who may support me in a future time of need."

"And you don't think that makes you less a monster than Edmund?" Claudette whispered.

"No, it makes me more pragmatic. I would rip apart any person who discovered our secrets and threatened my sanctuary. I would leave them bleeding and babbling insanely in a muddy ditch as a warning to others, if need be. I can be as much of a monster as Edmund."

Claudette dropped her hands from her knees, fear and pity mixing on her face. "But you don't enjoy it. Edmund does. He feeds off pain, Rafe. I know it, first hand. He watches you scream and licks his lips. He laughs as you whimper and beg. He *is* the monster. You don't even come a close second."

"So you aren't afraid that I'll rip your throat out if you so much as look at Lexi the wrong way?" Rafe asked, eyes narrowing as his body quivered with the need to pounce, to prove his dominance over this upstart vampire.

"I don't doubt that you could hurt me as much as Edmund did, or even kill me if given the proper incentive." Claudette stared at the ceiling, looking back into a darker time in her life. "But you wouldn't revel in the act. It would be a necessity, something that had to be done. It's Edmund's enjoyment of the suffering of other creatures that makes him a monster, something to wake up screaming and clawing at the very thought of his name."

"And that is why it stops here and now. I won't allow my people to continue living in that level of fear. We came here for freedom. We will have that freedom. There is no other choice." He gave Claudette one final warning, one final chance. "You will be either an asset to my fight or you will be a hindrance. You don't want to be a hindrance. I eliminate obstacles. Don't become one."

Rafe shoved off the floor, dusting his clothes, picking a few stray, blonde hairs from the dark fabric. He picked up the tray and looked down at the still prone vampire. "This is the part where you scurry back downstairs and get back to your job. We open in ten."

Claudette wobbled to her feet. Rafe watched her stumble away. It wasn't as though she needed to attract attention. Any man she wanted would be drawn to her vampire allure.

Rafe shook thoughts of Claudette from his mind the moment the woman ran past him. He lifted the tray to balance on his shoulder and tapped on the door. "Room service," he called through the solid wood, smiling to himself as he heard Lexi cursing as she fumbled with the locks.

The smile melted from his face as he saw the rage burning in his woman's eyes. For the second time that night, he put the tray down on the first table he found. "What's happened?" he asked, pulling her into a gentle, comforting embrace.

Lexi stayed stiff in his arms for a moment, before sagging against his chest, clutching at his arms. "I hate this. I just hate it."

Rafe felt his heart fall in his chest, bursting wide at her words. "Hate what? Hate being here with me?"

Lexi gave a weak chuckle, pulling back to grin at him. "No, that's about the only good thing that's happened to me in the last few days. I hate this situation, this soap opera that my life's become in the past two days."

"What's happened now?"

"I just got off the phone with the police. They've told me to close my shop. Not asked me, told me." Her voice held a panicked squeak, and Rafe noticed a wildness, a sense of desperation lurking behind her eyes. "I'm not allowed back for at least a week, maybe longer. Can they do that?"

Rafe wished it were otherwise, wished he could charge into the station and brainwash the lot of them. He could do it. He could make them all change their minds, but he couldn't afford to waste the energy, not now. But looking down at her tear-filled eyes made it tempting. "If they've declared it a crime scene, and especially if they feel it's part of the on-going murder investigation, yes, I believe they can."

"Damn it." Lexi pushed away, tossing her hands in

the air as she walked back to the loveseat. "Things were going great. Another month, two on the outside, and I'd have enough to expand, to go into true interior decorating, to get rid of all the kitschy tourist stuff my aunt started with. Now, who knows how far this will put me back."

At least this was a concern he could squash easily, not like the fear of Claudette. "Is that all that's bothering you? Because if it is, let me tell you something from one business owner to another. Human beings are ghouls at heart. Yes, you'll lose profits while closed, but the moment your doors open again, you'll be swamped. You'll make any missed profits up in the first few days."

"But they won't let me in, Rafe. Don't you understand?" Lexi plopped down, shoulders sagging. Her voice became lost, forlorn. "They've taken everything from me. I can't go to my home. I can't go to my work. What am I supposed to do, take up knitting or try my hand at origami? I can't sit around all day doing nothing. I'll go insane. They've taken my life from me."

Rafe sat down and took her hands, rubbing them to give them warmth. "No, it just feels like it. You're alive and well and spitting mad. Don't ever forget that. As long as you are conscious, you are alive. Those three women in the morgue, they are dead. You're inconvenienced. You feel useless and at odds, but you live."

Lexi pulled away to look up at him in shock. "Damn, that's a hell of a way to cheer a girl up."

"I'm not trying to cheer you up," Rafe replied, arching a regal eyebrow. "I'm trying to pull you out of a downward-spiral of self-pity. The question is, did it work?"

Silence filled the room as seconds ticked by, leaving Rafe to wonder if he'd gone too far. Finally, Lexi growled, "Yeah, now I'm not sure who to be mad at, you or me. But I don't feel powerless, just pissed off."

"Madam, we aim to please." Rafe placed his hand over his heart, inclining his head with a mischievous smirk. "Now would you like to partake in a wonderful meal, specially prepared for you by a flattered cook, who is most pleased that you chose to order her signature dish?"

"Really?" Lexi asked, eyeing the covered tray in a way that made Rafe feel a little jealous. "Why would she be flattered? It's not like I'm a restaurant reviewer or a producer at Food Network."

"No, but you are the woman who's dating the boss. It's always good to be appreciated by the boss."

She tilted her head, looking in askance. "So they think they can suck up to you through me? If I go downstairs right now, I'd get residual brown-nosing? I've never had anyone kiss up to me before, not even my own employee."

Rafe grabbed the food and started setting up the table. "That's the problem with hiring a friend. From my short conversations with her, I doubt Stella would know where to start when it comes to the great and time-honored tradition of gratuitous ass-kissing."

Lexi laughed, snuggling into the loveseat as Rafe waited on her. "That's for sure. I doubt she'd even recognize it if someone else tried to brown-nose *her*. Mind you, she has a hell of a bullshit meter, but she wouldn't realize they were trying to get into her good graces. She'd just figure they were after something, something she didn't want to give them."

"And in a way, she'd be right," Rafe replied, flipping open a linen napkin and smoothing it over Lexi's lap.

"True, but that's not how she'd take it."

"I understand better than you think, and it's a skill she'd do well to learn." He thought of how many young pups would be crawling after her, begging for favors, once Grant finally made his move. "Who knows what the future holds for her? Someday she might find herself in a position of power and will need to be able to tell who is telling her the truth and who is telling her what she wants to hear."

"So speaks the voice of experience?" Lexi asked as Rafe lifted the metal lid from her plate, letting the tomato and garlic scented steam fill the air.

"Anyone who tries to control an empire the size of the one I'm imagining has faced that problem before, many times."

"Aiming to become the next Rockefeller or Howard Hughes?" she teased, reaching for her fork.

"No, I was thinking more along the lines of Alexander or Caesar. Why aim low?"

Lexi's eyes sparkled with mirth. "Why indeed, oh Great Lord of Santa del Sol. I must say, with such high goals, you certainly picked a small place on the map to start with."

Because that's where Eldora told me to go, and no one argues with the Dark Lady. "Everyone has to start somewhere. I wanted a place that I could call home."

"Well, Santa del Sol's certainly good for that."

He could hear the pride, love, and personal history filling that single statement. Without his ability to scan this human's mind, he didn't know as much about Lexi as he would like. This was the perfect opportunity to find the key to use to convince her to join him. "You're very protective of this town and its people, are you not?"

Lexi took a huge bite of spicy pasta before answering. "They've been good to me. They saw through the stubborn, hard-nosed punk kid that I was and gave me a chance at a new beginning. There isn't a person here who doesn't remember the delinquent I was, yet they choose only to see the woman I am now. You wouldn't believe the amount of support I got after my shop was vandalized. People called the police, took me aside, and sat with me until they showed up. The people here care about each other and take care of one another."

"And you would do the same for any one of them?" he questioned, comparing her feelings for this town with his for his nest.

"In a heartbeat."

Rafe nodded and stored that piece of information for future review. He hoped it wouldn't come to it, but as long as Edmund lurked in the city, her city was in danger in ways that Lexi couldn't imagine in her darkest nightmares. She might think she was tough, hearing her talk about her misspent youth, but until she lay on a table while others feasted from her extremities and made long cuts down her back for amusement, she had no concept of being tough.

He hoped to keep her soft for the next millennium or so.

Rafe sat back in the opposite chair, arms and ankles crossed, and watched Lexi eat. It was the one thing he missed from being human, eating. He had no difficulties living off the blood of mortals, he overcame that hang-up in the first decade of his new life, but he missed the different flavors. He could still drink, in small amounts. The fluids passed through him without difficulty. But solid food sat heavy in his stomach, only to launch itself out at the most inopportune moments.

He knew of other, older vampires, who would taste food and spit it out, savoring the flavors without truly eating. He couldn't do it himself. It would be too difficult to know the taste once more, without being able to partake, a subtle form of self-torture. But he loved watching humans eat, savoring every bite.

He would take so much. Would the gifts he gave be worth the loss to her? Would she shrug off the sacrifices to embrace her new life, or would she grow to despise him for stealing pleasures from her?

Metal clanged against china as Lexi laid her fork down. "You know, while I enjoy the food and all, I could use some dinner conversation. You don't have to stare at me."

"I'm sorry, but I thought you wanted some time to your own thoughts."

Lexi picked her fork back up and stared down at her plate. She shuffled her food around without taking another bite. "Maybe. But I'm tired of being stuck in my head, tired of thinking about murder and mayhem. I'm sick and tired of having the same ideas whirling around and around in my brain."

She shoved her plate aside, standing. Rafe stared as she walked around the table and sat on his lap, wrapping her arms around his neck. "Can you think of some way for me to get my mind on something else, to stop me from thinking?"

"Oh, I might have an idea or two." Rafe stood, hooking his arms under her knees and lifting her to his chest.

"Hey, now, careful. I don't want to give you a hernia."

"From lifting something as light as you? I doubt it that you'd strain my back, much less anything else." He threw her up, so her body barely left his arms, then groaned as she fell back in place. "Oh no, I think I've ruptured my spleen. I can't feel my toes. Oh, how could I have been such a fool as to lift a gorgeous woman into my arms, intending to have my wicked way with her?"

Lexi slapped his shoulders. "Stop kidding, you freak."

Rafe groaned louder, staggering towards the bed. He tossed her into the center, watching her bounce twice. "Thank the stars there was a bed so near. I don't think I could have managed another step under the strain. I think I'm perspiring. Do you see the sweat upon my brow?"

"Nope," Lexi smirked, her eyes roving over his long body. "All I see is an idiot who might not be getting any tonight, but I don't see any sweat. I don't think you can sweat. It would ruin your perfect, debonair businessman image."

Rafe gasped, his hands going to his chest as though recovering from a blow. "You cut me to the quick, woman. Here I risk life and limb to impress upon you my manly strength, and all you can do is make fun of my efforts and threaten to take away my reward."

"I don't remember threatening you."

He wagged a finger in her face, enjoying his moment of play with her. "You insinuated that I would not have access to your desirable self. What is that, other than a threat?"

"A tease, a temptation, a way of getting you to take what has already been offered to you?"

Rafe felt his gums tingle. "You want me to take you? You want me to ravish that delectable body, to take you places beyond your imaginings?"

Lexi shivered, her eyes going dark. "Yes," she whispered, lying down with her hands palm up beside her head. Her pale form and flowing black hair contrasted against the red satin comforter, the perfect offering to a king of blood and darkness.

For being such an evil man and living the last few centuries bathed in blood, Rafe gazed down at the vision before him and realized that the creator must still care for him in some way.

Lexi was his blessing.

"Well, what are you waiting for, hot stuff? I can't be more obvious. Not without shimmying out of my clothes and doing a bump and grind."

Make that a naughty little blessing.

Rafe wasn't one to overlook a blessing. With a growl that was more real than Lexi imagined, he pounced.

She laughed, rolling away.

"Oh no you don't," Rafe said, grabbing her wrists and dragging her back. "You're mine, mine to do with as I please. You gave yourself to me. Now, you must live with the consequences."

"Ooh, I like it when a man knows what he wants."

"I know exactly what I want. You. And I intend on getting what I want."

Lexi squealed as he yanked her shirt over her head. He stared down at the bounty she offered.

When he didn't move quickly enough for her, she grabbed him by the ears. "Then get with the getting already."

It was going to be a long night.

Chapter Seventeen

Much later that evening, Rafe stared down at Lexi's happy, open face. He reached out to smooth one dark, sweaty curl back into place. She smiled, taking his hand and kissing his palm before cupping it against her cheek. Rafe pulled her nude body closer to his, soaking up her warmth, basking in the warm glow she gave him. "I have to go down soon, but I don't ever want to leave this place next to you."

"You're the boss. Can't you take one evening off?"

Not with a bloodthirsty monster stalking the streets, wanting nothing more than to rip the throat out of the one thing in this existence I'm beginning to love. "I can't. Not tonight. The club's popularity is growing so that it's difficult for me to take time off. When things get more settled, I'll have to turn over more control to Thane. In the meantime, I have to be indispensable."

Lexi sighed, exhaustion and satisfaction etched on every curve of her body. Rafe should know, as he spent hours putting them there. "You're good at that, being indispensable. I don't know what I'm going to do with all this time alone up here in bed."

"Is that what I am to you, a way to pass the time now that you can't go back to work?" Rafe teased, lost in the wonder of being able to do such a simple thing with a woman, lay in bed and joke. "I'm wounded, heart-struck. How could you be so cruel to one who wants only your happiness and pleasure?"

"If you can't tell that I want you for you, we really need to start over again." She rolled over, sliding her naked thigh between his. "I must have done something wrong, or you weren't paying attention."

Rafe groaned as her hot, little tongue ran the length of his chest and her nimble fingers coasted farther south. "Lexi, please."

"Please what?" she whispered, her hand dancing around the one place that wanted her attention the most.

He grabbed her wrist, his pelvis jerking towards her, wanting nothing more than to let her continue. "If you keep that up, I'll never make it back downstairs."

"And that's a bad thing?" she asked, batting her eyes.

"It is when I've already set up an evening meeting with some real heavy-hitters," he whimpered. "I already rescheduled once. I can't do it again."

Lexi's lower lip stuck out and quivered, but she couldn't keep the grin hidden for long. "I guess if you have to, I understand. But you better remember where we left off. I'll expect you to start in the exact same place."

"I will. There is no way I'll forget." He leaned over and kissed her passion-swollen lips, his fingers sliding across the place above her pulse that he'd so recently sunk his fangs into.

As their lips parted, Lexi sighed. "And to think, I wasted months avoiding you because of your offers to buy my house."

"Your home is safe from me," Rafe said as he slid out of bed and started gathering his scattered clothes together.

"Damn, talk about killing two birds with one stone. Now I really wish I'd known that sooner. You mean all I needed to do was sleep with you to get you off my back?"

Rafe smiled at her before pulling on his pants. "I didn't say I wouldn't get on your back, only that I'm no longer interested in buying your house. I'll work something else out, but I'm not limiting where my body goes in relation to yours."

Lexi's brow wrinkled for a moment before his words made sense. "Naughty boy."

"Only when it comes to you, my love." His shirt tucked in, he grabbed his socks and shoes and sat in bed next to her. It was a temptation having all that bare flesh so close to him, but he wanted these last few minutes near her. He needed to stock up on her presence in order to make it through the next hour or so without her.

Lexi's eyes roved from the hair her fingers had mussed to the feet he slid into his shoes, the heat of her gaze warming each body part it caressed. "No way do I believe you're an angel the rest of the time."

"Not an angel, no. But I'm not normally a lust-filled dark prince on my good days. My passions haven't run so hot for a woman before."

Lexi rolled her eyes. "Pull the other one."

"Truly. If I had ever felt this way before, I wouldn't be single."

With that little bombshell dropped, he walked out the door. As he closed the room behind him, he chuckled. The look of astonishment had been worth whatever myriad of questions she had waiting for him when he returned to her arms. He gave her a good half-hour to an hour before she came traipsing down to the club. She'd want to armor up in some outfit designed to give him a heart attack, if such a thing were still possible. He had plenty of time to meet with Grant and prepare for the siege that was sure to come.

With Lexi and Stella forming a bridge of blood between them, Rafe couldn't imagine a reason for the wolves not to side with him against Edmund. They had as much to lose, and their future queen would make them miserable if they allowed harm to come to her best friend.

Fate and mating seemed to be on his side.

Chapter Eighteen

Lexi lay in bed for a solid five minutes after Rafe left, his words echoing in her mind. He couldn't possibly have meant what it sounded like. They'd gotten to know each other only over the last week. She still had trouble believing how quickly they'd fallen into bed together, not that she regretted it in the least. But sleeping together and talking about marital status, like she could change his, that was going light-speed. Brakes needed to be applied, anchors thrown out to stop forward momentum before hitting the iceberg.

At least, if he meant what it sounded like. But he couldn't have. No man would say something like that, voluntarily, this early in. Not without judicious use of thumbscrews.

Would he?

Shit, she needed advice. Lexi swung her bare feet over the edge of the bed and staggered towards the bathroom she shared with Stella's room. As she reached for the door, she noticed the way her arm trembled and the goose bumps that covered her skin.

Clothes first. Can't visit without clothes.

She laughed at herself as she pulled a nightgown

over her head and tied the robe around her. Maybe *she* was the lust-filled idiot. Rafe didn't walk out of the room without his clothes on.

The man was dangerous.

When she got to the door on the other side of the bathroom, she knocked before she could second-guess herself. Stella was going to have a heyday with the information Lexi planned on giving her. But Lexi needed another perspective, a woman with a better grasp of the male psyche than she had.

Stella knew men.

And she looked like she knew them a hell of a lot better this evening than she had that morning. Rainbow-colored hair stuck out in every direction. Her cheeks and neck were whisker-reddened, and it looked like she had a bite mark on her shoulder.

Lexi leaned against the doorjamb and twirled the end of the sash on her robe. "Well, it seems that your evening has been similar to mine. Want to hash things out, share nookie notes?"

Stella rolled her eyes and yawned. "God, you want to talk. You want to take five and analyze everything. I can barely string sentences together yet, and you're already picking apart every move the poor guy made. Can't you do that by yourself?"

Lexi felt a momentary stab of pity, but shoved it aside at the thought of all the times Stella forced her to listen, in minute detail, about her latest squeeze. "Sorry, but this one's important, not my usual 'cold feet' monologue."

"It had better be. Grant left twenty minutes ago, but he kept at me all day and most of the night. I'm no longer bummed out that he hasn't made a move.

210

Instead, I can barely walk. I need some recovery time of my own."

Lexi grinned as Stella limped back to the bed, throwing herself across it with a groan. She plopped down beside her friend, smirking as the movement sent another pitiful moan from Stella's lips.

"Guess I wasn't the only one to get lucky this time, hmm?"

"You have no idea," Stella muttered into the bedding before managing to roll back over. "I can't decide if the man's an animal or a machine. He's wild, pouncing and biting, but making me want anything he does. Add that to the fact he has an unnatural recovery time and the stamina of a Timex, and you get the picture."

"Yeah, I noticed the nibble mark. Kinky."

Stella glanced at Lexi's neck. "You're one to talk. Looks like Rafe takes after Grant in some things."

Lexi wrinkled her brow, reaching for her neck. She felt a slight twinge and realized somewhere in the midst of passion, he'd either bitten her or given her one hell of a hickey.

Whichever it'd been, it certainly didn't feel bad.

"I need to talk. Rafe said something that threw me for a curve, and I want to know if I'm reading too much into it."

Stella groaned again, grabbing a pillow and holding it over her face. "Knowing you, the answer's probably yes."

"Give me a break." Lexi grabbed the pillow from her and tossed it across the room. "I need you to listen and give me your thoughts. Is that too much to ask?"

"Right now, maybe, but I'll give it my best. Shoot."

Lexi flopped down on her side with her head propped on her hand to get a good look at her friend. Stella's first reactions were always the best, and Lexi didn't want to miss this one. "We were talking about sex and lust, and he said he'd never felt like this with anyone else. I thought that was the normal line, what you say to the woman you just slept with and hope to sleep with again. That sounds logical so far, right?"

"Yes. It doesn't sound like you need me to tell you anything." Stella grabbed a blanket and snuggled in, closing her eyes.

"If he stopped there, you'd be right. But then, right before he left, he said that if he had ever felt this way before, he wouldn't be single."

Stella sat up, her covers falling to her lap and all trace of sleepiness gone. "He said that, exactly that?"

"Pretty much." Lexi took Stella's old position, looking up at the ceiling. "He said that the fact he was single proved that he'd never felt like this before. I know it's fast and all, but that sounds like a description of love to me, maybe even an opening to talk about commitment. I thought all guys were allergic to the L word, and you had to drag the C word out of them with the rack and bamboo under their fingernails. Am I reading him wrong?"

Stella shook her head, dragging her fingers through her hair. "Shit, I wish I were more conscious at the moment. It sounds serious. He's saying the same kind of things Grant told me last night, after a solid month of working on him. Damn, I'm jealous. I had to date a long line of losers, and then wait for the right guy to get the guts to say anything close to what Rafe told you. You don't date for years, go out with the man for less than a week and sleep with him at the drop of a hat. Then he falls over himself to make a vague declaration, but a declaration none-the-less. Life isn't fair. You do realize that, don't you?"

"I do now." Lexi sat back up, propping her chin on her knees. Her inside felt all twisted, unfamiliar emotions fighting it out with the butterflies in her stomach. "What do I say to him, Stella? Do I wait for him to make the next move, or is he waiting for me to say something?"

"Do you feel the same way about him, really? Is it more for you than sex and a nice dinner companion?"

Lexi let her knees drop at the seriousness in Stella's voice. This wasn't a slumber-party conversation between girlfriends. This was decision time. "Of course. Sex I can handle myself, with a little help from batteries. If I want a nice dinner companion, I can ask you out for pizza. But everything's happening so fast, with a maniac added into the mix to make things even more confusing. What if I'm not reading myself right?"

"Here's the easiest way to answer that question. If you don't take the chance with Rafe, if nothing else happens between the two of you from this point on, how would you feel? Would you regret it?"

Lexi didn't even have to think about her answer. "I would never regret being with him. I would regret losing him without having a chance to fight for him."

"Then there you go. You want a chance for more. Take it. Run with it."

Lexi nodded, her lips drawing out to a thin line. Even with her decision made, there was planning to be done, a man to ensnare. "I need help. I bought some drop-dead clothes, but didn't pack them when I got chased out of my house by the cops. I need an outfit, a killer outfit."

"Trying to say yes without having to actually say the words?" Stella teased.

"Yeah, do you have a problem with that?" Lexi asked, hands on her hips and eyebrows raised.

"No, not if you realize what you're doing. I'm all for the shock treatment, especially when it comes to male hormones." Stella dragged herself out of bed and made her way to the over-sized closet covering the entire back wall. "I'm sure I can scrounge you up something from my wardrobe. I never leave home unprepared, even when in the midst of a psycho-killer evacuation. I'm a little smaller and you're a tad taller, but that'll work to our advantage. Everything I own will be short and tight on you, the perfect combination for seduction. So, Eliza, my dear, put yourself into the good professor's hands. I'll make you a star."

Lexi smirked as she watched Stella practically dance around the room. "So, all you needed to get you up and moving was a makeover project?"

"No, I needed a makeover project with an immediate promise of gratification." She grabbed a small suitcase from the bottom of the wardrobe, sitting it on the bed before popping it open. A myriad of makeup dazzled the eyes. "I want to see Rafe's face when he catches the first glimpse of what I have in mind for you. Of course, you can't go alone, and I can't let myself be entirely out-classed. So I'll be with you, dressed to the nines as well. Maybe we'll both get our guys to pony up with the emotional commitment kudos. Sound like a plan?"

"Sounds like a plan. Just don't make me look like a Goth streetwalker. With an all-night club, like Nocturne, I'm sure Rafe's seen more than his fair share of that."

Stella tapped a makeup brush against her lips as she stared at Lexi. "I can't guarantee no street-walker look; tight and short, remember? But I can tone down the gothic ensemble and play up the punk. I can only work with what I've got on me. Too bad we aren't still at my place. I didn't bring that red number I told you about. That would've been perfect. Oh well, how do you feel about leather?"

"It looks nice, but is sweaty to wear." Lexi eyed her friend with suspicion. "I remember having to coat my legs with baby powder to slide into those pink suede pants I wore in high school."

"The one's you had to hold your breath and use a coat-hanger looped through the zipper to get on?"

"Those are the ones," Lexi said, smiling at the fashion nightmare.

"What did you ever do with those?" Stella asked, a dangerous speculation lurking in her eyes.

"Donated them to Goodwill," Lexi replied with trepidation.

Stella shrugged off her idea. "Guess someone got some *real* good will the next night, huh?"

"Did I ever tell you that you're awful?"

"Only every other day," Stella replied with a grin.

Chapter Nineteen

Rafe collapsed in a chair hidden from most prying eyes in a small alcove facing the stage. The night was almost over and no sign of Edmund. Worse yet, no sign of Lexi. Rafe had been certain she'd show up to torment him for his parting words. Maybe she didn't feel the same way about him. Maybe he'd made a mistake. Maybe fate had tied him to a woman who didn't want the connection, wanted nothing more than a few hours of sex-filled forgetfulness.

Maybe he'd sit here, drink his brandy glass full of werewolf blood and worry himself into oblivion. It wasn't as though anyone would bother him. The humans had left for the night. The only customers who remained were supernatural in origin, mainly werewolves. They knew what was happening around them. They realized the pressure Rafe was under. They would give him his time alone to plan and strategize. At least, that's what they thought he was doing, not moping around wondering whether a human woman liked him or not.

He was pathetic.

Suddenly, he saw the patrons turn as one to look

at the back hallway, the one that led to the sleeping quarters upstairs. A murmuring wave of appreciation washed through the masses as they whispered and nodded in that direction.

Rafe stood, unable to see from his secluded corner. The vision that met his gaze shoved his heart into his throat at the same time it jerked down his jaw.

Alexandria Hart looked like a wet dream come to life.

A short, black leather skirt wrapping around her thighs covered just enough to prevent indecent exposure. Black fishnet stockings framed the long line of her muscular legs, while stiletto heels threw her gait into a sensual roll. A hot pink t-shirt molded the top of her form. The gothic cut, with its low neckline and short, puffy sleeves, accentuated the bounty lying beneath the thin cotton fabric. Her long, jet-black curls formed a bouncy halo around her pale, delicate face. But her fire-engine red lips begged to be kissed.

Rafe didn't notice a similarly dressed Stella walking close on Lexi's heels. He had eyes only for his wonderful, seductive gypsy woman. A woman who could literally bring the dead back to life, or at least make him feel alive again.

Rafe didn't remember leaving his seat or crossing the dance floor. He hoped he did it at a normal, human-like pace, not his usual vampiric speed. His next conscious realization was that he stood inches from his woman, her hand clasped tightly in his own.

"You are so beautiful, you take a man's breath away, leaving him panting in awe." He raised her hand to his lips, placing nibbling kisses on each of her knuckles.

Lexi giggled under her breath, flinching at the sound. He thought her little habit was cute, but knew she hated the nervous, bubbly sound. Though he wanted to tease her about it, he didn't want to break the spell she'd cast over him and kept his mouth closed.

"That's quite a silver tongue you have there," she joked, lacing her fingers with his and stepping forward to place a hand against his chest.

"You would know the skills of my nimble tongue better than most, my sweet. If ever you wish for another demonstration, you have only to ask."

Lexi's eyes sparkled in delight as she raked her gaze across his body. "I don't think I need to do that much. You look ready to volunteer to me."

Rafe pulled her closer, letting her feel exactly what she did to him. "What can I say? You bring out both the beast and the slave in me. The beast wants to pounce, drag you upstairs away from other prying, male eyes, and have its wicked way with you. The slave wants only to bask in your presence, to worship you, and to gaze at your amazing beauty. Whatever you ask of me, if it is in my power to give to you, it is yours."

"Damn, you know how to knock a girl off her feet," she gasped, leaning into his embrace. "And here I spent all evening getting ready to do the same to you. It's not fair. I put all this work in, and you say five sentences to me and make my knees go weak."

"It's a gift, one I gladly share with you."

"You just want to watch my knees wobble."

Rafe let his eyes run over the length of her legs, imagining what they'd look like wrapped around his waist with those fishnets. "I must admit, you've made knee wobbling into an erotic experience. If this were another kind of club, I might hire you, if I could overcome my own territorial instincts."

The corner of her mouth lifted into a half smile as she stepped close enough for her breasts to rub against his chest, the heat of her skin apparent through the layers of cloth. "I make you feel territorial?" she asked, as her fingers walked up his chest to play at his collar.

Rafe's body trembled. He glanced around to see people studiously looking in the opposite direction. "You make me feel prehistoric. If you don't stop playing with me now, I'm going to embarrass myself in front of all my employees and customers. You wouldn't want to do that to me, would you?"

"Yes and no," Lexi replied. "I'd like to see your reaction, but I don't want to humiliate you."

"I'm glad to hear that." Rafe stepped back and took her arm, guiding her to his private table. He wanted to be as alone with her as he could manage, not ready to share her with his people. Not yet. "Let's discuss what you do want from me, shall we? I have some ideas, fantasies if you will, that I'd like to suggest. After our chat, we could dance the evening away or retire upstairs. I have meetings all day, but will see you again in the evening. How does that sound?"

"It sounds like you never sleep."

He thought of the darkness that closed over his senses with the rising of the sun, the complete emptiness that filled him until the sun set again. "I catch a wink here and there. Don't worry about me. I'll be more than energetic enough to entertain you."

Lexi laughed at his insinuation, but Rafe didn't

bask in the sound. Something else drew his attention. The hair on the back of his neck stood on end. A wave of power, familiar and strong, flowed through the club without any attempt at disguise. The ancient wanted his presence known, not hidden. This was an open challenge to Rafe's authority, to display such power in a place of sanctuary.

Edmund was ready to play.

Rafe stood, walking around the table to pull Lexi to her feet again. He scanned the area as he moved her to the opposite end of the club. "My sweet, there's going to be some trouble. Why don't you go into the back until I deal with it?"

"What's going on?" Lexi asked, glancing around the room. Every person, employee and patron stood frozen, staring at a small group marching in.

Rafe turned her face back to him, forcing her attention away from Edmund. He had to get her to safety, had to keep her from falling under the ancient's spell. "Some people who want to make trouble, that's all. I recognize one of them. I'd feel better, be able to handle him easier, if I knew you were out of the way."

A dark laugh filled the club, raking against nerves. Even Lexi gasped, holding her arms over her stomach as if bracing for a strike.

"Oh, don't hurry your little pet to safety just yet, Rafferty my boy," Edmund mocked as he took the center of the dance floor, other supernaturals falling to the side like a parting sea. "She's the reason I'm here, after all."

Rafe stiffened, closing his eyes so Lexi wouldn't see the darkness growing within them, surrounded by a web of blood-red capillaries. His fangs had already slid into place, peaking out past his upper lip.

If Edmund meant to take Lexi, it would be a fight. There would be no protecting her from the obvious. Rafe would guard her from the other vampire any way within his power and hope that she didn't hate him for it, didn't think him a monster.

"I'm sorry," he murmured, imprinting the look on her face in his mind, the last look of open acceptance he might ever see. He bent to place a soft kiss to her forehead before thrusting her behind him and facing his enemy.

He stood his ground, letting his own psychic shields fall to the wayside, filling the room with an aura of fear and intimidation. "You will not take her, Edmund. She is mine."

His stance only served to amuse the older vampire. Edmund snapped his fingers, his people spreading to form a semi-circle around him. The club fell silent, the only sound the beating hearts of the werewolves and the two human women. "I claim her as my prey, Rafferty O'Neill," Edmund said, his face a picture of peace and acceptance. He had the look of one who was seldom denied anything he desired. "I've stalked her for days now, leaving her presents to show my affection, to sweeten her blood with fear and terror. You will not come between me and my chosen meal."

A growl reverberated deep in Rafe's chest. His nails slid out into deadly talons, hidden beneath clenched fists. "She is my woman, and you cannot have her."

Edmund tilted his head, looking at Rafe with nothing short of amusement. "Do you think to fight me for her, boy? Don't you remember our last

221

encounter? If the sun hadn't risen, I would have killed you, bled you like a pig. Time alone saved you. Do you trust in time to save you again? If so, you're more a fool than I thought."

Rafe stepped forward, placing distance between Lexi and himself, hoping to draw the ancient's attention away from his woman and back to him. "You chose Lexi because you knew of my interest in her. That is a challenge to me, one I can't let go unanswered. If you take her, where will you stop? You will take my lands and people from me one piece at a time. I won't let it begin here with her."

"Maybe you're not as big a fool as I took you for." Edmund's smile widened even as he shook his head. "No matter. It won't change the inevitable. I have you outnumbered and out-classed. Give the human to me now, or later. The only difference will be how much flesh and blood you lose in the process."

With that, Edmund gestured to his followers. Two shadow vampires, young ones starved to the point of emaciation and desperation, took point in front of eight large werewolves wearing leather and spiked collars. The shadows quivered with repressed need, waiting for their master's signal. Snapping and popping filled the air as bones and joints began realigning themselves in the lupines.

Nocturne's protectors flew into action. Thane and Shanna appeared at Rafe's side, followed quickly by Lennox and Zachary. Claudette and Gemma took Lexi by the shoulders and dragged her to the back of the room. The majority of the werewolf patrons went to the back of the room as well, but seemed to be acting as guards for Stella as the five members of the Alphas stepped forward to join Rafe.

"My people stand by you in this fight," Grant growled as he pulled his shirt over his head. "My mate holds Alexandria Hart as her only family. As such, Alexandria Hart is part of my family and is under pack protection."

Rafe's gaze flicked to the other side, gauging their chances. "It's eight against five. It will take all of my vampires to handle the shadows. Can you take care of the werewolves?"

"Five free alpha wolves against eight vamp-bitten slaves?" Grant snorted, his face beginning to ripple with the change. "You're right in doubting the fairness of the fight. They don't stand a chance. You worry about your challenger, and we'll take care of ours."

Rafe clapped the werewolf on the shoulder, and then turned to face Edmund. He allowed his contempt to shine from his eyes. "Whenever you're ready, let's get this over with. Just try not to do too much damage to the club. I'd hate to delay opening tomorrow."

"You always were a cocky bastard. I told Eldora that she'd rue the day she decided to turn you instead of draining you dry and leaving you lying in a gutter."

"Less talk, more fight," Grant growled as his body started twitching and stretching.

Rafe launched himself through the air, talons and fangs bared. He heard a feminine gasp, but ignored it. His hands grappled with Edmunds shoulders, nails sinking deep into skin and muscle. He strained to reach Edmund's throat, rip it, and guzzle the powerful liquid. Fingers wrapped in Rafe's hair, Edmund wrenched him back.

Time slowed. Reality became fang and blood, pain and howls. Edmund snarled at Rafe, saliva dripping down his incisors as he swiped at Rafe's eyes. Rafe twisted, managing to keep his chin down and his neck protected. He felt a sting as the flesh on his cheek parted, but it was a minor wound.

Anger fed his strength, anger and fear. Rafe shoved Edmund back, landing on a table only to thrust himself into the air again.

Edmund waited, arms outstretched. Rafe hesitated for a moment, trying to reason out his opponent's strategy. Edmund was no fool. Why was he fighting with brute strength? Why hadn't he used any of his other vampiric powers?

Why was he being so easy?

Edmund glanced over Rafe's shoulder and smiled. Rafe took advantage of the momentary distraction, twisting and striking, raking his fangs across the other vampire's neck. Blood spurted, not pulsing with the beat of a heart, but pouring out to rain down on the combatants below.

A moment of triumph blazed through Rafe as Edmund pushed him back, his hand clamping over the wound. But when the other vampire's feet touched the floor, he looked up at Rafe and laughed. "Good shot, young one. First blood goes to you. But the battle is far from over."

He stared behind Rafe, still chuckling. Rafe glanced back to see what held Edmund's attention, what he found so amusing. Lexi and Stella stood, backs against the wall with their vanguard of vampires and were-wolves surrounding them. Lexi's wide eyes locked on

Rafe's floating form, the blood draining from her face as she touched the side of her neck.

"It looks like trouble on lover's lane tonight," Edmund chuckled, his wound healing with every passing second. "I'll leave you with your explanations. Maybe she'll accept them, but probably not. I wish you luck at convincing her that you aren't the monster that you seem. A difficult task, as you *are* the monster that you seem."

Rafe spun, hissing at the other vampire. Edmund's shoulders shook with the power of his laughter. "Oh, you should see the look on your face, so tragic and pain-filled. I couldn't have done better myself. And the fact that you've done this to yourself makes it all the more delicious."

Edmund snapped his fingers. The four surviving werewolves rushed to him along with one staggering, bleeding shadow. The rest had fallen under the claws and teeth of Rafe and Grant's people. Edmund arched an eyebrow. "Not bad. You fared better than I anticipated. But don't worry, I won't make the same mistake again."

As quickly as the siege had begun, it was over. But the aftermath, while not as bloody as Rafe had expected, was far more painful.

With the cracking of bone and cartilage, as well as a few pain-filled moans, Grant regained his human form. Not bothering to pick up his clothes, he rushed to his mate's side. Stella took one look at him, glanced down at the bite-mark vivid on her shoulder, and tore out of the room.

No one blocked her way, but a few smirks brightened the room as the alpha wolf gave chase to his mate. There were few doubts in anyone's mind how that hunt would end.

Rafe glided towards Lexi. He retracted his fangs, but saw how she stared at the wet blood shining silver in the artificial lighting. He reached one hand forward.

"Lexi, sweet, let me explain."

Amazement filled the air as Lexi's hand flashed out, slapping Rafe sharply across the cheek, rocking him on his heels.

Chapter Twenty

The sound of her slap echoed through the shock-filled silence of the club. Everyone stared at Rafe before scrambling out of the room, probably wondering if he was going to rip her throat open, too. Now that was a picture Lexi didn't want following her into her dreams, blood pouring out like a waterfall, drenching the people standing below. And the guy laughed about it.

This was a nightmare, and Lexi feared she'd never wake up.

It was stupid to hit him. He'd be pissed, to say the least. And he wasn't human. God knew what an angry Rafe was capable of, being a monster. Lexi didn't even want to think the word 'vampire'. Her stomach clenched at the thought that she'd slept with something that lived off of human blood. The first guy to come along and rock her world, and he was a vampire.

God help her.

Rafe looked up at her, his hand covering the cheek she'd slapped. He didn't look angry. Not at all. He looked sad, hurt.

227

Lost.

And whatever reaction she'd expected, it wasn't his next words. "I know I deserved that. I should have spoken to you sooner. You shouldn't have been forced to learn the truth in such a brutal manner. I'm sorry."

He was *sorry*. He tricked her, probably lining her up for his next midnight snack, and he was *sorry*. Lexi raised her hand again.

Rafe grabbed her wrist in a tight, but gentle, grasp. Determination lined his face, his eyes turning a midnight hue. Lexi shivered at his cold words. "Just because I deserved the first strike doesn't mean I will allow you to hit me again. I am not a punching bag, not even for you."

She struggled to break his grip, pull free. Her heart raced. Would he kill her? Had she slept with a murderer? "So what are you, huh? You're not human, that much I can tell."

"You know what I am," Rafe whispered, drawing her resisting body into him. "It's on the tip of your tongue."

She stopped fighting, shoulders sagging. What use was there in fighting him? He could overpower her without effort. Her mind refused to come to terms with the words that fell from her lips, truthful or not. "You're a vampire, a blood-sucking creature of the night. You're something out of movie matinees, not real life."

"I am what I am," he said, cupping her chin. "I can't be otherwise, no matter how much I might wish it. And I don't particularly wish it. It isn't a bad thing."

Lexi flinched, jerking away from his caressing fingers. Maybe she couldn't win, but she didn't have to give up without a fight. "You eat people, and you say it isn't a bad thing?"

"I take only what I must to survive. I don't kill needlessly."

"So what am I, then?" Lexi asked, ashamed at the pain tinting her voice. She thought he loved her, and she was nothing to him. How could she be? "Are you stocking up, putting aside a few meals to enjoy later?"

Rafe had the gall to look hurt again. It was her heart he was ripping out, and he had the nerve to look like she was hurting him.

"You're not a meal, Lexi," he murmured, his fingers digging into her shoulders. "I hope you realize that."

"Oh really?" she snapped, refusing to buy into his 'poor misunderstood me' routine. Flippant anger was her only refuge from the fear gnawing at the edges of her mind. "Then what about the bite mark on my neck? It *is* a bite mark, isn't it? You needed a quick pick-me-up after a long session in the sack. Is that it?"

Finally, anger flashed in his eyes. As she watched, they turned black with a fine, crimson webbing surrounding the iris. His fangs slid out, peaking from behind his upper lip. "How many times must I say it?" he hissed, pushing her against the wall. "Yes, I bit you. I confess to not having a great deal of control when it comes to you. I shouldn't have, and I knew it both times I bit you."

"*Both* times?"

Rafe ignored her question, staring into her eyes like a snake pinning its prey. "But I couldn't resist temptation. I couldn't resist you. I haven't been able to resist you since the first moment I laid eyes on you. I tried to keep it business. I tried to bend your mind to my will, get your house, and then stay the hell away from you. But I couldn't bend you. I couldn't even read you. So I had to talk to you instead, get to know you. And the more I got to know, the more attracted I became, until I couldn't resist you. You have no idea of the power you have over me."

"The power I have over you," Lexi snarled, eyes narrowing as she stepped closer, poking him in the chest with a single finger. "You're the supernatural monster boy. You're the one with the mystical mind powers, and don't think I missed the whole, 'I tried to bend your mind' bit. How do I know it didn't work, that my falling into bed with you quicker than it normally takes me to pick a pair of shoes isn't all some spell you cooked up?"

Rafe threw his hands over his head, daring to look like the offended party. "Do you see me holding a deed?" he growled. "Do you see me plowing over your home to clear the way to build a safe, high-security nest for my people? No, I believe I told you I'd given up, that you won. If I could control you, if I wanted you to obey my every whim, I believe I would have done a better job of it."

"God, do I ever pick them." Lexi stared at him, trying to see past the monster with fangs and glowing eyes to the man she'd fallen in love with. She couldn't have made love to something that saw her as little more than food. She had to have better judgment than that. But should she trust him, or her own common sense? "I should have my head examined. I can't even date in the same species."

Rafe shook her, his eyes flashing dangerously.

"Don't change the subject. You know you're not afraid of me. You don't think I'm a monster."

"Oh, and how do you know that, Mr. 'I can't see into her mind or bend her to my will?'" she taunted, the heat of her anger finally pushing back the chill of fear. "You're a monster. How am I supposed to look beyond that?"

"I don't know, but I do know you aren't scared of me. You hit me. You stand here and argue with me. What you haven't done is run. Even Stella ran."

"Yeah, well she just found out she'd been sleeping with a real dog." Lexi felt her heart leap as she remembered her friend's last gesture before leaving the room. The realization caused her heart to stutter. "Grant bit her. Shit, you bit me. We're going to be monsters, too."

Rafe couldn't meet her eyes. "With your friend, yes. An alpha werewolf bit her. With such a powerful being, transformation can only take one bite. A weaker wolf would've taken more than one, but Grant is anything but weak."

"What about me?" Lexi whispered, her fingers brushing against the mark on her neck. It couldn't be true. She couldn't be dead. She didn't feel dead. She wasn't craving steak tartar.

Rafe shook his head, dropping his hands from her and stepping back. His voice became carefully neutral. "No, you won't fall into a dreamless sleep at the rise of the sun. You won't awake with an insatiable hunger for blood. I took from you, but I did not give. Unlike lycanthropy, vampirism is a gift, something that must be offered and accepted. For you to cross-over, I would need to feed deeply from you, then you would have to drink from me."

"That's good," Lexi said, still rubbing her mark. The more she thought about it, the more it tingled and throbbed. There had to be more than he was telling her. "What does your bite do to me?"

Rafe turned away from her, staring at the empty stage. "Not much, not with your natural resistance and the small amount that I took from you. At most, if I needed to find you, you'd be easier for me to track."

Flashbacks of the hunchbacked little bootlicker in every Dracula movie she'd seen came back with gut-clenching clarity. "That's all. No weird food cravings?"

Rafe looked confused before he started to laugh. "No, you won't be eating insects or craving the life-force of spiders."

Lexi shuddered and sighed. *Gag much.* "Good. I'm not eating bugs for anyone not offering me a hundred thousand dollars or more to do it."

She looked at him, so forlorn and melancholy. He didn't look like the blood-crazed, hypnotic monster of legend. He still joked with her, found humor in his situation. How much of the man he'd revealed to her before truly existed, and how much was a mask? "There must not be anything that could gross you out."

He stared at the blood now coating the dance floor. "You'd be surprised."

Lexi refused to look down at it. If she did, she knew she'd freak out, the sight of that other vampire like Monty Python's Black Knight haunting her. Instead, she stuck to her more playful questioning. "Oh, I guess you can't be filmed, right? Or is that a myth?"

Rafe shrugged, shoving his hands into his pockets and rocking on the balls of his feet. "Myth, same with mirrors. It's not smart to be filmed though. You don't want your picture popping up fifty years later, and you still look the same."

"Or a couple hundred down the road."

"That wouldn't be to bad. Then you could always blame ancestry. I've used that one before. The 'I've always been told I'm the spitting image of my grand-father' excuse."

She stared at him, wondering for the first time how old he was. Talk about your May/December romance. "I can't believe I'm having this conversation."

"Believe it," Rafe replied, finally looking at her again. His eyes held a smidgeon of hope, but he held himself rigid as though prepared for a fatal blow. "I'm glad you're still speaking with me. I thought you'd leave me, not let me explain. I'm happy to find that I was wrong."

Lexi crossed her arms and glared at him. He was right. Whatever else she could say about her feelings for him, she didn't think he'd hurt her physically. Her heart was another matter entirely. Could a monster even feel real love?

"You're not forgiven. And the whole trust issue is definitely in question. But you've done nothing to make me afraid of you, not personally. And you've done your best to protect me, even tonight. I'm right, aren't I? I heard what that other vampire said. He was after me, and you fought him for me. They all did. Why?"

Rafe stepped forward, backing her against the wall again. "The werewolves protected you because of Stella. Grant is their leader and Stella is his chosen mate. If you are important to her, you're important to them all. Stella would lay her life down for you, and so would the wolves."

Lexi allowed him to overshadow her physically. It wasn't like she could stop him. But no way was she going to start letting him bully her verbally or emotionally. "What about you and the other vampires? Shanna and her guy are both vampires, and the two women who came to get me out of the way. They were vampires. Why did they stand up for me?"

"Because I love you. And they know I love you. They know that if I have my way, you will become my lifemate, my woman and my love for all eternity. They would lay their lives down to protect you, just as they would for me."

Again, Lexi's heart stuttered, but for an entirely different reason. "Your lifemate? You want me to be like you, live with you?"

"For all eternity, if you would do me the honor. I've been alive for over three hundred years, Alexandria Hart. In all that time, I've never met a woman who fascinates me the way you do. You make me laugh. You keep me on my toes. You look me in the eyes and match wits with me. I want you by my side, making each day worth living."

Rafe wrapped his arms around her, holding her against his chest. He rubbed circles on her back, calming her racing heart with his gentle action. "I know I'm asking a lot of you, more than you could dream. From my own experiences, I know what I'm asking you to give up, the things you will miss, both large and small. But I also know what I'm offering you. Eternal life. Powers beyond your imagining. Strength and senses, sights and sounds. But more than that, I'm offering you my life and everything I could possibly give you. I'm offering you whatever is left of my heart and soul."

"Do you still have a soul?" Lexi had to ask, fearing the worst.

His grip on her tightened, his arms shaking around her. "Honestly, I don't know. I didn't really know if I had a soul before the change. No one can answer that question until they truly die."

"Does the cross hurt you?"

"Personally, or as a race?" Rafe asked, laughing at her expression. "I haven't had a negative reaction to religious icons, any religious icon. Most of the younger vampires will tell you the same thing. That isn't true for the ancients. Whether it comes from their own beliefs, or if they've become so evil that the creator has completely turned his back on them, I don't know."

"So you can still go to church, still pray."

"I guess. I've never tried." He smiled and gave a self-deprecating chuckle. "In my own mind, I am flouting his law by still being alive after all this time. I haven't wanted to take the chance to find out for certain."

"At least you're honest now," she whispered, touching the corner of his mouth, tracing his dark smirk, trying to judge the fleeting emotions dancing across his face.

"I've tried to be as open and honest with you as I

could. But I didn't want to frighten you. I didn't want you to run from me, screaming into the night."

Lexi's heart ached at the pain filling his words. But there was more she needed to know, to understand, before she could even consider what he offered her. "Would it hurt?"

"The transformation? Some, but not a great deal." He gave her a coy smile, his eyes darkening in a natural, seductive manner. "And the bite itself can be quite pleasurable."

"Pleasurable?" Lexi would've stepped away if the wall wasn't at her back. Instead, she wrapped her arms around her middle. "I can't see how someone sinking their teeth into you could be pleasurable."

"You didn't seem to have any problem with it before," he taunted, caressing his mark with the tip of his finger.

She slapped his hand away. "I was blinded by passion."

"You aren't blinded now," he replied, stepping even closer. He slid a leg between her thighs. "How about a little test?" he whispered.

Lexi didn't know if she was up to this. "Sure you aren't a little hungry after your big fight? You know, looking for a quick snack."

All trace of humor faded from his angular face. "To my mind, you'll never be a quick anything. I do want a taste, to give you a small sample of what it would feel like if you gave yourself over to me."

Lexi's insides trembled, both with arousal and fear. She didn't remember it hurting, but did she trust Rafe not to hurt her? He could have killed her a hundred times before this night, but Lexi hadn't known that.

Before, she only thought she risked her heart, maybe some of her self-esteem. But not her life.

And yet, there was only one way to know for certain. If he was to be believed, Rafe could find her any time he wanted. She'd seen him fight the other vampire. He was inhumanly fast and strong. If he wanted to kill her, there was no way for her to stop him. She had to trust that he didn't want her dead.

Lexi took a deep breath, braced herself, closed her eyes, and tilted her head to the side.

She felt his breath first, warm against her neck. Being dead and all, she guessed he didn't have to breathe, but did it for effect, to blend in. But she didn't have long to ponder the intricacies of hiding a vampire in the midst of humanity. A quick, sharp pain brought her back to the present.

Lexi barely register the fact that it hurt before a warm, achy feeling flowed from her neck to her more private regions, starting a throbbing in a place she least expected it. She moaned, throwing her arms around him as the pleasure spread, causing every nerve in her body to become sensitive. Even the weight of her clothes on her body became a source of arousal.

Rafe's mouth left her neck, his tongue sliding across the sensitive skin, licking the last drops of the blood before he pulled away from her.

"Now that didn't hurt, did it?" he asked, a knowing smile cutting across his face.

"Well, that all depends on your definition of hurt. Right now, I have an achy, empty kind of hurt, deep inside. The kind of hurt that you could ease for me.

That's the point of the whole thing, right, to make your victim more receptive."

Rafe frowned. "I prefer thinking of it as a form of payment. You give me something I need, that I value. I should offer you something more than pain and terror in return."

"Okay, I'll give you that one. It doesn't hurt. It's scary when you know it's coming, but it sure doesn't hurt."

"Does that mean you'll think about what I said, what I offered?"

Lexi closed her eyes, taking deep, steady breaths to calm her nerves. "Don't rush me, please. Rafe, for all intents and purposes, you've offered to change my life and marry me in one swoop. Eternal life is a definite plus, but you've got to give a girl room to think. This isn't the kind of decision to be made lightly."

"Even if I were a mortal man wanting to spend the rest of my life with you, I would be anxious to hear your answer. I understand your need for time to consider, but there are issues at hand that you don't know about."

"That other vampire."

"That other vampire." Rafe rubbed her shoulders, resting his forehead on hers. "I need to know your answer by tomorrow night. If the answer is yes, we should go ahead quickly, so you have time to adjust before he returns for you. If the answer is no, we need to have time to find someplace safe to hide you from him until I have a chance to end this madness."

Lexi shivered, rubbing her hands up and down her arms. She almost wished he'd hold her, tell her that everything was going to be okay, even if it was a lie.

But she resisted the temptation of throwing herself on his mercy. "I understand. I promise to have your answer by sunset. I can't guarantee it'll be the answer you want, but it will be an answer."

Rafe finally stepped back, giving her room. "That's all I can ask of you. I'm grateful you're giving me this much of a chance. If you need anything, ask Patricia. She is my voice while I slumber."

He took her arm and led her back towards the guestroom stairs.

"You trust me to wander around up here while you're helpless, asleep downstairs somewhere?"

That comment stopped Rafe dead in his tracks. As he looked down at her, Lexi thought she could see his every dream in his eyes. "I have no trouble trusting you with my life, my sweet. Can you say the same?"

Chapter Twenty-One

To her relief, Lexi saw no one as she walked back up to the guest suite. All good little vampires must be tucked in their coffins, and the werewolves had to be exhausted after their big brawl. She was grateful. After the overload of information, the change in her worldview, she needed the alone time to adjust. She locked the door to her room, wondering if that would do any good.

Lexi sat on her bed for a long time, staring at the walls and trying to come to grips. Vampires and werewolves were real. Not only were they real, they made up a sizable portion of the population of Santa del Sol. She'd never be able to look at any of the other people in town the same way again. She'd be wondering what they had done on the last full moon and if they owned more than their fair share of razors. It surprised her that she wasn't more frightened. Modern TV must be doing its work.

Her boyfriend was a vampire, one who wanted to spend all eternity with her, literally. She didn't miss the fact that he really was the bloodsucker she'd once accused him of being. She'd meant it metaphorically when he harassed her to sell, and now look where she was. Could she give up living life as a human? She wouldn't have to face morning ever again, but she'd never have another good cup of java either.

And poor Stella. Her best friend was a werewolf now, and married too, if the word 'mate' meant what it sounded like. She wondered how her independent-minded friend took the news. Knowing Stella, handling the whole hairy once a month thing would go over better than the part where she got married and didn't even know it.

What had the two of them gotten themselves into?

Lexi stepped off the bed and went through the bathroom. She needed to talk, and Stella could probably use the time too. Hell, if Grant was still there, maybe she could pick his brain as well.

She had a huge decision to make, and she was scared to death of making the wrong one. It wasn't as if she could go back and change her mind if she turned out to be wrong. She didn't think there was a cure for vampirism

Grant answered her knock. Wearing only his jeans, his hair sticking out in all directions, and a goofy smile on his lips, it didn't take a brain surgeon to realize that she was interrupting.

"I'm sorry. I'll leave you two alone."

Grant grabbed her hand as she started to scurry back to her room. "You're not interrupting anything, not now. I want you to be the first to know that Stella's agreed to marry me."

"Not that I had much choice, since we already are married," Stella piped in, her voice dripping with sarcasm. She sat at the small table by the window, munching on pastries and sipping coffee. "Come on in, Lexi. I figure you're in as deep as I am. You've got to try some of these muffins. For a servant of the bloodsucking undead, their chef makes a mean banana nut.

"If you're certain," Lexi replied, eyes glued on Grant.

He smiled, his teeth looking perfectly normal. Then he tried to fold himself into one of the small, wooden chairs. The humorous look on his face was enough to make Lexi doubt that she'd seen him sprout hair and rip into other monsters.

"It's okay," he replied. "I could use someone else helping me run interference with Starry Eyes. She's still miffed about me not telling her."

"Miffed?" Stella growled. "I go to sleep thinking I've had the most amazing sex of my life and wake up a married woman. And what's worse is I'm married for most of a day before anyone bothers to tell me I'm married. You are *so* never going to live this one down, Fido."

Lexi snickered, finally taking the last chair, facing the window.

Grant shook his head. "I expected her to be pissed about me biting her. I couldn't help myself, but it's not an excuse. I made her a werewolf without even asking. But does she bitch about that? No. She's pissed about the mating." He looked over at Lexi for understanding. "I don't get women."

"You're not supposed to. That wouldn't be fair. We don't understand you, so you're not allowed to understand us." With that, Lexi took a huge bite out of a chocolate covered croissant with one hand and poured some coffee with the other.

"Well, it's nice to see you're still on solid foods," Stella quipped, passing the cream. "With my predicament, I was certain you'd be on a liquid diet by now."

"Nope. Unlike you, I have to bite him back to get changed. So I have until tonight to make my decision." Lexi looked down at the croissant with horror in her eyes as a tragic thought occurred to her. "Dear lord. This might be the last chocolate I ever get to eat. Oh, that's it. Immortality and great sex for a million years can't be worth giving up chocolate."

Stella winked at Grant. "See, I told you she'd take it well and land on her feet. She's already joking about it."

Grant didn't look as convinced, eyes filled with concern. "Lexi, this is a serious matter. I know Rafe feels you are his lifemate. That means a lot to a creature like him. Having a lifemate can mean the difference between life and death to a vampire."

Lexi stared at her hands, picturing them with hooked claws. She realized the truth, but didn't want to think about it, much less put her greatest fears into words. "I kinda thought they were already dead."

"I mean true death." Grant reached over to run his fingers through Stella's hair, the petting motion seemingly unconscious. "A vampire with a lifemate has something to live for, to hold on to. They tend to outlive all their peers. Rafe is very serious if he feels that you are his lifemate."

"What will he do if I say no?" Lexi asked, afraid of the answer. In her mind's eye, she could still see the other vampire, Edmund, with his throat ripped open.

243

"He believes you are his mate. He won't force you. Rafe has more honor than that, a rarity in a vampire." Grief filled Grant's face with his next words, shocking Lexi. "But he would only live a half-life without you. I wouldn't give him more than a decade before he walked out to meet the sun."

"He'd commit suicide?" she gasped, not even pretending to drink her coffee and nibble on pastries.

"He wouldn't be able to live without you." Grant watched Lexi's face. "It wouldn't be that bad. Being a supernatural being has its advantages. Longer life, powers beyond imagining, a phenomenal sex life."

"Not to mention, you get to be a queen like me." Stella threw in for good measure.

Lexi was still stuck on Grant's last comment when Stella's words finally registered. "Huh?"

Stella waved a hand in her mate's direction. "Grant here's pack leader, king of the local werewolves. That makes me their queen. Rafe is the leader of the vampire nest, their king. You'd be their queen."

Blood rushed away from her cheeks, leaving Lexi pale and drawn. "Great, just shovel on more pressure."

Grant had the good manners to look ashamed. "Stella doesn't know the half of it. She only knows what I told her concerning the werewolves. I haven't gotten around to telling her about Edmund."

"Who is Edmund?" Lexi asked at the same time Stella demanded, "You didn't tell me everything?"

Grant couldn't meet either woman's eyes. "I was going to tell you after you ate, Stella. I wanted you to have time to absorb what I'd already thrown at you."

Stella's eyes narrowed. She crossed her arms and

legs, glaring at her new husband. "Okay, I've absorbed. Start spilling the rest before I start throwing pastries at you."

Grant and stared down at his folded hands. "I don't know everything about Edmund, only what I've picked up from some of the younger vamps. They talk more than the others, and they're terrified."

Lexi listened silently, waiting for Grant to elaborate. Stella couldn't. "Okay, terrified vampires isn't a good thing."

"He is second-in-command to the woman who made them all, Eldora."

"A woman made them all, not Rafe?" Lexi asked, thinking of the pleasure shooting through her body at the feel of his single bite. A wave of jealousy lashed at her.

"No, Rafe's never made another vampire. His nest is made up of young, discontented vampires from Eldora's nest." Grant grimaced, looking at Stella for support of some kind. "It seems that Eldora put several of them under Edmund's direct control. From what I've been told, he's a complete sadist."

"And you're helping Rafe fight the guy off, right?"

A growl rumbled through the room. Grant's eyes took on an unearthly, feral glow. "Edmund killed one of my wolves, one I'd left watching your apartment after we left Lexi there alone. He also wiped the mind of the young vampire Rafe had left on guard. When he attacked a member of my pack, Edmund became my enemy as well."

"Someone died guarding me?" Lexi thought of that night, of waking, crying, on her knees. "The dream I had, the one with the man at the window. I didn't

245

think about it before, but it was the same man tonight. It was Edmund."

"Yes."

The pieces started falling together. "He's the one who killed the three girls. He's the one who left the body under my house. He's the one who vandalized my shop."

"Yes, yes, and yes." Grant's voice sounded scratchy, but his eyes had returned to normal. "He's doing everything he can to challenge Rafe's authority. By making public kills, he's proving that Rafe can't control the vampires in his territory. If he can't keep his vampires under control and out of sight of the mortal public, his nest will be put under the control of the nearest elder or ancient."

"And that would be Edmund."

"Give the girl a cigar," Grant gestured like a carnival barker but settled down to the story. "If Edmund takes over, it'll be the first time he's been given a territory of his own. He'll let loose a reign of terror unlike anything this country's ever seen. Santa del Sol will become a bloody wasteland, with Edmund sitting on his throne, salivating over the carnage."

"You're joking," Lexi said, panic causing her hands to tremble, sloshing the coffee in her cup.

"No, I'm not. If Edmund wins, no one, not werewolf, vampire, human, or other, will be safe. This whole town, hell, a thirty mile radius will be Edmund's private hunting ground, with everyone living in it becoming his plathings."

Lexi put her coffee down, almost missing the table as tears blurred her vision. "What can I do? These are my people, my family. How can turning vampire help in any way?"

"Do you really want to know?"

"Hell yes," Lexi jumped up and yelled without thinking about who and what she was addressing. At his raised eyebrow, she sank back into her chair. "Do you think I want to sit by and watch the people who've been kind to me all my life turn into walking blood buffets? How can I help?"

Grant shrugged. "If you become vampire, you help. You give Rafe something to fight for, something to call his own. Also, if you are a true lifemate, your mental strength will augment his, making him more powerful. On a political front, your involvement with him will cement werewolf support. You are Stella's family. She is our queen. You become the vampires' queen, and we become a solid front."

Not much of a choice. Don't join, and I live. Join, and Santa del Sol lives. "So if I die and become a vampire, chances are the good monsters win and my hometown lives?"

Grant didn't sugar coat her options. "Yes. Rafe wants Santa del Sol to be a sanctuary for all creatures. Here, you don't hunt. You don't feed. You don't fight. In this town, everyone is safe. With Edmund winning, no one is safe."

A fine shaking took control of her body. "And this is the only way I can help?" she whispered

"Unless you're a whiz with a crossbow or a powerful witch in disguise, this is the only way you can help."

Lexi hated this, hated Grant, hated Rafe, and hated knowing. But she couldn't go back. She wanted

247

nothing more than to be an interior decorator and part-time beachcomber, not a vampire queen. "And I thought Stella was the best salesperson in the world. She can't hold a candle to you. I have a lot to think about, don't I?"

"Yes. Your decision will affect more than you. Think about it carefully. What can you live with? What will keep you up at night wondering 'what if'? When you figure that out, you'll know what to do."

Stella stared at Grant, amazement stilling her fidgety frame. "Wow, Grant. That was deep and insightful. Makes me proud."

"What, you think I got to be king of the werewolves on brawn alone?" Grant reached over, lifting her across his lap.

"Well, yeah." Stella answered, wrapping her arms around his neck and cuddling closer.

"Guess you were wrong about a lot of things, hmm?" Grant growled before slamming his mouth over hers.

Lexi knew where this conversation was heading. "Well, I'll leave you two love puppies alone. Don't have too much fun."

Stella pulled back, licking her lips. "Why not? That's what got me here in the first place, and I'm enjoying the hell out of myself."

Lexi chuckled, but let herself out. Some things she could do without knowing, like what the mating rituals of the greater American werewolf looked like. But she was tempted to turn around and peek when she heard the howl, followed by the gasp and laughter, followed by the sound of dishes hitting the floor.

Nice to know they waited until she was out of the room.

Lexi closed the door behind her and walked back to the bed, collapsing across it. She was exhausted, but she didn't know if she should try to go to sleep. This might be the last day she'd ever see, the last sunrise and sunset.

There really wasn't a decision for her to make. The lives of everyone in her town weighed against her own. Not much of a choice. She wished she could go out and stroll down the boardwalk, watch the surfers and sun-worshipers one last time. On the bright side, the town looked its best after sunset, when the lights blazed.

And Stella was experienced enough to take over the shop during the day. Lexi could extend the nighttime hours to midnight, fitting in with several other shops. No one would think it strange, not if she moved in with Rafe. Everyone knew his hours were backwards, due to the club. If she wanted to keep the same hours as her husband, no one would think twice about it.

But even knowing she had no choice didn't help ease her mind, not as much as she would have liked. She stood on the edge of a precipice and was about to take the leap of faith.

Lexi walked to the window, pulling a chair up to it, and sat to watch her last day. She watched the tourists walking hand in hand. She watched the pretzel cart do a booming business around noon. She even watched the garbage truck come, back up into the alleyway, and empty the dumpsters.

When the sun sank beyond the waters, she'd never

seen such glorious colors. Blues, reds, purples, and oranges melted together into a spectacular show.

Ten minutes later, there was a knock on the door. Lexi closed her eyes and wrapped her arms around her waist. She stood slowly, dragging her feet across the carpet as she went to answer his summons.

Rafe stood at the other side, his question easy to read on his face.

Lexi said nothing, stepping aside and ushering him in. Rafe followed without a word.

He turned and started to speak. Lexi put a finger to his lips. She reached back with her other hand, pulling her hair aside and offering him her neck.

Chapter Twenty-Two

Lexi felt that momentary stab of pain as his teeth sank into her flesh. But like before, it couldn't overpower the sexual euphoria that flowed with every movement of his mouth on her neck.

Her body tightened while her legs trembled. She whimpered and writhed in his embrace, her arms wrapping around his waist, pulling him closer. She needed to touch him, to feel him as he fed from her.

Her fingers tore at his shirt, pulling the cloth apart as much as possible without breaking his hold on her. She began to feel light-headed as she ran her hands across his flesh, his chest warming with every pull on her neck.

Suddenly, her knees gave. She gasped as she started to fall, but Rafe swept her off her feet and carried her to the bed, never releasing her neck. Her heart trembled, fluttered, and struggled to beat in her chest. She was so cold. He was so warm. Everything dimmed, turning gray-tinged with sparkling lights.

Rafe pulled away with a growl, his nail slicing into his own neck. He pulled Lexi up, forcing her mouth against the cut. "Take life from me, my beloved, my queen. Drink and live."

It was a struggle to open her mouth, much less drink. She managed to swipe at the flowing liquid, capturing a drop on her tongue. It didn't taste like blood, not like it tasted when you got a paper cut and shoved your finger in your mouth. No, it tasted salty, but also electric, like sticking your tongue on the end of a battery.

With that single drop melting in her mouth, Lexi began regaining strength. She sealed her mouth over the cut and began a weak parody of his feeding, sucking in the life-giving fluid. She had no powers to make it pleasurable to Rafe, but he moaned and held her tighter as her mouth fluttered over his skin.

Her face felt flush. Her heart raced, threatening to pound its way out of her chest. A heat built in her stomach, stretching outward, burning at her every organ. She struggled to breathe through her nose, but her lungs wouldn't cooperate.

In a flash, she realized her body was dying.

Lexi fell away from Rafe, trying to scream, but unable to get the air necessary to do so. Her body twisted and shook, out of her control. Her stomach and intestines clenched and churned. Beads of sweat popped out all over as her body tried to cool itself from the fire raging deep inside.

Rafe stood up and left her clawing at the sheets. She lost the ability to track time, had no idea how long he left her in her pain-induced haze. When he returned, naked, he gathered her to him, picked her up, and walked to the bathroom.

A cool bath waited. He stepped in with her cuddled

in his arms and sank into the water. She managed to shriek as the icy liquid hit her burning skin. She wouldn't have been surprised to see steam fill the air.

But slowly, the icy feeling gave way to cooling comfort. Rafe's gentle petting and murmured words of comfort started to make sense, to slip past the mindless fever-induced mania. Her body relaxed against him, weariness and weakness overcoming the pain of her body changing into something else entirely.

As darkness embraced her, she wondered if this was what waited for her at each sunrise.

Lexi opened her eyes slowly, confusion and security warring within her. She had no idea where she was, but she felt safe wrapped in Rafe's arms. His cool lips whispered across her damp forehead while his hand smoothed her dark curls.

Everything rushed back to her, thrusting her out of her secure moment and into the truth of her future. Her stomach cramped, hunger clawing at her throat. She felt a quick sting at her gums. Her tongue slid over the new razor-sharp canines that replaced her normal teeth. She glanced around the room as a sweet, seductive scent filled the air, twisting her stomach even tighter.

Rafe rolled away from her, leaving her cold in her misery.

"Here, sweet. Drink. You'll feel better in a moment. Don't think, just drink."

Rafe tipped a cup against her lips. Liquid ambrosia poured past her tongue and down her throat. A warm glow filled her body, strength awakening in every cell.

Everything became crystal clear; every sound, every

scent, and every sight. As Lexi looked around Rafe's dark, masculine, and austere room, she could see every individual speck of dust gleaming and dancing in the air. Beyond the doorway, she heard a thunder of heartbeats, the humans and werewolves. It was as though with the death of her human form, the rest of the world gained greater life.

She stared around her, taking in every last color, each texture. But the most fascinating thing of all was Rafe. She couldn't keep her eyes off him. The very air around him seemed to shimmer with repressed power. His auburn hair held living flames of light and color, ever-changing. She longed to lap at his pale skin, let her tongue run over his body, absorbing the taste of his flesh as she remembered the taste of his blood.

Blood.

She took the cup from his hand, staring down into the life-giving liquid he'd offered her. Thick and red, it didn't turn her stomach as she'd feared it would, with her human sensibilities. It wasn't disgusting. It was magical, sacred. A gift as much as a necessity. Humans weren't cattle, not if they could produce such a simple, vital liquid.

Rafe must have misunderstood her fascination, reaching to take back her cup. "No one gave their life for your first meal. We have willing donors who supply us, for a price. Some take money, thinking their blood goes to a bank. Others are aware of who and what we are. They serve us for the protection we give them. Other creatures, such as the werewolves, donate to secure treaties with our kind, but that type of blood is too rich for a fledgling's first meal. The blood of those with magic can be like a drug. You must be careful not to drink any until you've more powers and years behind you. For most, it takes a decade or more."

Lexi gripped her supply like a junky, not willing to risk losing such a precious treasure until she'd drunk her fill. "I didn't think you'd killed someone for me, though I realize you would if you felt the need. No, I just never realized that blood could be beautiful. Before, it was something to avoid. It could carry disease, or it signaled danger, injury to someone. Now, I look at it and think of how powerful and amazing it is. It's a simple liquid that as a human I never thought much of, yet it is the basic building block of life. Without it, a human would perish. Without it, a vampire would starve."

Rafe turned and took a bottle to refresh her drink. "A vampire wouldn't starve. We don't die that easily. No, a vampire without blood would go mad."

"Nice of you to share that after the fact."

Rafe reached over for his own glass. "It will never be a problem for you, so I didn't think to mention it. You are my mate. It is my duty to provide for you, to be certain that you are never in need. As such, you needn't worry about starvation. It will not happen."

A fifties male mentality in a twenty-first century vampire. How quaint. "So, you'll provide anything I need?"

Rafe took a deep drink and smiled. "Anything within my ability, and my abilities are great."

"You know, most men would realize the danger in telling a woman something like that," Lexi teased. "And I will remember, every birthday and Valentine's Day. You do celebrate holidays?"

Rafe put his glass down and kissed her. "Not in centuries, but I haven't had a reason to celebrate anything until now. I can't tell you how much your decision to join me means."

Lexi swirled her glass, watching the thick liquid play against the cut crystal. She didn't want to see his expression as he answered her. "Grant said my joining you could mean the difference between life and death, my hometown's as well as yours."

Rafe didn't reply for a long time. Lexi wished she could read his mind, crawl into his heart and brain and see what was going on.

"It could be," he said slowly, as if weighing his every word. "Though I wish Grant hadn't said anything. I didn't want to influence your decision, not like that."

Then I made the right choice. No second thoughts. "These people mean something to me, yours and mine. This town is mine. If becoming a vampire helps you defeat Edmund and protect us all, then there wasn't much of a choice. But I have to admit, being immortal and having you at my mercy, my beck and call for all eternity, was a definite bonus."

Rafe took her cup from her, setting it on a table behind her back. He pulled her into his arms, curling his now warm body around her. "I hope you always feel that way. I hate to think you felt pressured to join me for any reason other than being with me, but I am not fool enough to throw the gift away. I'll spend eternity making it worth your while."

Lexi kissed his cheek. "And I'll spend eternity holding you to it. Now, do we get this show on the road or what? You can't tell me we don't have something other than lying around in bed to do."

Rafe smiled, his lips teasing hers. "Oh, lying around in bed sounds like much more fun than anything else I had planned, but you're right. We'll have to pick up here after the meeting."

Lexi closed her eyes, concentrating on the feel of the blood heating her veins and his words heating her body. "Oh, we will. You've got to work on keeping me happy and satisfied, remember."

"I'll do my best," he replied, giving a quick slap to her naked behind. "Now get up, lazy-bones. The others have been waiting for an official introduction since you made your decision last night. The sooner that's over, the sooner we can get back to more pleasurable endeavors."

"I like how you think." Lexi leapt to her feet, swaying as her body responded much more quickly than she'd anticipated, the room spinning. "Whoa, how do you manage to get around like this?"

Rafe was at her side before she could register any movement, his hand cupping her elbow. "Easy, love. Your body is stronger than you're used to. You need to take things slowly until you adjust. You'll hurt yourself and others if you're not careful."

Anticipation laced with fear filled her. "What can I do now?"

"We'll talk about that later," Rafe replied, pulling a black satin sheet from the bed and wrapping it around her. "For now, I had your clothing brought here from your home. Don't ask how. Human police aren't much of a deterrent against us. I'll leave you to get ready. I have to set up the gathering. Shanna will come for you in a few moments. She's volunteered to be your guide in this new life, as I'm too

257

close to you to be effective. You can trust her. She's been a close friend for over a century."

Lexi's felt the walls closing in on her. She clutched at his arm. He was the only safe harbor she had in this new world, the only one she felt secure with. "Shanna will bring me straight to you, right? I mean, she seems nice enough and everything, but I feel safer when I'm with you."

Rafe pried her fingers off him, raising her hand to his lips, kissing each one of her knuckles. "That is as it should be. Don't be long."

Chapter Twenty-Three

Lexi stepped into the large, circular chamber with Shanna at her side. Her insecurity mounted as she took in the crowd of people, all inhuman, waiting to greet her. Had she been able to eat solid food, the butterflies swarming in her stomach would've had her on her knees vomiting within seconds.

They waited to be introduced to a queen, and they were getting her. Talk about massive disappointment.

Shanna told her that everything would be all right, that all they wanted was Rafe's happiness and continued strength. Still, Lexi worked hard to at least look the part. When she'd picked out the dress to knock Rafe's socks off, this hadn't been the setting she'd pictured, but it fit the regal feeling of the occasion. A red carpet gown for a red carpet occasion.

At least she wouldn't humiliate him. Embarrass him, maybe. Humiliate, no.

Shanna had been very open about what all was at stake tonight, more open than Lexi felt comfortable with. If she didn't know how much was riding on this, maybe she wouldn't be as scared. Rafe and Grant both intended to introduce their mates and cement their treaty. Then they were to declare open war against Edmund and any he called his own.

So Lexi walked into the room, head held high and mimicking confidence she didn't feel while surrounded by so many people, creatures really, that she didn't know. She swept forward, her gown the color of sunset flowing around her graceful form. Rafe's eyes locked with hers, his eyes glowing with approval and desire.

The sound of so many hearts beating in such a small room sent Lexi's fangs sliding down, but Shanna made certain she'd drunk as much blood as possible before they came downstairs. She explained that satiating the hunger before approaching anyone with a beating heart was a must for a fledgling. Otherwise, the bloodlust became too strong and the fledgling attacked without thought, taking down any who stood between her and a meal.

Lexi could see how easy that could happen and was glad she'd followed Shanna's instructions. She saw Stella standing beside Grant and listened to their hearts beating in the same rhythm. Lexi felt her mouth watering, and a cutting pain shot through her. Her friend was food. If not for the fact that she'd fed so well, Lexi realized she would have been gnawing at Stella's neck.

If this was normal, how could a fledgling without a guide survive?

Rafe stepped forward, taking Lexi's hand in his and kissing it. He escorted her to the center of the room, taking his place beside Grant. The others muttered, but the overall noise level decreased as they realized it was time.

Rafe and Grant stepped forward, leaving Lexi and Stella a step behind. The two women looked at each other, feeling out their differences and similarities. Nothing would ever be the same for them, but they would face their new lives together as a united front.

Nice to know some things hadn't changed.

Rafe raised his arms, silencing the crowd. "Today, there is cause for celebration. Today two new members join our communities, giving hope for the future and bringing our people closer together."

Silence fell. Rafe took Lexi by the elbow and pulled her next to him. "I would like you to meet my first fledgling and my mate, Alexandria Hart. Many of you who have lived in Santa del Sol long enough may know her well. She has roots deep in this area, bringing community acceptance to our people as well as strength to me. She is the newest member of my nest, but will not be the last."

Thane and Shanna started the cheer through his people. Shanna had explained to Lexi that her conversion was proof of Rafe's power. Not only did he have a mate, someone to ground him to this life and supply him with extra power, her change showed that he was a powerful master vampire. Only a true master could create another vampire, even a perfect candidate, a human impervious to a vampire's control. A weaker vampire had the ability to create only ghouls, flesh-eating monsters with no conscience, no remorse.

Lexi's existence proved Rafe's strength and showed him worthy of leadership.

Grant stepped up beside Rafe, pulling Stella along with him. "But the vampires are not the only ones with cause to celebrate this night. The wolves have reason to rejoice as well. As leader of this pack, head alpha, I have found my mate. Stella Jones has accepted my mark and joined our ranks. Our pack now has an alpha bitch, a chance at continuing our line. And she joins our powers with that of the vampire, as she claims the mate of Rafferty O'Neill as family. Any family of a pack member becomes our family. Our queens merge our bloodlines, tying us together, joining our fates."

The chamber erupted in howls. The hair at Lexi's nape stood on end. She stepped closer to Rafe, her fangs lengthening and her nails growing to claw-like proportions in response to the threat. Rafe smiled down at her, lacing his fingers with hers and raising both their arms above their heads.

Cheers joined the howls, leading Lexi to believe the response was a happy one. She turned to a stunned Stella. Never had either one of them been so whole-heartedly and quickly accepted anywhere in their lives. Lexi realized that no one would be stupid enough to dissent in such a public forum, where they could easily be struck down. But she still expected some discontents to grumble at the very least.

Maybe this whole 'queen' business wouldn't be as bad as she'd thought when Shanna broke the news to her. She hadn't been completely taken by surprise, thanks to Stella and Grant, but she still planned on making Rafe pay for leaving the job of breaking the news to Shanna, not having the guts to tell her himself. But being queen didn't seem as scary as it had at first.

The group separated into two parts, a makeshift greeting-line. It might not have been a wedding in the sense that Lexi was used to, but Rafe and Grant had both made it clear what she and Stella meant to them, and the well-wishing and general butt-kissing commenced. She lost track of the different people she shook hands with and who kissed her cheek. She had a hard time keeping track of what species each person was. But in the end, it didn't matter.

Vampire or werewolf, they were all her people, all her family.

When she shook the last hand, her body sagged under the pressure of all the changes in her life. Rafe swept her into his arms and strode to the single door leading out of the club and back to the chamber. Laughter followed them. Had she still had the blood pressure necessary for it, Lexi would have blushed. She knew that everyone in that room knew exactly what Rafe had planned for her. Her only relief was the fact that Stella was in the same boat, except Grant slung her over one shoulder and stalked out of the room.

Lexi buried her head in Rafe's chest and held on tight.

It took no time at all to be secured behind the doors of Rafe's rooms. He placed her on the bed, and then went back to the security panel, closing the panic room. Her safety came first, but not last.

"Now, where were we before we were so rudely interrupted?"

Lexi pounced with eyes closed, hoping without vision the speed of her movements wouldn't make her as dizzy. All of her senses were now acute. She'd filled her hunger for blood, calming the beast she felt lurking inside her, but another hunger took its place.

The hunger for her mate.

Her arms and legs wrapped around a laughing Rafe as her lips locked over his mouth. His hands came around to cup her bottom, supporting her as he staggered to the bed.

Lexi abandoned herself to the madness of the flesh. It wasn't as though he resisted her, but it wouldn't have mattered if he had. She needed. She wanted. She took.

Her claw-like nails ripped the clothes from his body, shredding cotton and linen as though it were paper. He had more control, sliding her dress off her body with a flick of his wrist.

But even that second of separation was too much for Lexi. She whimpered and moaned, reaching for him, pulling him back to her. Instinct kicked in, and she struck. Yanking his head to the side by his hair, she sunk her fangs deep into his neck.

Rafe jerked and groaned, his arms wrapping around her and pulling her close. Lexi purred as she took everything she needed from this man she loved, comfort, desire, sex, sustenance, and safety. He gave her all without question, without regret.

She reached up with one hand and pulled her hair aside. As she fed, she tilted his head forward, inviting him to do the same.

Fire, of both pain and lust, slammed through her body as he completed the circle. They shared more than body and blood. They shared life.

His fingers caressed her body, bringing animal-like moans. He didn't even need to touch her. She felt his stroke before his flesh met with her own. The tiny hairs covering her body sent signals to her brain, sizzling her skin.

And then there was his scent. Passion and need had a smell. Thick, cloying, invasive, and masculine, it snaked through her nostrils, wrapping its way around her womb. She throbbed with need with each inhale. Add that to the smell of warm blood mingling, and her eyes rolled back in their sockets.

Even as Rafe joined their bodies together in that ancient rhythm, Lexi already realized what Rafe had told her. They made one another complete. They were a unit, unstoppable and inseparable.

They were mates.

Chapter Twenty-Four

Lexi woke the next evening, surprised to find she wasn't sore. They'd spent the entire evening making love, discovering each other. Lexi hadn't thought sex could get better than the first time with Rafe until she joined the vampire race.

There was something to be said for acute senses.

The faint sound of classical music echoed through the chamber as warm air flowed through to fight off any chill. Not that the cold bothered her anymore. But she had to admit, Rafe thought ahead.

Lexi curled into Rafe's nude form, resting her head on his bare chest. "Mmm, I never pictured waking up like this when I read *Dracula* as a kid. I always thought that you had to have the creepy, dirt-filled coffin thing going."

His rumbling laughter echoed in her ears. "Mr. Stoker was right about many things, but not that. Many ancients did such things to make an impression on superstitious peasants. It was never necessary, and certainly not comfortable."

"What about the burying yourself thing?"

"In an emergency, it is the quickest, easiest way to

hide from the sun. Thankfully modern conveniences make it unnecessary. I never did like worms in my underwear."

Lexi snickered, her hands roving over him. "No, that couldn't be half as much fun as having me in your pants, hmm?"

"Cheeky wench," he growled, squeezing her tight. "And to think, I'm going to have to spend eternity waking up to that smart mouth of yours."

Lexi gave him a sultry gaze, letting him see all of her desire shining forth. "You weren't complaining about my mouth last night. I seem to remember several compliments on the use of my mouth, followed by gasps, moans, and the occasional begging."

He licked his lips. "You can't hold a man to anything he says while a beautiful woman does wicked, wicked things to his body. I was under duress."

"And I thought you were under me. My mistake."

Rafe chuckled, his hands dropping to cup her bottom. "Oh love, how I wish I could stay here in bed with you all night, but we both need to feed and check the club."

"No rest for the wicked."

"Never. There's too much fun to be had. Now up with you."

Lexi stuck out her lip as she sat up and slipped on a long, red silk robe. Her body didn't miss coffee, didn't crave it, but she missed the morning ritual.

A tap sounded at the door. Rafe, wearing his own black satin robe, opened it, letting Patricia in. She carried a silver platter with two bottles and two glasses. She poured the crimson liquid, filling the room with the rich, life-giving scent.

Here was a new ritual to embrace, one Patricia should be happy about. When the woman first stepped into the room, heart beating, rushing blood through her veins, it was all Lexi could do not to pounce on her. Sensing her struggle, Rafe grabbed up a glass and handed it to her.

Lexi gulped it down without much grace, glaring down at the empty glass before handing it back to Rafe for a refill. Patricia scurried out of the room.

"Will it always be like this, an uncontrollable, tearing hunger that must be filled at once, or I'll take down the first living being I meet?"

"No, love. It will be this way for long enough, decades until you perfect your control. But it won't be always. In the meantime, I will help you, provide for you. You won't have to worry about turning into a monster and killing all in your path."

Rafe's sadness and guilt were easy enough to read, without the vamipiric mind powers she was told would be hers in time. Her self-pity didn't stand a chance against the self-loathing in his voice. "You did that, didn't you?"

He shrugged, turning away from her. "I didn't have a guide, not as you do. I had a mistress who wanted a new toy, and who amused herself by watching me cut a swath of destruction across the land. I don't want you to ever look back at your past and feel the same type of shame."

Lexi couldn't let him put this distance between them, couldn't allow his past to make him feel like less of the man he'd become. "No shame and no regret. I promise you that I'll not feel either. I made my choice and I will live with it. I'll learn to enjoy it.

I've already found much pleasure in it, and I've only been a vampire for a day."

"If it is only the sex, you could have stayed human."

"True, but you can't tell me it would have been this mind-blowing," she teased.

Rafe leered down at her, getting into the swing of things, following her lead. "Now you'll never know."

"If it gets any better, I won't have to worry about the burden of immortality. I'll be dead in a week from pure exhaustion."

He smiled at her. "Get dressed, minx. They're waiting for us. If we don't hurry, they'll know exactly what we're doing down here."

"Can't have that," she tossed over her shoulder as she headed for the closest. "They might get jealous."

A hive of busy bees couldn't have competed with the scurry of activity Lexi watched as she walked into the main part of Club Nocturne. Humans, vampires, and an occasional werewolf sped from one side to the other, cleaning, setting places, and doing sound-checks. Delicious smells bellowed out of the kitchen every time a member of the wait-staff opened the door.

Italian food, drowning in garlic and tomato sauce, became a small regret that sent saliva through her mouth, her fangs extending. The price one must pay for immortality.

Lexi closed her eyes, reaching out with her other senses. It was easier to adjust this way, take each bit of input one piece at a time.

She didn't need to breathe, so blocking out smells was easy. She concentrated on sound. She reached past all the sounds of heartbeats. Therein lay madness.

She listened to the clinking of glass and silverware in the kitchen. She listened to the whisper of the people walking by outside, few out this far down the board-walk at this time. She heard the sound of the carousel music five blocks down.

If she listened closely enough, she was certain she could hear the man selling pretzels across from her police-taped shop. She couldn't wait to go out, see her favorite town with her new eyes. How did a vampire see the surging waves? How did a vampire experience the mixture of music and babble?

She strained her hearing more, wanting to imprint her town upon her senses. Her brow wrinkled as she heard another sound, a closer sound, the sound of a car engine revving up. She didn't know what it was about the sound that caught her attention, what drew her. But something wasn't right. Something was about to happen that shouldn't happen.

She looked across the room and saw Grant standing near the doors. She flew to his side, grabbing him and throwing them both across the room.

They hit the ground rolling to the sound of breaking glass, shrieking metal, and crumbling concrete. People screamed. Rafe stood above her, his dark eyes sinking into her flesh.

"Lexi, are you hurt?" he asked, kneeling and brushing her hair back to check her face for injuries.

Grant answered for them both. "She threw me to the side before the car struck. We're both fine." He looked down at her. "It seems my pack owes you a greater debt then before."

Lexi smiled, but it faded as she watched the flood of creatures pouring through the new hole in the side of the club. This wasn't an accident. It was an invasion.

Rafe and Grant both turned to see what she stared at. Grant growled, changing as he stood to a half-beast form straight out of Hollywood nightmares. Hair rippled down his back. His legs popped as muscles and joints reformed.

The air around Rafe pulsed with power. His fangs dropped to full extension. His eyes took on an eerie red glow. His fingers lengthened, tipped with inch-long claws.

The humans ran for the safety of the underground chamber while vampires and werewolves charged forward.

"He's insane." Rafe snapped, eyes filled with blood and murder. "Human authorities will be flocking here in moments. He'll have to kill half the town to keep this quiet. Lexi, you and Stella go to my room. Lock it down. Once it's locked, no one can get in. You'll be safe there."

Rafe didn't wait to see if Lexi did as he asked, rushing into the fray, Grant at his side.

For a moment, there was a pandemonium of rushing feet. Then Stella crouched next to Lexi, pulling her up. "We have to get out of here. It's going to be a bloodbath."

"I'm not leaving," Lexi replied, jerking her arm free of Stella's grasp and staggering in the direction Rafe had gone. The smell of blood already filled the air, sending panic and hunger through every cell in Lexi's body. "If Rafe doesn't make it, I want to be here with him."

Stella stepped in front of her, arms held wide spread to block her from going to her mate. "You'll be killed."

"Do you think I want to live under Edmund's protection?" Lexi asked as she shoved at her friend. "You've heard the stories. You know exactly what he's like. I'd rather be dead."

"We're a distraction," Stella replied, but doubt edged her expression, taking much of the vehemence from her words.

"I'm supposed to make Rafe stronger. How can I do that in lock-down?"

Stella stared at Lexi. Her eyes glowed with anger and her face began to elongate. Stella had never backed down from a fight in her life and it didn't look as though she was starting now. "If I get killed, I'm haunting your ass. And after everything else we've seen this week, you can't tell me that there's no such thing as ghosts."

Lexi laughed, but the sound died in her throat as her friend changed before her eyes. Lexi might be the one with immortality, but Stella got the upper hand on cool changes. No way did the movies do werewolves justice. A thing like that couldn't be captured on film, not even with CGI effects. A computer couldn't make the air warm. It couldn't send electrical shivers up your arms. It couldn't touch that primitive part of the human brain that remembered fighting saber-toothed tigers and wolly mammoths, triggering a fight or flight response that sent every muscle clamoring for attention.

One of Edmund's wolves charged at them, his lips peeled back in a snarl showing his gleaming, blood-coated teeth. Stella and Lexi jumped at the same moment, attacking the wolf on both sides at once.

He never stood a chance.

Lexi went high, Stella low. Stella clawed at his unprotected stomach, spilling his warm intestines onto the floor. Lexi used her new strength to wedge his head up high enough for her to latch on and feast.

The flow of his blood through her veins sent power surging through her like shoving her finger into an electrical socket. She pulled away from the temptation, but too late. Her head swirled as she staggered back, falling flat on her ass. Bodies and blood surrounded her. Screams filled the air. But nothing mattered. Everything was fine.

It was like someone slipped ecstasy in her drink, propelling her from stone sober to sloppy drunk in record speed. If Stella hadn't stayed by her side, Lexi would've made an easy meal for any of the combatants.

She didn't move, absorbed in the feeling of raw power, until she heard a yip and thud close by her.

Claudette stood above the prone body of Stella, laughing. Lexi could hear her friend's heart beating, pounding against her ribs in a stronger rhythm than a human could manage. Lexi knew she was alive. Claudette smiled, teeth gleaming pink, before pouncing on her furry meal.

"What the hell?" Lexi screamed as she launched towards the woman who'd shown her to her seat at Club Nocturne on her first visit. Claudette was one of Rafe's people, a part of Lexi's new family. What was she doing helping the vampire who tortured and tormented them all?

Claudette didn't flinch. She buried her face in Stella's fur-covered neck and bit. Even semi-conscious, the action hurt enough for Stella to whimper and lash out with claws. Claudette pulled back, hissing, as they sliced into her cheek.

Lexi didn't hesitate. She grabbed Claudette by the shoulder, letting her new-found strength take over.

"Get your hands off me," Claudette screeched, dropping Stella to confront her new adversary. Her face contorted with rage as she coiled to spring. "It's all your fault. Everything would be fine if it wasn't for you," Claudette accused as she launched herself through the air.

Lexi stumbled back under Claudette's onslaught. Age and practice served the other vampire well as she grabbed Lexi by the throat and tossed her across the room.

"I could have been Rafe's queen," she screeched, stalking toward Lexi. "The wolves wouldn't be considered our equals, but pets for our amusement. I could have ruled. Instead, you force me to make deals with that animal, Edmund. But at least with him, I am secure in my place. He wants me and I can use him. Your death will guarantee my position."

Lexi didn't remember standing up, didn't remember crossing the few feet between her and Claudette. What she did remember was the sound, a quick snap, like the breaking of a twig, only louder.

The woman hissed, her clawed hands flailing. Her head hung loosely at her shoulders, facing just far enough in the wrong direction to make her problem apparent.

Lexi'd broken Claudette's neck with disgusting ease.

She looked down at her hands, not knowing whether to be amazed or repulsed. But she didn't have time to dwell.

Even injured, Claudette remained dangerous. She attacked without warning, shoving Lexi to the ground. Her fingers laced through Lexi's hair, pulling her neck to the side. Sheer desperation gave Claudette unbelievable strength. Lexi tried to grab her head again, finish what she'd started. She sliced her talons down the other vampire's chest, not able to reach high enough to score a vulnerable artery. But as she dug through Claudette's flesh, another thought came to her.

Lexi tore into the area above the bitch's heart. She ripped apart ribs as easily as she'd broken Claudette's spine. Hopefully, the movies hadn't lied about one thing.

Her fingers sank into the tough flesh of her opponent's heart at the same moment Claudette managed to sink fangs into her neck. Lexi squeezed and Claudette ripped.

Lexi watched the surprise in Claudette's eyes, the split second of humanity and relief before she sagged across Lexi.

Shoving Claudette's body off her, Lexi staggered to her feet. Her drunken dizziness gave way to a floating feeling, lightheaded. She looked at her feet, watching a red pool gather around her toes. Reaching for her neck, her fingers touched what amounted to a mass of raw meat.

So much for immortality.

Rafe ripped and clawed his way through the throng of werewolves and shadows to reach his goal,

Edmund. He'd finally given Rafe the reasons he needed to take him down. Driving a car through a building and then attacking, if that didn't prove to Eldora that Rafe had the right to use any means necessary to dispose of Edmund, nothing would.

Howls and shrieks filled the room. Rafe's gums ached from the blood-scent, filling him with the desire to feast on his enemies. But only one enemy stood out, one called to him.

Edmund stood at the far side of Nocturne, leaning against a wall and smiling at the damage he'd done, the havoc he'd caused. No one approached him, the fight fanning out around him like ripples in a pond. His people created a wall of carnage between Rafe's people and Edmund.

But Rafe didn't slow down. An enslaved werewolf stepped into his path, and Rafe snapped his neck. A ravenous shadow launched itself at him, and he sliced its throat with his talons. No movement or effort was wasted. He saved his energy for his ultimate goal.

Edmund.

"It took you long enough, leech. I was beginning to grow bored," Edmund taunted with a nod of his head and a smirk.

Rafe forced his shoulders to relax as he grinned at his adversary. "Please forgive me. It seems I've been a neglectful host. Let me make amends."

With a flash of movement, he leapt forward. He tore Edmund's cheek, extending his smile to his right ear, before landing back in the spot he started from.

Edmund's eyes widened, his fingers touching his open wound.

With his opponent distracted, Rafe jumped forward

again. His talon's caught Edmund's upraised arm, laying it open from wrist to elbow. Again, he flew back to his starting position.

Edmund crouched into a defensive position. With a spasm of raw fury, he launched himself at Rafe, scratching and clawing in indiscriminate violence. Rafe took the blows, flinching but not backing down. He felt each slice into his body, each parting of his flesh. But Rafe had learned to distance himself from pain after years of living under Edmund's constant torture. He took his blows and bided his time.

Rafe's calm response infuriated Edmund. He shrieked as he slammed Rafe to the ground, struggling to take his throat. In doing so, he released Rafe's arms.

Rafe reached up, grabbing Edmund's hands. With a decisive twist, he snapped the other vampire's wrists.

The damaged joints began healing immediately, popping back into place as Edmund growled and hissed. It came as no surprise to Rafe. That wasn't the point.

Delay and distraction.

Rafe flipped the other vampire over, straddling his body. Before Edmund realized what was happening, Rafe tore his throat wide open.

"How do you like feeling your own blood pouring out on the ground?" Rafe growled, leaning forward to lap at the flowing wound. "How do you like knowing you're helpless to the whims of someone else? How does it feel to know you are nothing but food for the one above you?"

Rafe reared back, preparing for a final strike, when

he caught sight of hair the color of the deepest night. Glancing over, he watched as Lexi stumbled to her feet after rolling the body of Claudette off of her. Blood poured out of a massive wound in her neck.

Her knees sagged and she fell.

No.

Chapter Twenty-Five

Blood. It was all she could smell, all she could think about.

Pounding heartbeats. Curses. Held too tightly. Endearments murmured against her hair.

Blood. Flowing past her lips. Pressure removed from her mouth. *I want.* New pressure, more blood. Smooth satin against the back. Cool body holding her close. Gentle fingers petting her head.

Another donor pushing against her mouth.

Time became an endless stream of blood and hunger. The sun was setting again when her eyes finally opened and she became aware of her surroundings.

"If you ever disobey me and do something so stupid again, I will save Edmund the trouble and kill you myself."

Lexi smiled, snuggling back into the warm body spooned around her. She held his arms around her waist, enjoying the simple pleasure. "I take it our side won."

Rafe's embrace strengthened. "For now. Edmund escaped."

"If I had the energy, I'd cuss," Lexi grumbled. "What happened?"

His body shivered against her, his arms shaking around her. He placed soft kisses on the crown of her head as one would do to comfort a child. Lexi suspected that he was the one in need of comfort.

"I never want to live through that again," he whispered, his voice tight with unnamed emotion. "I had him. One more strike. I only had to give him one more strike and all our problems would be over. Then I saw you. I saw Claudette lying dead across you. I saw the blood. I watched you climb to your feet only to fall. Everything in this world that held any meaning to me disappeared. Edmund ceased to matter. The nest ceased to matter. The fight ceased to matter. My life ceased to matter. The only thing in my existence that matters is you."

"He got away and it's my fault. Great." Lexi closed her eyes and leaned back, not wanting to see the accusation and disappointment in his eyes. He might think she was more important now, but he'd failed to take out Edmund when he had the chance. The other vampire would never leave it at that. He would be back for vengeance, killing again and again. Add Claudette's betrayal to the mix, and Rafe had to feel he'd won a hollow battle. Even cementing werewolf support couldn't make up for the losses.

Lexi stiffened as a different kind of panic shot through her. "Stella. Oh shit, tell me Stella's all right."

Rafe kissed her head again, pulling her closer. "Don't worry about your friend. She fared better than you did. After Edmund ran, his people weren't far behind."

"That's a relief. She promised to haunt me if anything happened to her. With everything else that I've seen lately, I wouldn't put it past her."

Rafe's chest shook as he chuckled. "No, a werewolf ghost is the last thing we want to add into the mix. You're lucky it didn't come to that. As it is, you are a hero to the pack. Most of your donors last night were lupines showing their respect."

"You'll have to forgive me if I don't sound grateful and all," Lexi replied, remembering the buzz she got from Edmund's wolf. She rolled over, wanting to gauge his expression. "But I remember you saying I should stay away from werewolf blood while a fledgling."

"It didn't stop you in the fight." He ran his hands over her naked body, the feel of his caress mixing with the touch of satin. "I don't know what the consequences will be for you, not yet. We share blood on occasion, but never in such large quantities. And never with a vampire so young as you. But we had no other choice. The vampires were occupied convincing the local police that it was only a car crash and not a battle scene. The majority of the human staff had run to their own safehouses. I, too, needed blood, and with deep wounds, fresh blood works best and quickest."

"So, I might start howling at the moon next month?" Lexi asked, trying to picture what a crossbreed might look like. It wasn't a pretty picture.

"No, you won't become a were-vampire. But if will affect the development of your vampire abilities. You will be stronger. You will be different. Beyond that, only time will tell."

Lexi could accept that. It wasn't like she had a choice, and it was better than being dead. "The long and the short of it is, it's not over."

"No, it's not over. Eldora will reprimand Edmund for his actions, but being on the other side of the world will limit her ability to bring him to justice."

"So, we have a rogue vamp running around in Northern California."

"For now," Rafe replied, his hands beginning an exploration that sent waves of arousal crashing through her needy body. "We will worry about that when it becomes necessary. In the meantime, I have other things that need to be explored."

"Yes?" she gasped in sweet agony as his fingers played over her most sensitive pleasure point.

"I want to see how fully-recovered my Dark Queen is."

A whimper fell from her lips as her body jolted. "And how do you propose to do that?"

He rolled her on her back, settling between her legs. "Guess."

Her eyes slid closed as Rafe's teeth sank into her neck. Ripples of dark pleasure shot out from the pin-points of erotic pain. Lexi's senses soared, opening to embrace the world around her. In the distance, she could hear the crashing of waves.

A dark, brooding man who loved her more than life itself. An extended family that included her best friend. Her hometown safe, for the time being. And soon, a mansion complex set on the beach where she could watch all the gorgeous sunsets her heart could desire.

Not a bad way to spend eternity.

www.ingramcontent.com/pod-product-compliance
Lightning Source LLC
Chambersburg PA
CBHW031001260626
47169CB00002B/646